Bill Kirton

UNSAFE ACTS

PfoxChase Publishing

PfoxChase, a division of Pfoxmoor Publishing
4972 Lowhill Church Road
New Tripoli, PA 18066 USA

www.pfoxmoorpublishing.com
www.pfoxchase.com

Unsafe Acts

Print ISBN: 978-1-936827-21-3
Digital ISBN (PDF): 978-1-936827-22-0
Digital ISBN (EPUB): 978-1-936827-23-7

Cover by Sessha Batto

First PfoxChase electronic publication: February 2012
First PfoxChase print publication: February 2012

Published in the United States of America with international distribution.

Dedication:

For Lesley and David, Sandra and Eric, Gillian and John

and this one's for

Catriona X

Bill

Chapter One

One hundred and fifty miles out in the North Sea, Ally Baxter pushed open the pressurised door leading from the accommodation to the walkway. He had to force the door hard against the gale which was driving hailstones half the size of golf balls against the steel of the Falcon Alpha production platform. As he clawed his way into the wind towards the drill floor, he held his head low to stop the lumps of ice slamming into his face. They pinged from his hard hat and he felt their impacts all down his right side. It was a bit early for it to be this bad. October was usually wet but the real cold didn't start gripping the rigs until November. Out here, though, production didn't stop for anything. A shutdown could cost millions and nobody wanted to explain that away to the bosses onshore.

Baxter was the platform's Chief Safety Supervisor. Part of his job, whatever the weather, was to make periodic checks on everything that was happening. Today, the roustabout crew were lifting casing joints onto the lower deck. These were pipes forty feet long and weighing one and a half tonnes each. On the best of days, slinging them on the crane was dangerous. In this wind, they'd be whipping about like straws.

He stood at the edge of the deck, angling himself to keep the hailstones at his back, and watched as Baz Jackson fought to slide slings over the ends of the pipe lying on the supports at his feet. The crane's boom swung round across the wind and lowered its loose, flailing cable. Jackson reached up to hook the eyes of the slings onto it. Immediately, Baxter shouted at him. Jackson didn't seem to hear and Baxter ran forward, signalling to the crane driver not to lift. He came up behind Jackson and tapped him hard on the shoulder.

"What?" yelled Jackson as he spun round.

Baxter pointed to the slings.

"They should be double-wrapped. You know bloody well," he shouted.

"No way," yelled Jackson. "It'll take twice as long. I'm wanting out of this stuff."

Baxter shook his head and again jabbed a finger towards the slings.

"If you don't double wrap them, they'll be on top of you and you'll be out of it for good."

He stumbled back as Jackson grabbed him by the front of his coveralls.

"You're just a waste of bloody space," he said, his eyes inches from Baxter's face.

"Do it," said Baxter, holding his stare. "If you don't, you're on your way home."

Jackson shoved him away hard, and told him to fuck off but, as Baxter watched, he wrapped each sling around the pipe once more before reaching up for the swinging crane cable, hooking them on to it and giving the crane driver the signal to hoist.

"Get out of the drop zone," shouted Baxter as the load was lifted and the pipe started twisting on the cable.

Jackson turned to give him the stare again, but duly stepped back from the area into which the pipe would fall if it slipped. Baxter went up to him.

"I don't give a shit if that lot crushes you, but I don't want the extra paperwork, so double wrap them and don't stand under the load, right?"

In reply, he got the mantra again.

"Fuck off."

Baxter turned and left him, knowing that he'd do as he was told. In the end, everyone out there knew that ignoring safety procedures was the quickest way to get put on the next chopper home.

Later, back in his small cabin, he sat at his keyboard, filling out the safety log for the shift. He noted the incident without stressing it. It was one of many and it was there for the record, protecting him, but there was no point in creating even more antagonism among the crew. Outside, the installation throbbed on and the wind screamed. He was glad that he'd soon be back on the beach away from it all again. Life offshore had always been difficult.

When he'd finished the log, he always opened a special file called Vicky and unloaded into it some of the specific pains and frustrations of his days. It was a sort of diary and part of the rituals he used to comfort himself amongst all the aggravation It was vague, stream of consciousness stuff, ranging from observations about particular individuals to opinions about the company and the way the platform was being run. The words were those of a natural victim, whining, moaning and generally using the file to get tiny revenges on his world.

He looked at the screen. His last sentence read, "…so it'll serve the bastards right when it goes up". He nodded, saved the file and copied it onto two memory sticks, one of which he put under some magazines in a locker, the other in his shirt pocket. He looked at his watch. One more night, then he could start getting ready for the trip back to Aberdeen.

****

DCI Jack Carston had just come out of the shower and was getting into his pyjamas. His wife Kath whistled at him and he adopted an unashamed Superman pose. His pyjama trousers fell around his ankles.

"I've changed my mind," said Kath.

Carston laughed and hitched up the trousers. The truth was that Kath's first impulse had been legitimate. Carston, in his late forties, still looked good. His waist was beginning to thicken a little but there wasn't much flab anywhere else. Apart from the laughter lines beside his dark eyes, his skin was smooth and unmarked. What made him even more attractive was that he didn't realise that he was. He pulled on his trousers and sat on the bed.

"Are you rushing out again this evening?" said Kath.

"Not necessarily. Why?" said Carston.

She came to sit beside him.

"Good," she said. "We can talk about the show."

"What show?"

"At the Warehouse."

"Oh no, bloody hell," he protested. "Another two hours of superdarlings and crap sandwiches."

"You mean crab."

"I mean crap."

She leaned against him. He put his arm round her shoulder and kissed her on the temple.

"Dot wants me to take some publicity shots," she said. "I said I would and that we'd go to the preview."

"When?"

"Saturday afternoon."

"Out of the question."

"Why?"

"I'll be busy."

"Liar."

"And I'm a philistine."

"You're a yob."

The tone of their conversation was bantering, but it concealed a real difference. The Warehouse was a small local theatre, of which Kath's friend Dot was the administrator. The three of them got on very well together but Carston rarely understood the sort of experimental shows that Dot seemed to favour. He once had to sit through an evening in which a solo performer had a dialogue with an electric razor. The climax came when the character suddenly reached into a cupboard, produced a shaving brush, then broke down into either floods of tears or hysterical laughter; Carston had been unable to say which.

He moved his hand and began trailing his fingers around her breast.

"OK," he said. "What do I get if I come with you?"

"Put it this way," said Kath, pushing his hand away. "If you don't come, you'll get nothing."

He pulled her so that they both fell back onto the bed.

"It's a deal," he said.

****

Late the following afternoon, the Bristows S-41 came down through the drizzle that had drifted in after the hailstorms, hung ten or so feet above the runway for a few seconds, then eased further down to settle on its wheels and start trundling towards the main reception building. Inside it, the workers from Falcon Alpha looked out at the hangars, the wet tarmac, the other aircraft. They were impatient with this last, slow ritual. The two weeks of pent-up

4

hungers in them made them eager for pubs, women and families, more or less in that order.

It was a Wednesday and this was the heliport at Dyce in Aberdeen, the busiest in Europe. Midweek was changeover time. As the men from Falcon Alpha grabbed their bags and were directed by the ground crew towards the terminal, others were moving in the opposite direction.

The Falcon Alpha team trooped out to the waiting minibus. Passengers from most of the other oil companies took off their survival suits and left them in the stores at the heliport but Anstey Oil, the operator of the Falcon platforms, preferred to keep theirs at a base on the nearby Kirkhill industrial estate.

Rick Bole sat beside the driver. It was a sort of right. He was a big, bald, loud-mouthed maintenance engineer with attitude. He'd spent time in Perth prison for assault and frequently behaved in a way that suggested that they could probably expect him back soon.

"Come on, you dozy sods," he shouted to Jim Gellatly and Mike Milne, who were still standing on the pavement lighting cigarettes. "You're wastin good bevy time."

Gellatly and Milne squeezed into the back, slid the door shut and the driver set off for Anstey's.

"Make it quick," said Bole.

As the minibus turned onto the main road, Gellatly nudged Baxter and said, "Oi, Ally. You on for Bell's tonight?"

Baxter shook his head.

"Bloody Swan more like," growled Bole from the front seat.

Baxter turned to look out of the window and said nothing.

"Is that where you're goin then, Rick?" asked Gellatly, with a wink at Milne.

"Fuck off," said Bole.

The four of them lived in Cairnburgh. The Swan was the town's only gay bar. No-one knew why it had been chosen but, gradually, the town's gay community had staked their claim on it and the barman, who was a straight, middle-aged guy from Laurencekirk with a wife and two daughters, realised that his profits were beginning to depend on them more and more heavily.

"Used to be a good pub," said Gellatly.

"Yeah, if you fancy a pint of Aids," said Bole.

"Do they get dykes there, too?" asked Gellatly.

5

The question was directed at Baxter. He said nothing. Once again, Gellatly had to nudge him to get his attention.

"What?" said Baxter.

"In the Swan. Many dykes there?"

"How should I know?" said Baxter.

"Careful, she's probably got the rags up," said Bole.

"Wanker," said Baxter.

Bole's impulse was to swing round and punch him but his bulk made it impossible. Baxter leaned back into his silence. If it ever came to a face-off between himself and Bole, he'd be lucky to come second. But he wasn't afraid of him. He was used to bullying. Ever since the first suggestions that he was gay, he'd had to take verbal and physical abuse from everyone anxious to establish their own straight credentials. If he'd shown any fear, it would have made them worse, so he'd chosen silence.

When they got to Anstey's, Bole was first out. He slid back the door, grabbed Baxter by the front of his survival suit, dragged him out and slammed him against the side of the minibus. The others made protesting noises but they didn't try to intervene. It would have been like putting your hand into the blades of a turbine.

"You ever say anything like that to me again and I'll pull your fuckin tongue out," said Bole.

Baxter looked him straight in the eye.

"You're a wanker, Rick," he said. "You can beat the shit out of me but you'll still be a wanker."

He only just managed to get the words out before Bole's right knee came up into him and his left hand started slapping his face from side to side. Baxter sagged forward, nausea washing up from the pain in his groin. He lifted his hands to protect himself, but Bole's slaps and punches knocked them aside and his right hand pushed harder in Baxter's chest. The van's door handle dug into his back. The van driver sat helplessly, waiting for them to finish and move away.

****

Vicky Bryant was finding it difficult to keep smiling. The man in the driver's seat had been telling her for nearly half an hour what turned him on. She'd been forced to listen as she rubbed away at him trying to stir some life. He was in his late fifties and smelled

6

strongly of booze, fags and sweat. She'd already tried going down on him but even that got no response and she was glad when he grabbed her hair and pulled her head back up so that he could look at her face as she rubbed away.

She saw the time on the dashboard clock. Past five already. She had to pick Billy up from her sister's soon. He'd need feeding and cuddling a bit before she took him back there again so that she could deal with her evening punters. She worked harder. Her wrist ached, but the man was beginning to make the right sort of noises, his breathing was getting faster, shorter. She ignored the ache and pumped fast and hard.

At last, with a death rattle noise from the man and a clenching of his teeth, it was over. She continued to move her fingers, slowly now, until he opened his eyes again, looked at her and said, "OK. Now piss off."

She'd made sure he'd paid her up front so she was glad to get away from him. He'd parked in a yard behind the cinema, so she had only a short walk to her bus stop. As she turned onto the pavement, she heard the man start his engine and pull away towards the street beside the canal. She'd been working since one o'clock and earned just sixty pounds. Unlike her last client, the job was getting harder all the time.

****

After the fast initial outburst, Bole was soon breathing heavily and moving slowly. He dropped his left hand to grab the other side of Baxter's survival suit and lunged forward, his bulk crushing Baxter against the van and forcing his back against the door handle. Baxter was finding it hard to breathe. Bole had opened cuts on his eyebrow and at the corner of his mouth. Their faces were inches apart and Baxter could smell and taste Bole's rasping, smoke-tainted breath.

"I'll kill you, you bastard," said Bole. "Useless faggot."

Baxter clawed at his wrists. Bole banged him back against the van again.

"Don't you ever try it with me again," Bole went on, his voice rising. "I'll swing for you. If you—"

His words were stopped as Baxter suddenly snapped his neck forward and brought his forehead down onto Bole's nose. Bole felt

7

the crunch of gristle and the flow of warm blood over his lips. He stepped back, caught by the surprise of it, tears streaming from his eyes, his hands pressed against his face. Baxter stood up, refusing to feel his own wounds, waiting for the reaction he knew was coming. Bole shook his head, wiped his hands on the front of his survival suit and jumped at Baxter, knocking him to the ground and rolling on top of him. Gellatly, Milne and the others began to pull at Bole, trying to get him off. It took three of them to prise his fingers from Baxter's neck and drag him away. He was screaming and swearing at all of them.

"Come on Rick," said Gellatly. "Knock it off."

"I'll knock you off, you bastard. Let me go."

"No, come on, pal. He's not worth it."

Bole continued to heave and strain towards Baxter, who was slowly getting to his feet.

"Anyway, he's bleedin, look," said Gellatly. "Don't want to catch Aids, do you?"

It was an inspired comment. Bole dabbed at his nose and looked at the red streams trickling from cuts on Baxter's face. He took one step forward, raising a bloodstained hand to stop the others grabbing at him again. The other was pointing straight at Baxter's face.

"You're on borrowed time," he said.

Baxter managed to hold his stare but reckoned he'd said and done enough to make his point. With a final "Bastard", Bole turned to go inside. Baxter dabbed at the wounds on his face with his fingertips and, very slowly, walked in after him.

As the men queued to hand in their survival suits, they could see two of the company's bosses through the glass partition behind the counter. They were looking at some papers and Hugh Nicholas, the Finance Director, was pointing at something and shaking his head. The person with him, Dick Hamer, was a small man, too skinny to show off his expensive suit to any effect. His shining bald head made him look much older than his thirty-eight years. He was Anstey's Assistant Director of Human Resources. Nicholas towered over him. At thirty-two, his bulk was still muscle rather than fat. His thick, black hair was long but well cut, just brushing over the white collar of his Oxford shirt as he lifted his head to look through the glass at the new arrivals.

Bole threw his suit onto the counter with the rest. The storeman checked the name tag, put another tick into his book and continued carrying armloads of suits through to hang them on their labelled racks. All the time, Gellatly and Milne were talking of booze. The topic of the Swan had come up again.

"OK, OK," said Gellatly. "If you're so interested, why don't we give it a try?"

"What? In amongst a load o' shirt-lifters?" said Milne.

"Why not?"

"I've got too much respect for my arse."

The thought of Milne's arse brought a chorus of disgust.

"Yeah, we should give it a try," said Bole. "Get Alice over there to take us in."

The tension snapped back into the air. Baxter hadn't yet taken off his survival suit. He was busy filling in the paperwork that his job demanded every time he came ashore. He said nothing.

"Might liven up the evening a bit. What d'you reckon, Alice?" said Bole, moving over to him and slapping him on the back. Hard.

Baxter turned to look at him but said nothing. Bole kept his arm around Baxter's shoulders as he said to the others, "Told you. She's menstruatin."

Nicholas had come through from the office and was watching it all.

"Not on the premises, eh?" he said.

Baxter looked at him, shrugged Bole's hand away and took his papers to the counter. There, he banged them down and pushed them across to the storeman.

"Hang on to these for me, will you, Joe?" he said. "I'll come back and finish them later. Once the crap's been cleared away."

He turned, pushed Bole aside and went to take off his survival suit. Bole was ready to explode. If he'd already had a few drinks inside him, he'd have risked giving Baxter a few more slaps, even with Nicholas there, but it wasn't worth disciplinary action from the company. He gave Nicholas a stare to let him know what he thought of his intervention then turned to where Baxter was sitting.

"Keep out o' my way tonight, ya bloody poof," he said, before turning to the others and saying, "Come on. Let's get a few in before we go home."

They all began to troop out to the car park. Most other companies' workers took taxis or buses or were picked up by their wives, but Anstey's people had what they saw as a perk in the form of company cars. It was one of Nicholas's innovations. The men who'd just left for the platform drove the cars into work and the incoming shift took them over for their fortnight. Only supervisors had their own individual cars; the rest had to share, but Nicholas had sold the idea to them as a privilege and a benefit. In fact, maintaining a limited fleet which was permanently used was cheaper than providing transport vouchers and raising wages to the level they were supposed to be at. Nicholas's rise in the organisation had been built on similar schemes in almost every area of costing. He had the knack of finding savings and making them look like hand-outs.

"Couple of jars in the Skean Dhu?" said Bole as he shoved the key into the door of a red Nissan Primera.

"Aye, OK," said Milne and Gellatly, whose status meant they had to share an old Sierra.

They saw Baxter coming out and heading for a green Renault Laguna.

"And if that dickhead comes in," said Bole, loud enough for him to hear, "I'll break his bloody neck."

****

Billy Bryant had managed to get most of his Mars bar inside him but the bits he hadn't were getting spread more and more thinly over his skin, his clothes and the toys he was banging together. Most of his face was smeared with sticky brown daubs, and the crevices in his toy cars, guns and dolls were accumulating a rich bacterial culture medium as he fingered and sucked them. He was lost in his world of noise and colours, temporarily satisfied with the chocolate he'd scoffed and having frequent shouted conversations with bits of plastic.

His mother, Vicky, hardly heard him. She was used to the background he provided and filtered it out with little effort. She hummed along with an old Beyonce hit on Northsound Two as she drew black lines around her eyes, lifting them into feline slants at the corners and trying to recreate the look that had been so effortless not much more than a year ago. She'd changed as soon as she got home but the clothes she'd put on still advertised her trade. The black, leather-look skirt clung across her buttocks and reached just a few inches below them. The shiny pink nylon top had a huge scoop neckline and was tight enough to show not only her breasts and nipples but also the continuous valley created by her bra strap and the little folds of spare flesh down the sides of her ribs and at her waist.

She was singing because tonight's first client was one of her regulars. Normally, it was straight back out onto the street at the mercy of whoever drove along. Her beat was down by the canal with all the others. Waiting there was always a lottery, especially since the competition had been getting so much younger. Vicky knew that she only had maybe two more years left before she'd have to charge so little that it wouldn't be worth it any more. She'd been trying to save to get out into some normal job but the early debts she'd built up were still hanging around her. Luckily, she'd never got into drugs so, unlike most of the girls she shared the pitch with, there was no crushing imperative that would keep her on the streets. But Billy would soon be getting more and more demanding and, when he eventually went to school, she wanted desperately to be able to take him to the gates with the other mothers and, well, just be normal.

Regulars were one of the ways of stepping outside the worst aspects of the job. There was less danger, either of physical assault or of them leaving without paying. And sometimes, like with tonight's guy, they talked a lot and it was like being part of a normal couple. The comfort was as illusory as the exoticism her appearance offered to the punters but it beat standing in the darkness, waiting for God knows what to step out of the mist and ask how much.

Billy was getting fed up with the lack of attention and started to whine. She hardly noticed it but suddenly jumped as the phone rang. She swore because it had made her drag the eyeliner a bit too far. She was ready to give the caller an earful but her mood changed quickly when she heard his voice. It was unmistakable; a reedy, urgent tone which came from the throat rather than the diaphragm. Each sentence was preceded and punctuated with audible intakes of breath as if he were salivating rather than speaking. It was the vocal equivalent of a flasher's Mac.

But it belonged to no dirty old man. Dave McEwan was in his mid thirties and had a way with women. So much so that he'd managed to acquire a stable of twelve of them which he ran in Cairnburgh. He caught them young, sweet and ready for love and either switched them on to dope, crack and the rest or promised them marriage. Whichever route they ended up taking, they found that sex with him began to extend to "favours' for his mates and that the balance between the two soon shifted as the number of his mates grew. Even as they still listened to his promises, most of them knew very early that McEwan was just a pimp but by then, they already owed too many favours, too much money or were well into even worse dependencies. Some were just too afraid to break away.

"How come you're not out working?" he asked.

"How come you're phonin if you thought I would be?" she replied, her tone already guarded.

"Hey, hey," he said. "You're a bit uppity, aren't you? You want to watch your mouth."

"My punter's comin at half seven," said Vicky, already apologising even though she'd done nothing wrong.

"I thought it was half eight."

"Aye, it was. But he phoned. Wanted to change it."

"So he's calling the tune now, is he?"

"No, but—"

"I'm the one who says when you meet him, not him. Getting too picky he is. More trouble than he's worth."

"Sorry, Dave, but he—"

"That's no bloody good, is it? Saying sorry. Just get rid of him quick."

"Why?"

"What d'you mean, why? 'cause I said so."

"Aw, Dave, you know he always wants to talk. He's never in a hurry."

"I don't give a fuck whether he is or not. He takes up too much of your bloody time. You could have two or three in the time you spend with him."

"Not tonight, Dave. Not in this rain."

"You trying to tell me my business?"

Billy's whining had increased in volume. It was harder for her to shut it out.

"Your business?" she said, stressing the first word by way of protest. "I'm the one who's standin out in it."

"Yeah, and you'd better remember why. So get shot of him quick tonight, right?"

"Why?"

"Bloody hell, what is this? Since when do I have to tell you why? Just do it."

Vicky said nothing. She looked at Billy, whose face was now red under the chocolate and who was managing to cry bitterly and yet produce no tears.

"Get him out of the way, get a few tricks in on the street, then get back to the flat by quarter past nine," said McEwan. "You've got another punter. He'll be picking you up outside the flat around twenty past. So get some bloody graft in. And no hanging around with lover boy, right?"

Vicky gave a huge sigh. She wanted to tell him where to shove his punters, all of them, but he'd picked up the tab for her debts and, for a while longer, she belonged to him.

"Right?" said McEwan again.

"I suppose so," she said.

"There's no suppose about it," he said, his thin voice whistling with anger, as he sucked in his short, drenched breaths. "And if you don't like it, we'll maybe get rid of Mr Wonderful altogether."

"OK, OK," said Vicky, irritated now by Billy's noise and by McEwan's threat. "Who's the new guy?"

"Never mind that. He'll be there at twenty past. Make sure you are, too, right?"

"Right," she replied.

It had been a long time since she'd had the right to ask questions or have any say in the trade she got. McEwan knew everything about her and had built her dependency on the loans he'd given her. He was the boss. They both knew it. She was just an item of his stock. Recently, he'd been making noises about her reliability. He didn't like the fact that Billy had to be catered for and that she wasn't on permanent call. Their relationship, if that's what it was, had developed an edge and he was continually testing her. She didn't like some of the things he'd been getting her into and this abrupt order to meet an unscheduled stranger seemed like yet another potential abuse.

"Don't mess it up," he said and she heard the line go dead.

She put the receiver back and went to pick up Billy. He was still cranking out his dry-eyed crying but she had to try to calm him at arm's length rather than with a cuddle. His skin was much too sticky to hold against her outfit.

****

The house belonging to Darren Baigrie and Paul Gallacher was out at the west side of Cairnburgh. It was a semi-detached granite villa with most of its original features intact. The two men were quiet and gave the neighbours nothing to complain about. Baigrie and Gallacher smiled when they met them in the street, said "Hello" and kept their house and garden neat, tidy and altogether worthy of the middle classes amongst which they'd chosen to nest.

It was probably just as well that few of the neighbours had been inside the house. The front room, visible through the window, was relatively restrained. It had lots of paintings on the walls and heavy velvet curtains. Just inside them, a tall sculpture of a naked woman dipping her toe into water seemed to take up a lot of space. Around the walls were chairs and sofas covered in heavy brocade, through which ran thick traceries of gold. It was a room which looked affluent, if a little overstated. Baigrie, who was responsible for it all, had shown no such restraint in their more private quarters. The dining room at the rear was a temple to his many influences. Indian motifs predominated and the ornaments ranged from tiny statues of the Buddha and various elephant gods to a full sized Indian dancer carved out of ebony. Red, gold and black were the principal colours and six small lamps in recessed holders threw a soft light across the linen-covered walls. It was like the waiting room of a brothel with pretensions.

Baigrie was in the kitchen, where rust-coloured Satillo tiles blended with almond worktops. Copper-bottomed pans hung and shone along one wall, dishes and cooking utensils splashed bright primary colours on shelves and in holders and, to provide some drama, the cooker, fridge, freezer, microwave and dishwasher were all the same deep, glossy black.

Baigrie was thirty-one, a good-looking, slimly built man just under six feet tall. He was wearing a turquoise jacket with matching trousers by Dries Van Noten, an outfit which had set him back nearly fourteen hundred pounds on their last visit to Amsterdam. His short hair was startlingly white. His dark, sea-blue eyes seemed to move very slowly over the things he looked at. He took a bottle of orange juice from the fridge and drank from it. As he was putting it back, he heard Gallacher coming downstairs.

"At last," he called. "You're getting worse, you know."

Gallacher came in and stood at the door, his hands outstretched.

"Worth it, though, wasn't it?"

He was four years older than Baigrie, taller and carrying a bit more weight. His dark, curly hair was cropped as closely as his partner's and his face was tanned and lean with deep lines curving down beside and past his lips. He wore black Armani jeans and a black moleskin shirt. Baigrie looked him over.

"No," he said.

Gallacher smiled.

"Now then," he said. "I've just got a couple of things to see to at the office first, then I'm off to the Swan, where I intend to get mildly pissed. Or even paralytic. Wanna come?"

"Sweet-talking bastard," said Baigrie.

Chapter Two

Vicky sometimes found it hard to believe that Baxter enjoyed the sex she gave him. Each time he arrived, they kissed like a normal couple, she gave him a drink, then almost immediately got to work. Sometimes his orgasms were noisy; usually, though, they were short grunting gasps that could just as well be expressing pain as pleasure. The best was when she'd finished. They'd just sit and talk and he'd be as happy to listen to her woes as he was to tell her his own.

Tonight had been slightly different because she'd had to clean up the cuts on his face and be very careful with the bruises on his chest and back. The handle of the van had left a blackish stain over his left kidney. The residual effects of Bole's knee in his groin also made sex a very tender business and her caresses had to be feather-light. He didn't want to talk about what had happened, saying only that he'd been thumped by "a primitive bastard". This had led on to more chat about what he'd been up to offshore on the latest trip. She'd listened and nodded and even asked questions now and then to keep him going. Now, though, it was half past eight and she was beginning to get anxious about getting him away. Dave wanted more tricks before she saw the new guy.

"I've got to be careful," he was saying. "Got to cover my back. I've got it all on file, though. Dates, times, everything. I'm not taking any chances."

Vicky was at the mirror, combing her hair. She said nothing.

"And those stupid buggers'll have it coming soon enough," he went on. "They'll be out on their arses before the New Year. And they'll get bugger-all in the way of severance or redundancy."

He laughed.

"I'll be OK, though. You can stick with me. I'll look after you."

"What're you on about, Ally," she said, flicking at the hair over her forehead.

"You wait. You'll be surprised. Tell you what, what d'you want for Christmas? Go on. Anything you like."

Vicky looked at him. He spread his hands, inviting her to answer.

"Alright, a car," she said.

"No bother," said Baxter. "What sort?"

"I don't know. Any sort. French one. Sexy one."

"It's yours," said Baxter. "We'll get it in … five, six weeks."

"Aye, right," said Vicky, turning back to the mirror. "If I had just one of the things I've been promised, I'd be a rich woman."

"This is straight. I mean it," said Baxter.

Vicky looked at her watch again.

"Look, Ally, I'm sorry, but I promised Mandy I'd fetch Billy early tonight. D'you mind?"

The enthusiasm he'd shown when talking about her present dropped away and she was surprised to see sadness in his face.

"No. It's OK," he said, after a pause. "I've got to see this guy anyway. Might as well get it over with."

"Trouble?" she said.

He shrugged his shoulders and touched his hand to the cuts on his face.

"Might be. Dunno. Just something I need to sort out."

He stood up. She took his jacket from the hook behind the door and helped him into it. It was like dressing Billy.

"I mean it," he said. "About the present."

Vicky nodded.

"I'll remind you," she said. "When are you coming again?"

Baxter shook his head.

"Not sure. Week after next probably. Maybe during the day on Wednesday. Before I go offshore again."

"OK. I'll be here," said Vicky.

As he left, they kissed again, dryly, quickly, like a long-married couple. It was the last time.

****

17

"That bloody tee-shirt he's always wearin," said Bole. "You know. The one about the sky-divin crap."

"Yeah," said Milne, his lids closing slowly and opening again with each word. "'Sky Divers go down faster'."

"Yeah, that's it," said Bole. "Now what the fuck's that mean? I mean, 'goin down' – that's bloody blow-jobs, innit?"

Gellatly laughed.

"What a prat," he said.

"Yeah, so, if Baxter's so proud of goin down fast, it proves it. He's a poof. Right?"

"Right," said Gellatly.

"He can't be," said Milne. "I mean, he's away to have a shag."

"Huh, so he says. D'you believe him?" said Bole.

"No, but some o' the guys says he's got a bird he sees every time he comes home."

"Bloody fairy story, that is," said Bole.

"Fairy's the word," added Gellatly.

All three of them found this very, very funny.

As arranged, they were in Bell's. Gellatly had arrived first, then Milne, who'd paused briefly at home to have sex with his wife. They waited a long time for Bole. It was almost nine o'clock when he came through the pub door, agitated and already well-lubricated. The evidence of Baxter's head-butt was still clear around his nose. It was bruised and his eyes were badly bloodshot.

At first, their conversation turned around some of the things that had happened during the past couple of weeks on the platform. The way they saw it, the folk sitting onshore in front of computer screens knew bugger all about exploration and production, but the guys offshore were sitting on top of pressures and substances that could launch the whole bloody platform higher than a space shuttle if things went wrong.

It was easy for Bole to associate it all with Baxter. As Chief Safety Officer, he was seen to belong to the other side of whatever the argument was. He was constantly holding up their work to make them fill in bits of paper, double-check that they'd isolated systems, put on gloves, hard hats, ear defenders and the like. And, of course, he was the channel through which all the directives came from all the other authorities who knew fuck-all about the job—people like the Health and Safety Executive.

"It's all he's fit for," said Gellatly. "Gettin in the way."

"Poofs offshore are a bloody disaster area," said Bole. "Canna do the work and always thinkin about the arses all around them. Bloody perverts."

Perhaps the most remarkable thing about the conversation that followed was that the three of them never questioned whether homosexuals would find them attractive. All three were carrying too much weight, Bole and Milne were, respectively, bald and very balding and the skin on Gellatly's face looked as if he shaved it with a cheese grater. And yet their assumption was that Baxter and his like would find them irresistible simply because they were male.

"What d'you reckon?" said Bole, at last. "D'you think he'll be down the Swan?"

"Ally?" said Milne.

"Aye."

"Could be."

"Aye," said Bole. "And even if he's not, some of them'll be there."

They looked at each other.

"What d'you think? Worth a trip?" asked Bole.

Milne looked into his glass then drained it.

"Definitely," he said.

****

Carston had had yet another of those days which once again made him wonder whether he'd chosen the right job. It was partly his fault because he'd let the various bits of paper and emails pile up and, as usual, had to force himself to start reducing the backlog. But it wasn't just today. In the past month or so, he'd had to spend more time than he wanted stuck at the Burns Road headquarters of the West Grampian police. Not that there was anything wrong with the place; it was some of the people there that got to him. And he itched to be outside, with space to breathe and think, and preferably with something to exercise his mind a bit more.

Until recently, the station had been like a cosy little club, with just him and his sergeant, Jim Ross, leading the team. But Superintendent Ridley had started poking his nose in more and more and had even drafted in one of his moles to keep tabs on them. Andy Reid was untutored in the ways of CID but still managed to tie himself up in most of the cases that came their way and send reports upstairs to Ridley. Carston's tolerance levels had been severely tested by him ever since he'd arrived.

Going home to Kath was nearly always a pleasure. Sometimes, his preoccupation with a case generated sharp, satirical observations from her about his unsuitability for marriage or indeed any normal relationship, but usually it was a relief to pour a couple of glasses of wine and just relax with her into their habitual mood of rarely taking anything too seriously.

The meal had been as delicious as usual and they were watching the Channel 4 news. There was an item about Japanese tourists in Edinburgh. As Carston watched their tiny Geisha-like steps and listened to the shrill excitement of their chatter, he shook his head and said, "Glad we don't live there."

"Where, Edinburgh?" said Kath.

"No, Japan."

"Why?"

"Well, look at their breasts—they're like ping pong balls hanging from their collar bones."

"Pervert," said Kath.

Suddenly, in close-up on the screen, Joanna Lumley was smiling her enormous smile with its multi-storey teeth. Kath tapped Carston on the thigh.

"Not a word," she warned.

"At least she's got tennis balls."

Kath's response was stifled by the sound of the doorbell. Carston heaved himself up with a "Shit" and went out to the front door. When he opened it, his heart sank. A couple stood smiling broadly at him as if they'd known him for years and were delighted to see him again.

"Good evening, sir. How are you?" said the man.

He was immaculately dressed, with short blonde hair and a smile that made Lumley seem toothless. His colleague had a heart-shaped face. Unfortunately, the heart was upside-down, the point at the top accentuated by her jowls and two ill-advised hair bangs. In stark contrast with her colleague, her clothes didn't fit well. She looked clean and fresh enough but the overall impression she gave was of a trainee bag-lady.

"Lovely evening," she said, pointing at the sky, presumably to help Carston understand the remark.

"Can I help you?" said Carston, although the pamphlets they were holding told him right away why they were there.

"We just wanted a quick word about our Lord Jesus," said the woman, indicating herself, her colleague, then the things they were carrying.

"I'm afraid I don't—" Carston began.

"Don't be afraid," said the woman, shaking her head. "Our Lord washes away fear." Her hand scrubbed an imaginary stain from the air. The urge to tell them just to piss off was strong, but Carston used his alternative strategy.

"Problem is," he said, "speculative abstractions based on a monotheistic premise lose credibility in the face of existential angst. Even Kierkegaard leaves me cold."

He was pleased to see the couple look at one another, their smiles narrowing significantly. Before they could regroup, he pointed down the road.

"Tell you what," he said. "Down there, just around the corner, you'll probably find a guy out in his garden talking to a bush. It's Jimmy McCloy. Take no notice of the bush, he's always talking to it. Needs to know he's got a friend on the street somewhere. He'll be pleased to listen to you."

The couple, sturdy with faith, stood their ground. Luckily for Carston, the phone in the hall started ringing.

"Must go," he said. "Bye. God bless you."

He shut the door and grabbed the handset. It was Sandy Dwyer, the desk sergeant at the station.

"OK, Sandy," said Carston. "What is it?"

"Couple of complaints. Two so far," he said. "Woman reported a fight outside JJ's, the clothes shop in Market Street and we've had a call about an assault in the public lavatory in Provost Sinclair Drive."

"JJ's. That's the gay place, right?"

"Yes. Stays open till ten most nights. And we know all about the lavatory."

"Speak for yourself."

"Looks like queer-bashing," said Dwyer. "I thought you should know. I've sent a car, but it's probably too late. They're away by now."

"OK," said Carston. "Who's there?"

"Spurle and Fraser."

21

"Right. If you pick anybody up, get Reid in," he said. "You'll need a CID sergeant and he needs the experience."

"Right, sir," said Dwyer.

Carston put the phone back and went in the flop down beside Kath again.

"My soul's just been saved," he said.

"Thank God for that," said Kath.

****

The complaints Sandy Dwyer had received were about Bole, Milne and Gellatly. On their way to the Swan, Milne had suggested that a quick detour via a couple of known gay hang-outs might be fruitful. It was. They'd caught two customers leaving a clothes shop and got in a few kicks and punches before the men managed to run away. Then they'd found a lone teenager waiting just inside the tiled Victorian entrance to the public lavatory in Provost Sinclair Drive. There was no way for him to get past them and he'd been thrown down the steps and around the interior, cracking against washbasins and walls, before they eventually stuck his head in one of the pans and flushed water over him again and again. Milne noticed after a while that he was limp and, suddenly afraid that they'd actually killed him, he'd pulled the others away and reminded them that their real target was at the Swan. After a few parting kicks, they staggered back up the steps. The teenager lay still, waiting for the silence that would tell him that he was alone. At last, he got to his feet, found his mobile and called some friends to come and get him.

In an alleyway just two streets away from the Swan, they'd met a couple of men walking along hand in hand. By the time they'd finished, one of the men was bleeding badly from four separate scalp wounds and the other had a fractured left ulna and a dislocated finger.

Opposite the Swan, just minutes later, Jeannie Campbell sat at her window and watched the three separate fights going on in the street below. Milne was grappling with Gallacher and seemed to be losing. Gallacher was drunk, but slightly less incapable and certainly in better condition. He spun Milne into a headlock and was squeezing so tightly that Milne could feel the blood pounding in his ears. Gellatly was holding another man by the hair and punching at his face, bringing the head down to meet each blow. Bole had

22

thrown his opponent, Baigrie, to the ground and was kicking him in the back.

Jeannie had seen other fights. She'd lived in the same house for thirty years and the Swan had never aspired to respectability. Over the years, though, things had become nastier. It used to be stand-up fist fights which degenerated into wrestling bouts as the fighters got tired, but nowadays it was bottles, knives, chains, bits of metal – whatever was handy. She watched as Gallacher dragged Milne to a lamppost and charged his head against it. Milne let his body slump and pulled Gallacher to the pavement. Gellatly's man was on his knees, his hands trying to grab the fist that was still being pistoned into his face. Baigrie tried to roll away from Bole's boots. As he was pushing himself up, Bole ran at him and landed a kick on the right hand side of his face, splintering the bone beside his eye and lacerating his right eyeball. He fell back and lay still. Bole stopped, breathing hard, then managed just two more kicks before he felt his arms grabbed and pinned behind his back. It was the uniformed police sent by Sandy Dwyer in response to Jeannie's call; their arrival probably saved Baigrie's life.

Sandy had logged the call at ten forty-seven and, after phoning Carston, had called through to warn DCs Spurle and Fraser to be ready to question the men being picked up.

"I've called in Sergeant Reid, too," he said.

"Oh good. We'll be alright then," said Fraser, with leaden sarcasm.

He and Spurle were glad that there was going to be some action. It beat the paper-pushing they were having to do.

"It's like a bloody epidemic," Dwyer was saying. "Fourth call there's been since half nine."

"OK, sarge, we'll get set up," said Fraser.

As he started getting out the charge sheets, Fraser filled Spurle in on the few details Dwyer had given him. The fact that Reid would be responsible for any action they took against the people they brought in created conflicting responses. He knew less about CID procedures than they did and his past record suggested that cock-ups were always on the cards. The thought that they could do a night's work only to have Reid send the perpetrators on their way again was irritating but, for Spurle at least, the knowledge that Carston would be more upset than they were by Reid being in charge gave the situation a little spice.

****

It was past eleven and Mandy knew that she'd soon be getting a call. Mandy was Vicky's sister and young Billy always got left with her in the evenings when Vicky was working. If business was good, he sometimes stayed there all night but Vicky always let her know when that was going to happen. Mandy worked part-time in Tesco's and lived on her own in a small council flat. She had two children of her own but hadn't seen her husband for eighteen months and was glad of the extra few quid that Vicky slipped her for baby-sitting.

Billy was asleep in a cot in the corner and, when the phone rang at twenty past eleven, Mandy grabbed it quickly so that the noise wouldn't wake him.

"Mand? Sorry. Just got away. I've got a couple more punters still to do, too. OK if Billy stays?"

"Aye, no bother," said Mandy. "Business good then?"

There was the slightest of pauses.

"Don't know 'bout good. New guy tonight. Wants to be a regular, accordin to Dave. Bastard."

Mandy waited. She knew Vicky would tell her more if she felt like it. Or needed to. She sounded tired tonight, though. In the end, she sketched, in flat, weary tones, the time she'd spent with the new client. He'd taken her to his own place. All the usual domination gear was there. He'd started out by saying he was wicked and needed to be punished, but after she'd flicked a riding crop against his bare thighs once or twice, he'd grabbed it from her and reversed roles. It was the first time that had ever happened. McEwan was good to her in that way. Apart from anything else, he didn't want his merchandise marked. This punter had caught both her and McEwan out and he was too big to stand up to once he'd started.

"I s'pose I was lucky in a way," said Vicky.

"How?" asked Mandy.

"He hasn't marked me too bad. And it doesn't hurt much any more. If I'd tried to stop him, he could've killed me."

"You should get out o' that racket while you're still breathin."

"Yeah, Mand. But he did pay well over the odds."

She'd tried to put a smile into her words as she spoke but the strain in her voice made it obvious that the experience had hurt her mind as well as her body and that this was the sort of regular she could do without.

They talked for nearly a quarter of an hour in the end, alternating details of Vicky's evening with chat about what Billy had got up to. The inconsequentiality of it all soothed away some of Vicky's stress and helped her to set herself up for her next client. She promised to pick Billy up the following afternoon and Mandy rang off and switched her attention straight back to the film she'd been watching on television. It was the story of a wannabe beauty queen somewhere in Montana who had to work the farm and look after her alcoholic father at the same time as she practised deportment and elocution. Things were not looking promising for her and Mandy's sympathies were much more acutely engaged by her than they had been by her sister. The trouble was that Vicky's stories were sometimes a bit bleak. And anyway, they were happening in Cairnburgh, not Montana.

****

Andy Reid was tall and neat. He was in his mid twenties, but looked younger. His black-rimmed designer glasses made his brown eyes seem bigger. His hair was well-cut and gelled carefully into place and he always dressed immaculately. The charcoal Hugo Boss jacket he'd put on to come in when Sergeant Dwyer had called him was only matched in class by the ecru wild silk Kenzo suit of Robbie Findlay, one of the men who'd been arrested. The jacket's dark elegance contrasted with the flamboyance of the Kenzo. It also had the advantage of not being soaked in blood. In fact, each of the five men he'd spoken to had the same problem. Bole, Gellatly and Milne were in jeans and tee-shirts so the brownish stains seemed less obtrusive, but Gallacher and Findlay had gone to some trouble with their outfits and the Kenzo suit was effectively a write-off. Baigrie was at the Bartholomew Memorial hospital, where surgeons were working to rescue his eye.

Reid had tried to be systematic, sifting his way through their claims and counter claims one by one to try to establish the facts. Gallacher and Findlay's version was that they were drinking quietly in the Swan with Baigrie when Bole had come over, picked up Findlay's pint of lager and poured it into his lap. They'd started fighting. It had spilled out onto the street and Bole and his pals had waded into them with fists, feet and bottles. The other three had obviously had much more to drink but insisted that the pint had been knocked over accidentally and that, when they left, they were set upon by Gallacher, Findlay and "all their poofy pals", as Milne put it.

Reid was more inclined to believe Gallacher and Findlay but there were plenty of cuts and bruises on the oil men's faces, too, so the fight had obviously been a two way business. He didn't like the sloppiness of it all. It was just a wee bit of pub brawling, an unimportant event which could bring him little credit and plenty of strife. He could charge them all with assault and breach of the peace under section 2 of the Criminal Justice (Scotland) Act and keep them in the cells overnight for Carston to deal with in the morning, but that would simply confirm Carston's opinion of his uselessness.

He was back with Bole again, the recorder running and Spurle sitting beside him offering little in the way of help. On the table in front of him, he'd laid a page of notes about the other reports of trouble earlier in the evening. There was little doubt that they were connected but he didn't know how to bring them together.

"Where were you before you went to the Swan?" he asked.

"All over the place. Why?"

"Where exactly?"

"Fuck knows. We're just back onshore so we went out for a bevy."

"What time did you leave home?"

"Dunno."

"How'd you get to the pub? Bus? Taxi?"

"Uh-uh. Car."

"Your own?"

"Uh-uh. Company's. Nissan Primera. Blood red. Beauty."

His lids opened and closed slowly and his pointing finger sketched gestures unrelated to his words. He had no idea he was setting himself up for a drunk-driving charge on top of everything else. Spurle could see that it was all a waste of time.

"One of your pals says you were drinking in Bell's earlier," said Reid.

"Uh."

"After that, did you go to Dunstan Street?"

"Could've."

"Provost Sinclair Drive?"

26

"Uh."

"Back Wynd?"

"Uh. All the same, the bastards."

"What d'you mean?"

"Bloody poofs, innit? All the same. Used to be laws against stuff like that."

Spurle leaned forward. He was tired of listening to this.

"You better start concentratin, pal. This doesn't look good for you. We're talkin DUI, breach o' the peace, assault, GBH, wilful damage, all sorts."

Bole turned a ponderous head to let his eyes wander over and around Spurle's face.

"It's a lawyer then, right?" he said.

"What?" said Reid, as the word "lawyer" leapt out at him.

"Need the company's lawyer," said Bole. "Better ring Anstey's."

The name of a major oil company combined with the thought that its lawyers might become involved flashed an alarm in Reid's head. He switched off the recorder. So far, he'd done everything by the book, but if bigger forces were about to be unleashed, he wanted time to think about it all and make sure that nothing could reflect badly on him.

It was well past midnight. Realistically, the chance of getting anyone at the company's offices was slim and the likelihood of their lawyer being either available or interested was even more remote. Reid knew that calling up some company executive in the middle of the night could seem like over-reacting, but he also knew that, if he left any loopholes, Carston would have a field day with him. He needed to cover all the bases and get his own responses logged and timed. He went through to the foyer and got Dwyer to look up Anstey's number and dial it from the front desk. The call was answered by the night security guard. Reid identified himself and asked to speak to someone who could put him in touch with the legal department.

"This time of night?" said the guard.

"Sorry," said Reid.

"I've got two mobiles you could try. They're for emergencies really but, you bein the polis, I s'pose it's OK."

He recited the two numbers. Reid thanked him, rang off and dialled the first. After a longish wait, it was answered by Nicholas and his abrupt "Yes?" made it obvious that the call wasn't appreciated.

When Reid established who he was talking to and realised that he was well up in Anstey's hierarchy, he immediately apologised for disturbing him and suggested that the call was prompted more by concern for the company's reputation than by the legal demands of Bole and the others. His deference seemed to be appreciated by Nicholas, who quickly overcame his initial irritation at being disturbed and listened carefully to Reid's résumé of the evening and the part Anstey's employees had been playing in it.

"I see," he said at last. "Bit tricky for you. S'pose they're in a bit of a state."

"The worse for wear, that's for sure, sir," said Reid.

"Can't it wait till the morning?"

"I'm sorry, sir. If I want to keep them here, I'll have to charge them."

There was a pause as Nicholas considered the options.

"I'll drive over now, then," he said at last. "I'll be there in about half an hour."

He rang off without waiting for a reply and Reid turned his attention to Gallacher and Findlay. So far, they'd been consistent and their testimony certainly seemed to corroborate one another's stories. He went to interview room three, where Fraser was sitting silently with Gallacher. Reid switched on the tape, logged the restart of the interview and sat beside Fraser. Opposite them, Gallacher was weary and nervous. He was frowning and tapping his fingers against his thigh.

"What now?" he said.

"You say you were in the pub from eight o'clock?" said Reid.

Gallacher nodded.

"And the first you saw of them was when the fat one came over to you."

"I don't know for sure. Look, I'm trying to remember." He shook his head. "I think there were two guys pissin against the back of a car."

"What sort of car?"

Gallacher shook his head again.

"What colour?" asked Reid.

Drink and trauma were combining to jangle all Gallacher's memories.

"Wasn't red, was it?" asked Reid.

"Could've been."

"D'you remember the make?"

"They all look the same."

"Could it have been a Nissan Primera?"

Gallacher nodded.

"Could've been."

As they went over the fight details again, Reid was patient and painstaking but nothing was emerging which could help him make up his mind. Gallacher knew nothing about the other three incidents, Reid couldn't see how to connect them and it was becoming clearer all the time that the five people he was holding needed to sober up before any real progress could be made.

****

Vicky was against the wall of the car park. Her punter was sucking at her mouth, his breath rancid and his unshaven chin scratching across her skin. Hard, grunting sounds came from him as his tongue probed round the inside of her mouth and his right hand clutched at her breast. Her skirt was high on her hips and he was thrusting his groin hard against her, making the pain from the weals on her back hotter and sharper as he ground her against the wall.

"Get it out, then," he said, his mouth still gnawing at her lips.

Obediently, her mind miles away, Vicky reached down for his zip and teased and pulled at him to try to speed things up. Despite the cold, she could feel the sweat on him. His grunting breaths came louder and he pulled slightly away from her to give her more room to work. She pushed herself away from the wall, eased him round so that it was he who was leaning against it and dropped to a squat in front of him. As she let her hands and mouth take up the rhythm she knew would soon release her, she was surprised to find her thoughts shifting to Ally Baxter. Even though she used exactly the same techniques with him, there was a tenderness in their contact that made them less transactional. Maybe he meant it. Maybe he would get her a car. Maybe he'd somehow get her away from McEwan and she'd be able to stand at the school gates at half past three waiting for Billy to run out to her.

The punter grabbed her hair and began to thrust hard at her face. He was nearly there. It'd soon be over. Thank God.

****

When Nicholas arrived and introduced himself as Anstey's Finance Director, Reid apologised again and admitted that he was no further advanced than he'd been when they'd talked on the phone.

"It's not just an isolated incident," he said. "There've been three other fights."

"Three?"

Reid outlined the separate incidents.

"I see your difficulty," said Nicholas. "Well, d'you think it'd help if I had a word?"

"I'd be grateful if you did, sir," said Reid.

They went down to the interview rooms, where Nicholas spent upwards of twenty minutes trying to get some sense out of Bole, Milne and Gellatly. He was wasting his time. Bole was aggressive, Gellatly kept scratching at his pock-marked face and opening up old spots and blemishes. Milne was coughing all the time and spitting the results into a brownish hankie which he then stuffed into his pocket. None of them added anything to what Reid already knew.

"Sorry. Not much help, that, was it?" said Nicholas, when they were back in the office.

"No, I'm sorry you've had a wasted journey," said Reid.

The mutual politeness, apparent respect and civilised tone of their exchanges contrasted sharply with the filth and aggression of the people in the interview rooms. It made it much easier for Reid to decide to sweep the problem away. He belonged in cleaner surroundings with more reasonable people. As he said his smiling goodbyes to Nicholas, he felt the satisfaction that a fellow decision-maker had heard and approved of the course of action he'd chosen.

Chapter Three

The following morning, another decision-maker, DCI Carston, was much less accommodating.

"Let them go?" he said, making no attempt to hide his anger. "Let the buggers go? When they've been beating the shit out of people right across town?"

"We don't know that, sir," said Reid, his voice quiet, defensive. "We only picked them up at the Swan. There was no corroboration to say that they'd been at the other places."

"No? So how d'you know there were incidents in..." He looked at a note on his desk, "Dunstan Street, Provost Sinclair Drive and Back Wynd?"

It seemed a strange question to Reid.

"There were reports. People saw fighting."

"And?"

"Well, nothing. They were separate incidents."

"Listen Sergeant. Each one happened in a place known to be favoured by the gay community, right? Each one involved drunks and gays setting about one another. Their timings and locations make it very likely that they were perpetrated by the same people on their way from Bell's to the Swan. There are eye witnesses to each incident."

"But none of them actually linked them, sir. There was no hard evidence which—"

"Moorov's Doctrine," said Carston.

"Sir?"

"Of course, you've never heard of it, have you?"

"No sir."

"Well learn," said Carston. "If you've got a series of similar offences closely related by character, circumstances or time, and you've got different witnesses to each one, you can treat that as corroborative evidence. They're all part of a single course of conduct. You could've charged them on that basis. Pity your knowledge of CID work's so bloody thin, isn't it?"

Reid thought of pointing out that Spurle and Fraser had been with him and said nothing about this doctrine thing but decided to save it until he related the whole incident to Ridley.

"You did know that one of the men assaulted in Mill Road was taken to casualty?" said Carston.

"Yes, sir."

"And that he's still there."

"Well, I hadn't got round to—"

"You haven't got round to anything very much, have you? If he's severely injured, he'll have lawyers in our faces asking why we let the other buggers go."

Reid said nothing.

"And the blood they had all over them, stuff that might give us some useful DNA, that'll all be gone now, won't it? So well done, Reid, you've left us with bugger all."

Some of Carston's anger came from the nature of the offences. They'd had periodic bouts of queer-bashing in Cairnburgh and very few of his colleagues gave them much priority. Often, those responsible were treated with sympathy and almost congratulated on doing something which, according to many, was a perfectly healthy male response to deviance. The consensus seemed to be that gays deserved it.

"Right. Let's see what we can salvage, shall we?" he said. "First, you get Fraser and Spurle back in. I know they were on the late shift but that's tough. You get together all the information you've got, tart it up in your bloody computer and you tell the radio, press and telly that we want to hear from people who saw any of it. Think you can do that?"

"Yes, sir," said Reid.

"Do it then," said Carston, waving a hand to send him away.

As the door closed behind Reid, Carston swore to and at himself. He went to his favourite place at the window and looked out at the usual lines of cars, filling the air with the throb of their exhausts and the beat of their sound systems. Right from the start, he'd over-reacted to Reid. The man had been foisted on them by Ridley, which was enough to justify their suspicions, but Carston's dislike of him was unreasonable. He resented him more for what he represented than for what he was. Carston knew that his own sneers and insults were out of character but there was some sort of need in him to keep on producing them. He wondered why. What was going on? The male menopause or something? Surely not. Kath would have noticed that and said something about it.

He sat down, tried to push thoughts of Reid and the night's assaults out of the way and turned his attention to proformas on staff evaluation. His enthusiasm for that was such that, when Ross came in a few minutes later, he closed the whole bundle and put them into his out tray.

Ross went straight to the coffee machine and started pouring himself a cup. He lifted the pot by way of asking whether Carston wanted any. Carston shook his head and leaned forward to answer the phone which had started ringing. It was the duty sergeant.

"I've got one of the men who were in here last night, sir," he said. "Just come in. Wants a word with somebody. I thought you'd maybe—"

Carston interrupted him.

"Yes, right. Who is it?"

"Name of Gallacher. Says he's in a hurry. On his way to work."

Carston looked at his watch. It was nearly nine thirty. Alright for some.

"Gallacher?" he said, searching through the scribbled notes on his desk.

"Yes, sir."

"OK, John. Give me a couple of minutes. Put him in three. Tell him I'll be right down."

Gallacher was pacing up and down the small room when Carston arrived. He was wearing the standard office workers' gear; dark grey suit, pale shirt, red tie. Its ordinary respectability made the bruising on his face look even worse. Carston introduced himself and offered Gallacher a seat.

"No thanks," he replied. "I'm not staying long."

Carston sat down at the table.

"Won't mind if I do, though, will you? I'm older than you."

Gallacher shot him a quick glance. People found it difficult to tell when Carston was being sarcastic. Quite often he was. Not this time, though.

"You wanted to see me?" he said.

"Depends," said Gallacher. "Are you in charge of last night's stuff?"

"Stuff?" echoed Carston.

Gallacher pointed at the bruising on his face.

"Yes. Stuff," he said, a little anger breaking through. "The pillocks who did this. The pillocks who may have blinded the guy I live with."

His features were tense, his teeth clenched and the tautness of his flesh made the dark creases in his face seem deeper. He was obviously under lots of stress and Carston didn't want to increase it.

"Blinded?" he said, with some genuine concern.

"Yes. I was up at the hospital this morning. They wouldn't let me see him last night after we eventually got away from your sergeant. Darren's probably going to lose the sight of his right eye. Got splinters of bone in it. Thanks to those bastards."

"Mr Gallacher," said Carston. "I appreciate how you feel but no charges were made. There wasn't enough evidence for us to—"

"Go and look at Darren," said Gallacher. "There's your bloody evidence."

"Well, it needs more than that."

Carston could see that Gallacher was ready to interrupt again so he hurried on.

"Maybe if you told me about what happened. If I heard it first hand—"

Gallacher's head was already shaking.

"No," he said. "I've been through it too many times with your lot already. Nothing's changed. Except Darren and I went out for a quiet drink and now he's only got one eye left."

"So why did you come in this morning?" asked Carston.

Gallacher made an obvious effort at controlling his anger.

"Because I'm sober. I'm thinking straight. And, after seeing Darren, I wanted to find out what you were doing about it."

Carston spread his hands, mentally cursing Reid all over again.

"We're still investigating it. If we get some more evidence we'll be able to—"

"Evidence?" said Gallacher. "OK, I'll give you some evidence. Those bastards, the ones who set about us, were animals. And if they're trying to say we started it, let me tell you a bit about Darren. He wears fancy gear, camps it up, but he'd never, ever start a fight. He'd run a mile to avoid one."

Carston nodded his head.

"I believe you, but that's not exactly evidence, is it?" he said. "Unless there's something else you can tell me, something concrete, I don't see what—"

Gallacher stopped his pacing, looked at Carston and sighed.

"No. Par for the course. Only a bit of queer-bashing, isn't it?"

Carston sat back in his chair, controlling the impulse to bark back at him.

"There's no 'only' about it," he said. "If that's what it is, we'll give it the same attention we give to every case of assault. But I can't go to the procurator fiscal with a gut feeling. He wants proof."

It was Gallacher's turn to nod. A slow movement, expressing resignation rather than agreement.

"I understand what you're feeling, Mr Gallacher," said Carston. "As far as I'm concerned, everybody gets the same protection from us. Sexual orientation isn't a factor."

Gallacher smiled.

"It is from where I'm standing," he said.

"Look," said Carston, "we're still on the case. I've got officers out looking for witnesses, and I'm going over the whole incident while it's still fresh."

"Sure," said Gallacher. His tone was sarcastic. "Well, before you decide whether you're going to charge me or Darren, I suggest you go and have a look at him. Maybe it'll help you to concentrate your mind a bit."

"Mr Gallacher," said Carston, patiently. "I am concentrated, believe me. And we will be talking to your friend."

Gallacher gave a little laugh.

"And don't forget," Carston continued, "you're one of the ones we brought in last night, so there may well be more questions for you to answer, too."

Gallacher's face held the smile.

"Yes," he said. "I bet there will."

Carston stood up.

"Well," he said. "Is that all?"

Gallacher looked at him and held his gaze.

"Yes. It probably is," he said at last.

Carston opened the door for him and showed him through to the front desk.

"Will you be late for work?" he asked as they got to the door.

Gallacher looked at his watch.

"Yes," he said, lifting his hand to touch the bruising on his face. "This'll keep them quiet, though."

"Where d'you work?"

"Dillinger's. Offshore contracts office."

Carston remembered the Anstey connection.

"The guys you were fighting with, they work offshore," he said.

"Yes, along with thousands of others."

Carston smiled.

"You don't know them, then?"

"I know they're just back from Falcon Alpha. It's an Anstey platform. We do stuff with them. Project management, contractor liaison, that sort of thing."

"Big client," said Carston.

"One of the biggest," said Gallacher.

Carston held the door open.

"I know it's hard to believe," he said, "but I get as sick and angry about queer-bashing as you do. If that's what it is, I'll deal with it."

Gallacher stopped and looked at him. Carston's sincerity was obvious in his eyes and face.

"OK. Thanks," said Gallacher. He waved a hand to indicate the station and the people in it. "You're outnumbered, though."

"I'm a hard bugger," Carston replied with a smile.

Gallacher nodded and left, his shoulders straightening and his pace picking up as he set off for work.

Back in the office, Ross was at his computer.

"Got half an hour or so, Jim?" asked Carston.

Ross looked up.

"Aye. What's up?"

"That guy. Gallacher. His…" He hesitated, not knowing how to designate Gallacher's partner and feeling a flush of annoyance at his own uncertainty. "pal's at the hospital. He says he's in a bad way. Nobody's talked to him yet. I think it'd be an idea if you did it."

"Right. You want me to go now?"

"Yes. I'm trying to salvage something from Reid's cock-ups. The sooner the better."

****

For a change, McEwan was talking gently to Vicky. It was a bit like the old days. They were in her flat. Billy was in his chair, concentrating hard on yet another Mars bar. Vicky was lying on her bed, naked but for her pants. Beside her sat McEwan, his fingers trailing lightly over the weals across her back and sides. He was a small man. His permatan was much too golden for late October and his thinning hair had bleached highlights. Under the dark arch of his eyebrows, his eyes were hollow and he still affected designer stubble. The light from the single bulb hanging shadeless in the middle of the room accentuated the contrasts in his face and made it look like a panda's. His butter yellow shirt clashed with his black chinos and grey Nubuck boots. On each wrist he wore a thick gold chain..

"I didn't know. Honest," he was saying. "You know that, don't you, darlin?" His voice was quiet, but still had its characteristic, throaty urgency.

Vicky nodded her head against the pillow.

"Sick bastards," he went on. "You're worth more than that. Much more."

His fingers slid up to her neck and began the light massaging that he knew she liked. She moved her shoulders and sank deeper into the bed.

"This is like Inverness," she murmured.

He had no idea what she was talking about.

"That night in the Grange, remember?" she went on. "By the Caledonian Canal. The room with all the flowers and towels and wine."

"Yeah," he said, vaguely remembering a long ago night full of sex and variety.

"You were so … nice then."

"I'm nice, now."

She smiled.

"Aye, but it was … I don't know. Like we was married."

"Christ, Vicky. Wasn't that bad, surely?"

Her smile became a laugh, then a cough. He looked at the marks left by the punter's whip and at the swell of her buttocks inside her white pants. He felt no desire at all. The thought of all the others who'd used her body robbed it of the attractions it had once held. But he knew that he owed her for the beating she'd taken and that fucking her would be seen as a proof that she was more to him than just a source of income. His hands continued their gentle easing of the soft flesh at the top of her back. She sighed contentedly.

"Tell you what," he said. "One good thing's come out of lover boy."

"Lover boy?" she said slowly, her voice far away.

"Yes. Last night. What's his name? Baxter."

"What?"

"He may be a pain in the arse, but he knows his women. He's recommended you to one of his mates."

Vicky lifted her head from the pillow and looked at him. He leaned over, kissed her on the cheek and coaxed her back down again with his probing fingers.

"I got a phone call. Bloke said Baxter had told him about you. He gave him my number. Said you give the best blow-jobs he's ever had. Well, he's right there anyway."

She lifted her left arm and dropped it over his thigh, bending it so that her hand was in his crotch.

"He wants to come here and see you. What d'you think?"

Through her drowsiness, Vicky knew that she was being softened up. Dave never asked what she thought of punters or whether she wanted to meet them. But, just for today, she could pretend.

"Whatever you like, Dave," she said.

"No. Only if you think it's OK," he said.

He leaned and kissed the scars on her back.

"I mean, we don't want any more of this sort of shite. Do we?"

"What if he calls again?"

"Who?"

"The guy who did it."

"I'll tell the bastard what I think of him. Don't worry. He won't be back. I'm not interested in perverts."

The fact that Vicky didn't react to his words showed how effective his gentleness was being. In the time she'd known him, he'd sent people to her whose needs would make interesting entries in any encyclopaedia of sexual excess. She'd had to paint her skin with substances ranging from honey to industrial strength insect repellent, her hands, lips and tongue had explored places and things unfit for consumption or even contemplation, and time and time again, she'd worked hard and long to drag decrepit passions from bodies too old to generate their own.

"So what do you think then?" asked McEwan, sliding his hand underneath her body now to begin the caresses that she knew were the prelude to sex.

"If you think he's OK," she said, lifting her left hip slightly to give him access to her.

"Yeah. No bother. Not this time. He'll be here tonight. About nine. That OK?"

"Mmm," she said, more aware now of his fingers inside her than of his words. Her hand felt for him and started to squeeze and stroke.

McEwan closed his eyes and recalled the French student he'd picked up the previous weekend. She was small, dark and incredibly sexy. Memories of her soft, responsive body soon began to have the effect that Vicky's hand was failing to achieve.

Billy was still only half way through his Mars bar.

****

Jim Ross was thirty-four years old, married with two daughters. His rugby-playing days were over but he'd kept his athleticism and ease of movement. He was tall, slim, with hair which was just a light enough red to stop it being ginger. His pale blue eyes were flicking nervously around the ward as he sat by Baigrie's bed. He felt uncomfortable on two counts. First, he always hated being in hospitals. The sounds and smells of it all seemed foreign. He had never himself had a serious illness and felt slightly ashamed to be so healthy amongst so much suffering. It was like being an intruder in an alien white world.

The second source of discomfort was the fact that he was with Baigrie. Ross was no homophobe, but he was nonetheless uncomfortable in the company of homosexuals. He wanted to treat them in the same way that he treated everyone else but, by simply making the distinction, he was separating them, categorising them.

Whatever the reason, his own shyness or some residual rugby club conditioning, he was usually wary and embarrassed. When he'd confessed as much to his wife, Jean, she'd joked that it was probably because he was a latent homosexual himself. It didn't make him laugh.

What made it worse today was that Baigrie's condition made his sexual preferences totally irrelevant. His face was horribly swollen and bruised and thick bandages were holding a huge pad tight over his right eye. The other eye was very bloodshot and reduced to a slit by the swelling of his left cheek. His arms, lying on the top sheet, were pale, thin and badly discoloured with more bruises.

He was still very drowsy from the effects of the previous night's surgery and the analgesics he'd been given. Ross felt that he was wasting his time.

"Your friend Mr Gallacher came to see us this morning," he said. "He's very concerned about you."

Baigrie smiled weakly.

"Poor Paul," he said. "Always worries. He'll never admit it, but he does."

"How much d'you remember about the fight?"

Baigrie shuddered and turned his head away on the pillow for a moment.

"Nothing," he said quietly. "We were there. Just ... having a wee drink. I think we went outside the pub. Then, next thing I know, I'm here. Hurting all over. And with this ... turban on."

"D'you not remember who else was involved?"

"No. Not really. I think there was a fat guy. Yes, there was. He was the one ... I don't know really, though."

"What about him? The fat guy?"

Tears began to form in the slit which was Baigrie's left eye. As he spoke, one ran down the side of his cheek.

"Oh God. The usual testosterone. Name-calling. Same old stuff."

"Can you remember anything specific? Anything he said? Or did?"

Baigrie closed his eye. More tears ran from it. He lifted his hand and pointed at his face.

"This is what he did."

Ross felt bad at his own insensitivity.

"I'll tell you a secret," Baigrie went on, beckoning Ross towards him with a feeble wave of his hand. Ross leaned nearer.

"I'm gay," whispered Baigrie. "So it'll happen again."

His voice faltered as a small sob broke through his words. Ross looked towards the door, wanting a nurse to come in and tell him it was time to leave.

"I'm sorry, Mr Baigrie," he said. "It's just that we haven't got much in the way of evidence. We need to find out as much as we can from those who were there."

"I can't help you," said Baigrie. "I want to. I really do. But there's nothing. Maybe it'll come back, but—"

"If it does, will you let us know?"

Baigrie nodded. Ross decided to cut his losses. He stood up.

"Don't be surprised if folk don't say much to you," said Baigrie.

"I'm sorry?"

"At the Swan. They don't have much time for you and yours."

Ross nodded, then stood up.

"Anything I can get you before I go?"

Baigrie turned his head so that he could look at Ross with his good eye.

"What did the doctors tell you about my eye?" he asked.

Ross was taken aback.

"Nothing," he said. "I didn't ask them."

Baigrie nodded.

"No. Not your concern, is it? Oh don't worry," he went on when Ross started to protest, "I don't mean you don't care. I mean you've got other priorities. Paul will be here at lunchtime. He'll find out. He'll tell me."

Ross was standing by the bed, no longer wanting to be there and yet unwilling to leave. Baigrie noticed his discomfort.

"I've got lovely eyes, you know," he said, with a smile.

Ross's discomfort deepened.

"Goodbye," said Baigrie, the smile broader now.

Ross nodded down at him.

"Goodbye. I'll look back when you're feeling better."

"You'll be very welcome," said Baigrie. "Are you married?"

Ross frowned slightly at the question.

"Yes," he said.

"Pity," said Baigrie.

****

Ross's discomfort at the hospital was nothing compared with that of Carston in Ridley's office. Their encounters were never friendly and today, Ridley thought he had a legitimate grievance.

"This Moorov doctrine," he was saying. "How do you expect Sergeant Reid to have that sort of information to hand? That's what he's with you for, to learn."

Carston was concentrating hard on being polite. It was difficult faced with the evidence that, once again, Reid had gone running to Ridley to complain.

"Yes, sir," he said.

"Two of your constables were there. They must have known about it. Why didn't they say something?"

"It was Sergeant Reid's show, sir. He has his own methods."

"And?"

"They're not easy to fathom sometimes. DCs Spurle and Fraser probably thought he was taking a different approach. He is a sergeant, after all. It's hardly their place to put him straight."

"On the contrary, Carston. Today, it's cooperation, communication."

He was speaking like a manual again. Carston couldn't resist replying in kind.

"Yes, sir, but they can only be deployed within the constraints of devolved responsibilities and proactive line management procedures."

He left a pause. Ridley looked at him.

"Surely?" Carston added.

Ridley had suffered this sort of thing from Carston many times. The garbage he spoke always managed to sound legitimate and Ridley didn't like to risk being caught out in case it was. He changed tack.

"What's the state of the enquiry?"

"Which one, sir?"

"The queers."

"Ongoing, sir. Difficult to pin things down. Sergeant Reid's omissions have left big gaps."

"Right. Get him working on it as of now."

"Sir?"

"I want him to be a real contributor to your team. That means giving him more responsibility. Treating him with the respect his rank deserves."

"With respect, sir," said Carston, without respect, "his record so far hasn't been all that encouraging."

"Maybe some assistance from you and the others could have helped."

"We've been pretty busy. There hasn't been time to baby-sit."

Ridley tapped the pen he was holding sharply on the pad in front of him.

"Spare me the gibes, Carston. Reid's a good officer. You're lucky I assigned him to you."

"Yes, sir."

"I'm considering transferring Ross."

The suggestion alarmed Carston.

"What for, sir?"

"To make room for some new blood. Break up your cosy little partnerships."

"I thought cooperation and communication were encouraged."

The pen tapped angrily again.

"Not if they get cosy. Not if they restrict productivity."

It was a baseless criticism. "Productivity" had been fine before Reid arrived but Ridley would never acknowledge it.

"So, let's raise Sergeant Reid's profile. Starting with these queers. Let's get it cleared out of the way."

"Yes, sir," said Carston, fighting hard to keep his anger down.

"What's the next step with them?"

"Sergeant Reid's getting a press handout ready to see whether there are any witnesses who haven't yet come forward."

"Good."

"But I wouldn't hold out much hope."

"Oh?"

"No. We've already had a couple of calls. Customers in the Swan who left when the oilmen arrived."

"Ran away, eh?"

"Yes, sir."

"Typical. We spend too much time and public money looking out for them. It's all very well being liberal but it's not cheap. They don't deserve the levels of protection they're getting. They bring it on themselves anyway."

43

"Sir?"

"The way they are. Provocative, blatant. It's no wonder they get attacked."

Carston said nothing. When Spurle and Fraser came out with that sort of comment, he could dismiss it as part of their general lack of development; when it came from a senior officer, it was not only depressing, it somehow consecrated and legitimised the attitude. Carston had had years of it now. He'd learned to live with it, but in recent months, his tolerance had been slipping. Bigotry had seemed inevitable under Thatcher and her heirs and Blair's lot hadn't done much to change things. But he was an optimist and always hoped that, some day, words like compassion could be used openly and with some hope of being understood. On the other hand, maybe he was just having a mid-life crisis. He decided to ask Kath about it that evening.

"...shouldn't they?"

Ridley had been droning on. Carston had no idea what he was being asked about but Ridley's expression showed that he expected him to agree with whatever it was.

"Without a doubt, sir," he said.

Ridley looked sharply at him. Carston's tone hadn't been as emphatic as the words demanded. Carston nodded to himself to indicate that he was still pondering the absolute rightness of Ridley's unheard remark.

"Fine," said Ridley. "Get cracking with Reid, then. Let's see if we can wrap up this queers business. No hanging about, eh?"

"Right, sir," said Carston briskly, already at the office door. "I'll put it in his capable hands. Should be sorted by this evening."

He closed the door behind him before Ridley could react.

****

The dog was black and white. There was a lot of border collie in its breeding but plenty of other things, too. It kept looking back to see if its master was following it. Sometimes it waited for him to get right up beside it, then it cocked its head on one side, raised an eyebrow and managed to create an expression that looked affectionate, vulnerable and inquisitive. It was the sort of doggy look that advertisers of minced offal love to stick on their labels and in their television commercials.

44

Its owner was a man of about sixty. He wore a long tweed coat, a thick scarf and a wide-brimmed black trilby. He turned out of Provost Sinclair Drive into a back lane that led towards his home. The dog foraged ahead, stopped, looked back, then hared off again. It had been out of sight for a long time when the man heard it barking.

"Badger," he shouted. "Stop it!"

The dog took no notice. The man quickened his pace, wanting to stop the noise, aware of the anti-dog sentiment that was becoming more and more prevalent. He reached a smaller lane leading off the first. The dog was darting in and out of a group of dustbins, his tail wagging, his barks coming in bursts of three or four.

"Badger," the man shouted again.

The dog turned to look at him, stood his ground and barked some more.

The man went to drag him away from whatever he'd found. As he drew level with the dustbins, he saw a pair of feet sticking out of a pile of spilt garbage. He bent, grabbed the dog and slipped its leash on, then stepped forward to see the rest of the body. It was partly covered by black plastic bags. The head, though, was visible. When he saw it, the man turned quickly away and was violently sick at the base of the wall.

The dog barked again.

Chapter Four

Over the years, Cairnburgh's councillors had been careful to preserve the town's reputation as one of Aberdeenshire's urban jewels. There had been none of the Sixties' architectural vandalism in the centre and in most of its residential areas, the side streets were lined with trees, many of which had grown into fine specimens which dwarfed the houses around them. As Ross drove him to where the body had been found, Carston looked out at the yellowing leaves, dripping with the October mist, and felt a strange comfort that winter would soon be back. It was a feeling which had grown only in the past couple of years. He still loved the long summer evenings and the days when dawn broke at four o'clock, but, perversely, he also delighted in having to wrap up well before leaving home and sitting inside warm buildings while winds sliced icily against the windows outside.

Walks with Kath in the hills and glens of the Cairngorms and Royal Deeside were pleasures in any of the seasons, and the huge skies of north east Scotland were almost always spread with tones and tints which begged to be painted. Not today, though. Today was one of the grey ones: grey granite, grey pavements, grey skies. Even the leaves took on a muddiness as they lay in the dribbling gutters. There were plenty of them among the rubbish strewn around the bins where the body lay. Seagulls had been at some of the black bags and dragged out vegetables, the leftovers from sticky, brownish meals and lots of soggy cardboard packaging. Sergeant Julie McNeil, the only woman in Carston's team, had been the first to arrive. She'd calmed the man who'd found the body and driven him home, realising that it would make sense to get him away from

46

the scene, which was still causing him lots of distress, before asking for a statement.

Brian McIntosh, the police surgeon, was making his usual slow examination when Carston and Ross ducked under the blue and white tapes. The two of them stepped carefully across to look at the dead man. He had no face and, indeed, his head had been so badly beaten that his skull had lost its shape. He wore a blue tee-shirt with "SKY-DIVERS GO DOWN FASTER" across its front. His jeans and the flesh inside them had been split and slashed around the crotch.

"Are we going to be able to identify him?" asked Carston, as McIntosh looked up and nodded a greeting.

"Alistair Baxter," said the doctor, turning back to his task again. "The SOCO's got his papers. He had his wallet in his back pocket."

"Useful," said Carston.

"So's this," said McIntosh, leaning back so that Carston could look over his shoulder.

McIntosh had pulled the top of the tee-shirt down. Along the top of the chest and up into the throat someone had cut the word "FAGOT".

"Figures," said Carston.

"Why?" asked the doctor.

"Last night, some guys from a rig went out for a bit of gay-bashing. This was on their route."

"Interesting," said McIntosh.

"Why?"

"He worked offshore, too. Had his MAPS card with him. Safety Officer for Anstey Oil."

The name struck Carston and Ross at the same time. They looked at one another. Ross nodded.

"Three of them. Last night," he said.

"Too good to be true," replied Carston.

McIntosh looked up at them.

"What is this? A Masonic ritual?" he asked.

Carston grinned.

"Sorry Brian. No, it's just that three of the gay-bashers worked for the same outfit. Anstey."

McIntosh raised his eyebrows.

"Your lucky day," he said.

He flicked back through the pages of the pad he was using and looked at a note.

"I'm estimating he died between eight and eleven. Does that tie in with what you've already got?"

"Spot on," said Carston. He turned to Ross again. "Kick Reid's arse, Jim. Get him to pull that lot back in. Grab the clothes they were wearing, too."

"Right sir," said Ross, turning away and taking out his mobile.

"And when they get to the station, get them all to write faggot. You never know."

He took a step nearer McIntosh and squatted beside him.

"Anything else, Brian?"

"Well, you can see for yourself what they've done to his head. Lots of mutilation of his rectum and genitals too. In fact, as corpses go, this one's pretty articulate."

"Meaning?"

"None of the cuts has bled much. Except for the skull."

"So he was dead for a while before they did all this," said Carston, gesturing towards the mutilations.

McIntosh pulled at his beard and looked at Carston with a grin.

"You're learning, Jack," he said.

"You're a good teacher," said Carston.

McIntosh looked at the body again.

"Doesn't help with your theory about the gay-bashers, though."

"Why not?"

McIntosh pointed at the area around the body.

"He wasn't killed here."

The two of them stood up. Carston's eyes wandered again over the black bags, the rubbish and the body. He saw what McIntosh meant. There was very little blood around. He nodded slowly and recreated the scene in his mind. It was too calculated to be part of the casual mayhem of gay-bashing, and yet it had all the classic ingredients.

"Bit of misdirection going on then, eh?" he said.

"That's your business. Wherever they killed him, though, it wasn't here. The only thing they did here was the mutilating."

"OK, Brian. Thanks. How busy are you?"

McIntosh smiled, then tutted.

"You'll get it as soon as it's ready," he said.

Carston returned his smile, nodded to him, took a last look around the scene and started back towards the car.

It wasn't raining. There wasn't even much mist about, but the air was drenched and the pavements shone. The leaves spread over them looked like a layer of old, dark, oily skin flaking away from the ground. Carston wiped the moisture off his cheeks and pulled the collar of his black overcoat higher. The time of death, the location and the nature of the man's injuries brought the crime directly within the framework of the previous night's rampage by the people Reid had sent home. McIntosh's comments on self-evident facts seemed to break the connection, but the links were still there. They all worked for Anstey. And even if it wasn't gay-bashing, somebody had certainly tried to make it look as if it was.

Ross was waiting for him beside the car. Carston gestured for him to get in and went to open the passenger door. He looked at the houses on each side as Ross reversed to a wider part of the road.

"Get all these checked, Jim," he said. "Find out when they last used the dustbin area. See if any of them know him. The usual."

"Right, sir," said Ross as he turned out into Provost Sinclair Drive.

"Did you get Reid on it?"

"Aye, sir. The Anstey guys'll probably be at home. The other two'll be working. He's sent the lads out for them."

Carston snorted.

"The bugger ought to be out getting them himself. He's the one who cocked it up." He stopped as thoughts of Reid got between him and the murder. He wasn't in the mood for him. He took out his mobile and hit the button to call the station. When he was put through to the CID room, it was McNeil who answered.

"Julie, how'd you get on with the guy who found the body?"

"OK, sir. He's fine now. Be telling all his pals about it tonight."

"Get anything useful?"

"Not really. He was just walkin the dog and found it."

"OK. Listen, is Supergrass there?"

"Sir?"

"Reid. Is he there?"

"Yes, sir. D'you want to—?"

"No. Definitely not. Tell you what I do want, though. Take him to Aberdeen with you. I want you to go to Anstey's."

"OK, sir. Checking up on the three guys we had in, is it?"

"Better than that. The guy we've just found worked there, too."

He heard a low whistle from her.

"Yes. So get some of the basics. Did they all know each other? Did they drink together? Anything you can."

"Right, sir."

"They just came back onshore. We may need to go out to the platform. Warn them about that, too. Find out when they've got flights going out."

"Right, sir."

"And don't let Reid do anything to bugger things up."

Carston could hear the smile in her voice as she answered, "No, sir."

"Get on to it, Julie. See you later," he said.

As he tucked his mobile away, Ross looked across at him.

"What?" asked Carston, when Ross said nothing and just turned back to look at the road.

Ross shook his head slowly.

"You and Andy Reid," he said. "One of these days, you're going to get yourself into bother because of him."

"Bother? I'll bloody kill him if I get the chance."

****

Gallacher was using his lunch break to visit the hospital. In the cold, grey October light, Baigrie looked even worse than he had earlier. The ripening bruises, the swellings, the bandages and the burst blood vessels in his left eye combined to make him seem incredibly small and fragile against the mounds of white pillows on which he was lying. Gallacher had to work hard to hide his anger.

"You look bloody awful," said Baigrie.

"Not as bad as you," said Gallacher. "Treating you OK, are they?"

Baigrie looked at a nurse sitting at a table at the far end of the ward, next to the door.

"Aye, they're fine." He paused and, without looking at Gallacher, added, "They're not telling me very much, though. About my eye."

"I asked a doctor on the way in," said Gallacher. "They don't know yet. Not till they take off the bandages."

"Oh. Right," said Baigrie, his voice quiet, flattened by his anxiety and the need for reassurance.

"Have the police been?" asked Gallacher.

Baigrie smiled and nodded.

"A sergeant. Not a bad guy."

"What did you tell him?"

"Nothing. Nothing useful anyway. I still don't know what happened. Just that fat bastard. And before that. The other one. In the tee-shirt—" He stopped as the memories brought back his tears.

Gallacher took a tissue from the box beside the bed and dabbed gently at Baigrie's left cheek. Baigrie lifted his hand and stroked his soft fingers over Gallacher's. He looked at him and smiled.

"Watch it," he said, his head turning to indicate the man in the next bed. Gallacher turned to look at him too. He was red-faced with short, yellowish hair combed straight back. His eyes met Gallacher's and Gallacher knew immediately what Baigrie meant.

"Good morning," Gallacher said, with a wide smile. "Are you well?"

The man muttered something inaudible but unmistakably disapproving and turned his back on them.

"The bobby who was here told me you'd been in to see them," said Baigrie. "What for?"

"Trying to get them to get their fingers out," said Gallacher. "They let those bastards go last night. No evidence. Bloody rubbish."

Baigrie was shaking his head.

"Christ, Paul, you still surprise me," he said.

"Why?"

"What sort of evidence d'you want them to find? It's just another punch-up, isn't it? I bet you gave as much as you got last night."

Gallacher's anger flashed, in spite of himself.

"Don't start, Darren. I'm not just standing back from that sort of shite."

Baigrie reached his hand out to tap gently on Gallacher's forearm.

"I know, I know. But they'll find as much evidence against you as they do against them. Probably more. You know that, don't you?"

Gallacher sighed deeply, pushing his anger away again.

"You know your trouble?" he said.

"What?"

"You're too bloody reasonable altogether. What's it like being a model citizen?"

"I don't think you'll ever know," said Baigrie.

There was no point in talking about the police or the previous night any more. It only served to reopen Baigrie's anxieties and relight the fuse of Gallacher's anger. Instead, they both tried to lighten the mood, Gallacher describing the reactions and comments of the people at work when they saw his bruises and Baigrie outlining a theory he'd been developing which equated hospital efficiency with the relative thickness of nurses' tights.

"It's true," he said, his face and body conveying the fact that he seemed to be serious. "The matron, or head nurse or whoever she is. Big woman. Huge. And she's got these things like army blankets wrapped round her legs. God knows what it must be like further up. You don't only see her coming, you hear her coming." He made a regular, scraping noise in his throat, like marching feet. "Thighs rubbing together. Enough friction to boil an egg. It's a question of energy."

"What is?"

Baigrie half-turned on the pillows, eager to make his point clear.

"She's wasting half of hers just dragging her legs past one another."

As nurses came and went, Gallacher and Baigrie talked themselves back into the comfort of their relationship, mutely reassuring one another that the assault at the Swan had done no fundamental harm and that, once again, they'd proved to be survivors. At one point, the red-faced man asked them to keep the noise down. Gallacher looked at him, then got up slowly, took the two steps to the side of his bed and put his hand to the man's neck.

"Want me to snap your head off, granddad?" he said, his tone low and chill.

The man looked into his eyes and believed that he meant it. He pushed Gallacher's hand away and once more turned his back to them. Gallacher patted him on the shoulder and tucked his blanket in, pushing his hand deliberately against the man's back and sliding it downwards.

"There. Comfy now?" he said.

The man didn't move.

"Enjoy that, did you?" asked Baigrie, when Gallacher sat down beside his bed again.

"Incredible," said Gallacher.

"Gay necrophilia," mused Baigrie. "Contradiction in terms, I'd've thought."

"Don't you believe it," said Gallacher.

He was pleased that he'd come. Baigrie's mood was so much better than it had been earlier. Ever since they'd first met, the four year age difference had seemed more like twenty. Baigrie's need to be loved was overwhelming. From the start, he'd done things to test Gallacher's constancy, perversely trying to prove that trust was always betrayed. He'd swing from contentment to despair at the slightest provocation and it had taken several years for him to believe that Gallacher really did love him and that he did have a basis on which to build some security. By then, he was in his late twenties and it was the first time in his life that he'd felt safe. He never liked to spend too much time separated from Gallacher, who, in turn, was flattered by the unqualified faith being invested in him and constantly entertained by Baigrie's sometimes outrageous inspirations. He was happy to protect Baigrie and equally happy to know how much he was loved.

It was just when he was beginning to regret that he'd have to go back to work that the cocoon they'd managed to weave around them in the ward was comprehensively destroyed by the arrival of DCs Fraser and Thom. They'd checked at Dillinger's and been told where they'd find Gallacher. The nurse sitting at the table had pointed out Baigrie's bed to them and they'd strode up the ward, looking revoltingly robust amongst all the paraphernalia of weakness it contained.

"Mr Gallacher?" said Fraser.

"Yes."

"We'd like you to come to the station with us. Few more questions. About last night."

Gallacher looked at Baigrie. His expression showed that all the good work of the visit had been undone. The anxiety and fear were back. Gallacher stood up and looked at Fraser. He was about the same height but seemed to have only half the policeman's muscles.

"What for? I told you everything. There's nothing else," he said.

"Only a body," said Fraser.

Baigrie made a noise in the back of his throat and put his left hand up to his mouth.

"What d'you mean?" asked Gallacher.

"Let's go to the station, eh? Talk about it there."

"Have I got a choice?"

"No," said Fraser.

Gallacher heard a laugh. It was the red-faced man, who'd listened to everything. His first impulse was to grab him and shake him, even with the two constables there. But his concern was for Baigrie, who was having difficulty handling the news. Gallacher took a long, deep breath and stepped across to the other bed again.

"It's alright, Dennis," he said to the man. "They don't know about you. And we won't tell them, darling."

The smile vanished from the man's face.

"Who's Dennis?" he asked.

Gallacher turned back to the policemen.

"Sad, isn't it?" he said. "Bad enough when they're like Darren and me, out in the open. But when they have to book upstairs rooms in the Swan, like Dennis here, and go in and out the back door, it's bloody tragic."

He was rewarded with a smile on Baigrie's face. He leaned over and kissed him on the lips.

Fraser and Thom both turned away

"See you soon," said Gallacher. "There's nothing to worry about."

"Come back as soon as you can," said Baigrie, grabbing his wrist.

Gallacher nodded and stood up. Fraser and Thom were looking, with considerable distaste, at the red-faced man.

"They should all be locked up," said the man.

"Bloody pervert," Fraser said to him.

"Ready, gentlemen?" said Gallacher.

He walked away with the two policemen.

"Hey, I'm not gay," the man in the bed shouted after them.

"Yes he is," shouted Baigrie.

****

54

McNeil and Reid made a fine-looking couple. He was as neat as ever in an Agnès B jacket and blue-tinted Lacoste glasses, she wore a navy blue suit over a cream-coloured shirt that looked cool enough to be silk. Her face was pale and framed by cropped red hair. Its peculiar attraction lay in the fact that her features were perfectly regular until she smiled, when her lips rose higher on the right to create a lop-sided grin. It looked like a come-on, but wasn't. She was five-feet-six tall, with small, high breasts. Her shape from the waist down was so right that it always brought small pleasures to the men in the squad as they watched her moving about the office.

Even though Reid had been a sergeant longer than she had, her greater experience of CID work gave her the edge on their trip to Aberdeen. Carston had implicitly put her in charge of the visit to Anstey's and Reid was content to stand back and let her take the lead.

As Assistant Director of Human Resources, Hamer was the first point of contact for anything involving the company's personnel. They were sitting on two low, black leather chairs in his office. He'd taken refuge behind his desk, a long slim affair on which files, trays and the usual desktop gadgets were stacked with seeming care and precision. He was wearing a cashmere Aquascutum jacket which drooped on his narrow shoulders. Reid, who took great care with his own wardrobe, wondered why someone with such an unprepossessing shape bothered to drape it with such expensive items.

Nicholas had been called in to join them and greeted Reid like an old acquaintance. McNeil noticed, then dismissed, the fact that Reid's reaction was to transform himself instantly into Uriah Heep. As he shook hands with Nicholas, he bowed slightly and expressed what appeared to be untrammelled delight at seeing him again.

He sat quietly as McNeil filled in the details of the investigation, interrupting her only twice when she touched on things he and Nicholas had already spoken of in Cairnburgh the night before. Hamer listened, making notes on a pad, asking questions and shaking his head at each new revelation. When McNeil described the various incidents, all of them involving gays, he made disapproving noises but, rather than deplore the activities of Bole and the others, he seemed more concerned with the effect it might all have on the public's perception of Anstey Oil. However, when she described, in unflinching detail, the state of Baxter's body, he paled and fell silent again.

"Perhaps I should have got Michael out of bed after all," said Nicholas.

Hamer looked across at him. Michael Long was the company's lawyer.

"Bole asked for him last night," explained Nicholas. "That's why the sergeant phoned me. Thought we ought to know about it."

Reid smiled and nodded.

"They weren't exactly a good advert for Anstey," he said. "Could have been a bit embarrassing for you."

"Very thoughtful," said Hamer.

"Still, it's gone beyond that now, hasn't it?" said McNeil, annoyed that Reid had taken the pace out of the interview. "We're dealing with murder, not a company promo."

"And you think it's connected with what went on last night?" asked Nicholas.

"That's what we're trying to find out, sir," said McNeil. "But it does seem quite a coincidence that your men were in all those places, that Mr Baxter was killed there, and that he—"

"He wasn't killed there," Reid interrupted, stressing the "there". "The murder was somewhere else. He was just dumped there."

McNeil couldn't believe it. Reid wasn't thick and yet he had no instinct whatsoever for correct CID procedures. If she didn't stop him, he'd blab out all the evidence they had so far and it'd be in the evening papers.

"When did you last see Mr Baxter?" she asked, swallowing her anger and forcing herself to be businesslike.

"Yesterday evening," said Nicholas. "They all came ashore."

"Everything normal, was it? No sign of anything … out of the ordinary?"

Nicholas shook his head. Hamer looked at him.

"There was a fight," he said.

"Oh yes," said Nicholas.

"A fight?"

Hamer leaned forward in his chair and straightened the pad on which he'd been writing.

"Yes," he said. "Bole and Baxter."

"It was nothing," said Nicholas. "They were always having a go at Ally. It's happened before. It's got nothing to do with last night. Can't have."

"What do you mean, 'Having a go' at him?" asked McNeil.

"He's a Safety Officer," Nicholas began.

"A good one, too," said Hamer.

"So?"

"When they do their job properly … it makes them unpopular sometimes."

"Why?"

"The other men just want to get on with the job. Some of them don't see the need for the forms they have to fill in and sign. Sometimes their work's stopped while the safety team test things. It just … builds up, I suppose."

"I thought safety was a priority nowadays."

"It is. Absolutely," said Hamer, so quickly that it was obviously a conditioned reflex. "The men know it, too."

"Depends how you do it, though," said Nicholas. "You see, Ally already had a reputation. The other guys tease him … used to tease him about being gay."

"Was he?"

Nicholas shrugged.

"How should we know?" he said. "Personally, I don't think so. But it made it worse for him."

"Yes, and his man-management skills were sorely lacking," added Hamer. "I don't think he ever tried to be diplomatic."

"So you're saying he had some enemies," suggested McNeil.

"No. Certainly not. Not enemies. That's much too strong."

Nicholas smiled.

"You can't work offshore if you've got enemies there," he said.

"But people 'had a go' at him," insisted McNeil.

"They took the mickey, that's all. The usual sort of thing. Happens all the time."

McNeil was aware that they were getting lots of information and wished she was working with Fraser or one of the others. Even Spurle. Reid was sitting quietly, a smile on his face most of the time, listening to the two men and nodding as if he agreed with everything they said. No wonder Carston resented having him in the team.

57

She finished making a note and took them back to the fight between Baxter and Bole, asking them exactly what had happened and what was said. They seemed anxious to help but offered only vague, general versions of the incident. Each of them seemed keen to play down its significance. Neither of them mentioned that Bole had threatened to kill Baxter.

"So it all fizzled out and they left separately," said McNeil at last.

"I'm not sure about it fizzling out," said Hamer. "But it certainly stopped. And yes, they left."

"Not right away, Dick," said Nicholas.

Hamer looked at him.

"Baxter came back in," Nicholas went on. "He just went out to his car then came back to finish his paperwork."

Hamer was already nodding.

"Of course," he said. "But, as the sergeant said, they did leave separately."

"So what time was all this?" asked McNeil.

"About half past six," said Nicholas. "Baxter went soon after the others. Then he came back in more or less right away. I think he just waited till Bole and the rest had gone."

"Who else was here?"

"The two of us and Joe Taggart, the storeman," said Hamer.

"Did Mr Baxter stay long?"

"No. Just filled in some of his reports and left. Couldn't have been here more than fifteen minutes."

"Some of his reports?" said McNeil, stressing the first word.

"He had a date," said Nicholas. He smiled before adding, "with a woman. Said he'd be back later to do the rest. After he'd seen her."

McNeil looked up at him. He shook his head and pushed back his thick, black hair.

"That's what he told us," he went on. "Don't know if it was true."

"What d'you mean?" asked McNeil.

Nicholas looked at her and spread his hands to indicate that the reason was obvious.

"So you do think he was gay," she said.

"Does it matter?" asked Hamer.

"I think when we're dealing with a murder which ties in with queer-bashing, it's fair to assume it might," said McNeil, only just managing to keep some respect in her voice. These people were so concerned about the bloody company that they couldn't see the value of the information they had to give. Or maybe they just preferred not to.

"Did he come back?" she asked.

"He must have," said Hamer. "The reports were all filled in and processed on Thursday morning."

"Any idea who this woman was?" said McNeil.

Hamer shook his head at once. Nicholas frowned a little as if he was trying to remember something.

"No, but I think she was maybe a prostitute."

Hamer looked sharply at him.

"Why d'you say that?" asked McNeil.

"Just one or two things he said. I may be wrong."

"And he left here at six forty-five to meet her."

Nicholas and Hamer looked at one another and nodded.

"About that, yes," said Hamer. "I left soon after. I was home by seven thirty."

"And you, sir?" asked McNeil, looking at Nicholas.

"I didn't hang around either. Had to check the changeover details with Joe Taggart. We left around eight, I'd say."

"And then I disturbed you at home," said Reid.

He'd been silent for so long that his voice surprised all of them. Nicholas flashed him a smile.

"In the event, I'm glad you did," he said. "It was bad enough when it was just assault, but now—"

"Yes, it's just as well that the company's been involved from the start, isn't it?" said Reid.

"Yes," said Hamer. "And, of course, we'll cooperate at every step."

"Good," said McNeil, pushing aside the feeling that she'd stepped into a feelgood brochure and looking to regain control. "Now, do Mr Baxter and the others have lockers or cupboards here?"

"Yes. Everybody does."

"Right. Before we go, we'll lock and seal them and I'll arrange for a squad to come and clear them. We'll want all the survival suits the men on that Wednesday flight were wearing, too."

Hamer made a note on his pad. McNeil didn't wait for the question he was obviously about to ask.

"And we'll need to visit the platform. The one Mr Baxter worked on. Can that be arranged?"

Hamer looked at Nicholas, who thought for a moment, then nodded.

"Any idea when you'll want to go?" he asked.

"Soon as possible," said McNeil.

Nicholas took out a pocket diary and jotted a note in it.

"Leave it with me," he said.

"And we'll need to talk to your workforce."

Nicholas gestured towards Hamer.

"Over to you, Dick."

Hamer sighed and shook his head.

"Which ones?" he said.

"Anybody who had any dealings with Mr Baxter. Maybe some of the others, too."

"When you're ready, liaise with me directly. I'll arrange it."

It was dark outside and the thought of a forty minute journey with Reid was depressing. McNeil knew that the information they'd collected would be a solid basis for more investigations and decided to leave Hamer and Nicholas while they were still being cooperative. She stood up. The three men did the same.

"Well, I'm sorry about all this trouble, gentlemen," she said, "and I'm very grateful that you've been so understanding and so helpful. I'm sure DCI Carston will be in touch very soon."

She waited while Reid told Nicholas how nice it was to have met him again and Hamer how much their meeting had delighted him. As she drove away and turned south to pick up the main road to Banchory, Reid started talking about Anstey and the successes it had had in the past five years.

"Sets the benchmark for the rest," he was saying. "Quality control procedures, tight budgets. It's a model. There was an article in the Financial Times about the Falcon field which—"

McNeil listened, unable to understand how he could switch his attention off their case and onto the promotional trappings of just another oil company without a flicker.

"D'you know how many barrels of oil they exported in the first year of operation?" he said.

"Andy," she said. "I don't care. Shut up."

Chapter Five

Spurle had had plenty of bad days in the cells and interview rooms at the station. His abrasive machismo had provoked drunks and hard men to lose the place and attack him. His Precambrian attitudes to issues from politics to marriage frequently drew scorn and insults, even from his colleagues. And his constantly renewed need to let those who outranked him know that he was at least their equal led to regular, embarrassing bollockings from the authorities he questioned. Today, though, he was more than usually furious.

"Like a bloody knockin shop here," he said as he came into the squad room to fetch more interview sheets. "Pooves everywhere. I'd lock 'em all up and throw away the key."

"That's the way, Spurley," said Fraser. "Hang the bastards, eh?"

"Alright for you. You're not havin to interview the sods. I'm chokin wi' all the perfume down there."

As usual, there was no substance to his complaint. As well as Bole, Gellatly, Milne, Findlay and Gallacher, there were five other men in the interview rooms. They'd come forward in response to a request for information that had been broadcast on BBC Radio Scotland's news bulletins during the afternoon. One of them had been in the Swan the previous night and seen some of the fight. It was he who'd sparked Spurle's initial reaction. He was wearing a black satin stretch jacket by Helmut Lang over a pale yellow Gucci and Prada shirt and, before coming to the station, he'd dabbed on a hint of Yohji, from Yohji Yamamoto.

It was the combination of this light fragrance and the unsuitability of the outfit for a Thursday afternoon that had reminded Spurle that he was being forced to spend time with gays. The questions he asked and the manner of their delivery were far from objective and only succeeded in making the interviewees clam up or give answers designed to increase his discomfort even further.

He was muttering "bastards" over and over to himself as he looked for the interview sheets and didn't hear Carston come in through the door which he'd left open.

"Problems, Spurle?" asked Carston.

Spurle didn't bother to turn and look at him.

"No," he said.

"No, sir," snapped Carston, surprising both Spurle and Fraser.

As Spurle turned to look at him, he saw Carston's finger pointing at him. It was shaking.

"You've done enough damage for one day. Don't add to it or I'll kick your arse back on the beat. Fraser, let's go."

He started back downstairs without waiting for a reaction.

"Jumped up pillock," said Spurle, leaning to search in the filing cabinet again.

Fraser got up and, as he passed him, he trailed his hand lightly over his bum. Spurle straightened again as if he'd been electrified.

"Fuck off," he shouted, a blush already in his face.

"You love it, really," said Fraser, with a laugh.

He caught up with Carston but made no attempt to say anything. Carston was still seething with whatever had triggered his comment to Spurle. They were on their way to interview room four, where Gallacher was waiting for them. Carston had already spoken to Bole, Milne and Gellatly and heard the same claims of innocence they'd made the night before. When he'd told them that it wasn't just the fight he was asking about, but murder, their protests lost some of their anger and took on more of a whine. Bole in particular had become restless and his aggressive gestures had given way to smaller, more nervous movements.

The revelation that the victim was Baxter put them all in a complete turmoil. Their answers lost coherence, their stories were revisited and all sorts of new timings and locations were produced. The confusion this caused was becoming a characteristic of the case. Each new discovery bound them all more closely together and yet seemed too convenient to be a reliable explanation. Carston was careful to let them keep all their options open but he realised that their drunkenness the previous evening had muddied their recollections. On top of that, they'd used the time they'd had between their release and being picked up again to try to tighten their version of events. Another triumph for Reid.

Carston shuddered as the name came into his head.

"You got them all to write 'faggot' when they came in?" he asked Fraser, as they walked along.

"Yes, sir," said Fraser.

"And did they all spell it correctly?"

Fraser hesitated.

"With a double 'g'," said Carston.

"Yes, sir. I think so," said Fraser.

Carston nodded as they came to the door of room four.

"OK," he said. "Let's see if we can get any sense here then."

Gallacher was pacing up and down, watched warily by the uniformed constable who was standing inside the door. Carston nodded his head at the constable, who was glad to get a break. As the door closed, Gallacher stopped and looked at Carston.

"Well?" he said.

Carston gestured towards one of the chairs at the table.

"Sit down," he said. It was only just short of being an order.

After a small hesitation, Gallacher did so. Carston and Fraser sat opposite him.

"Shall I switch on?" asked Carston, pointing to the tape recorder beside them. "Or is there anything you'd like to say off the record before we start?"

"Record it. All of it," said Gallacher. "I've got nothing to hide. What I do want to know is why the bloody hell am I back here?"

Carston switched on the tape, identified himself and the others and sat back in his chair.

"D'you know a man called Alistair Baxter?" he asked.

Gallacher was still for a moment, then he shook his head. Carston pointed at the recorder again.

"No," said Gallacher.

"Are you sure?"

"Positive."

"He used to go down the Swan," said Fraser.

Gallacher looked at him.

"And?" he said

Carston was irritated by Fraser's question.

"OK," he said. "We'll get back to Mr Baxter in a moment. Let's talk about last night."

Gallacher's reaction showed what he thought of going through the same things all over again.

"For Christ's sake, I've said it all," he said wearily.

"Not to me. I want to make sure it's straight."

He turned over some sheets of paper which he'd brought with him, lifted one out and laid it apart from the others.

"This is the statement you made. I'd just like to go over some of it."

Gallacher heaved a great sigh, which conveyed exactly what he thought of the idea. Carston smiled humourlessly and asked a series of simple, direct questions based on the typescript in front of him. Gallacher's answers were short, even abrupt, but most of them confirmed the story he'd already told. The whole interview was easy, businesslike and showed Gallacher in a good light. It had the effect of soothing away Carston's anger as it progressed.

There was a clear contrast between Gallacher's evidence and that of Bole and the others. It wasn't just that his version of events was radically different from theirs, it was the details he supplied. For Bole, the people he'd been fighting with were undifferentiated poofs; Gallacher, though, remembered faces, clothes, words and expressions that were used, and things like the pattern of the ring one of his attackers had been wearing. If it ever came to court, he'd be a good witness, whether he was in the dock or not.

Things changed suddenly when they got to the point where Gallacher and Baigrie left the pub together and first saw the three oilmen.

"Hang on. I thought you said one of them came into the pub," said Carston.

Gallacher sighed again.

"I was pissed," he said. "I'm trying to remember, OK?"

"Go on," said Carston.

"Right."

Gallacher wrinkled his brow, put his head back and searched his memories again.

"We went out and saw two guys pissing against the back of a car."

"Would you recognise them again?"

"They're the guys who attacked us."

"Go on."

"Then ... the fat one got out of the car—"

Carston interrupted him.

"I thought he was in the pub. That's what you said last night."

"Did I? I don't know. I think he was in the car."

Carston looked at the notes.

"Shit," he said, but so low that the recorder didn't pick it up. He looked at Gallacher again.

"D'you remember what sort of car it was?"

"Er… Red one, I think. Yeah. Red one. Japanese job. Toyota, Nissan, something like that."

As he spoke, Carston was nodding.

"Right," he said. "Let's leave that for the moment. What were you doing before you went to the Swan?"

"I was at home."

"Anybody else there?"

"Yes. Darren. We got home from work just before six and left for the Swan just as the news was starting. Nine o'clock."

"And you don't know Alistair Baxter?"

"Never heard of him."

It was Carston's turn to sigh.

"Who is he?" asked Gallacher.

"Was," said Carston. "He's dead. Killed last night. Dumped with the garbage."

"Why're you asking me about him?" asked Gallacher after a slight pause.

Carston stood up.

"All part of the same investigation, Mr Gallacher."

"Can't be. There was only me, Darren and Robbie Findlay involved. And the three lunatics."

Carston thought about this, then gave a small nod, looked at his watch, recorded the fact that the interview was over and switched off the machine. When he and Fraser were outside the door, he swore loudly and stalked back up to the squad room. He phoned through to the front desk and told Sandy Dwyer to get his team together and send them up for a briefing. Fraser sat at his desk and buried his head in the papers he'd been checking when Carston had first arrived.

Carston went through to his own office, looked out of the window and tried to calm himself by watching the cars streaming past and the comings and goings of Cairnburghers. It was true; he was much quicker tempered than he used to be. Ross's wife had once called him the coolest member of the squad and Kath had often been infuriated by his reluctance to get worked up about things. But the slow, laid-back individual of those days seemed to have been replaced by a crotchety old bugger with the shortest of fuses. Was it middle age? He really must ask Kath.

The door opened and Ross came in.

"Any good?" asked Carston.

Ross had been talking to the people who'd responded to the broadcast. He shook his head.

"None of them's got anything definite. Not sure they'd be able to identify anybody. They're all willing but not much good."

"It's so bloody sloppy, Jim," said Carston. "And our lot are making it worse."

"How?" said Ross.

Carston waved a hand.

"I don't want to think about it now. I'll say it at the briefing. Are they there yet?"

"Still waiting for Julie, Andy, Bellman and Spurle."

Carston sat at his desk. Ross logged on to his laptop.

"D'you think I've changed, Jim?" asked Carston.

"How?"

Carston shrugged.

"I don't know. More ratty. Older."

Ross smiled.

"We're all older."

"Yeah, but seriously. Have I?"

Ross gave it some thought.

"Maybe. Hard to say. You let Andy get up your nose a bit."

Carston felt the urge to say that that was entirely justified but he held back.

"Why're you asking anyway?" said Ross.

"Dunno. The job seems harder somehow."

"Harder?"

"Yeah. I used to be more … sure of it. Right and wrong."

"That's a hard one," said Ross.

"Yeah. Sometimes I just feel like a crabby old bastard."

"Well, that hasn't changed."

Carston smiled and shook himself free of the thought. "How are you managing with these gays?"

"It's hard." Ross said, and went on quickly to forestall the joke he knew Carston would make. "In fact, it's like what you just said—

about right and wrong. With these guys, I can't help myself. I feel awkward."

"Yeah. Me, too," said Carston. "It's going to get in the way if we're not careful."

Ross nodded his agreement.

"Maybe I could try a bit of research," said Carston.

"That sounds a bit dodgy," said Ross.

"Not that sort. No, I mean Kath's friend, Dot. The one who runs the Warehouse."

"What about her?"

"We're supposed to be going there on Saturday. Half of them are bent. I could get the inside track. Talk to them."

"Get the feel of things," offered Ross.

Carston laughed and reached for the phone.

"You rugby players," he said.

He dialled and Kath answered almost at once.

"Hullo?"

Carston smiled.

"This is an obscene phone call," he said.

Ross looked up. Carston winked at him.

"You should've reversed the charges," said Kath. "I wouldn't mind paying for a bit of obscenity from you. It's been so long."

"Don't nag. I'm phoning aren't I?"

"Yes. Well, what do you want?"

"Nothing. Just a chat."

There was a definite, deliberate, expressive silence.

"Well? Go on then. Chat."

"Alright. You win. I don't know how to chat."

"Well, thanks for ringing. Bye."

Carston smiled.

"Before you go," he said. "This play at Dot's place."

"Yes."

"What's it about?"

"It's by a Welshman."

"What's it called?"

"Go Gentle."

"Go Gentle? Sex, is it then? As in 'Be gentle with me, darling'?"

"No, death. As in 'Do not go gentle into that good night'. Dylan Thomas."

"So it's about dying?"

"Might be. It's experimental."

"Bloody hell. An experimental play about death. And it's Welsh! I must love you a helluva lot."

"You do."

"That's true. Any chance of us talking to the actors before or afterwards?"

"Is this you being satirical?"

"No, I mean it. We've … we've got this case … The gay guys. I wanted to—"

"Come out?"

"No. I don't know, get some ideas. Try to … I don't know."

"So you want to meet the cast?"

"I can't believe I'm saying this, but yes."

"OK. You've remembered that I'm going there tonight to take some photos."

"Yes. I might be late, though."

"I'll leave your dinner in the oven. It's the stuff marked 'For external use only'."

"My favourite. See you later."

"Bye, Jack."

"Bye love."

Carston put the receiver back.

"I don't know why she stays with you," said Ross.

"My sex appeal," said Carston.

The two of them smiled but Ross's words had an edge of truth for both of them. In Carston's case, the joking had helped him out of his mood but the thought of being kept away from home by the new workload was unpleasant. He loved spending time with Kath. Of all the people he knew, she was not only the one he loved, she was also a very good friend, the only one he allowed inside himself.

As he was thinking about her, one of the toxins to which she was the antidote came into the room.

"We're all ready, sir," said Reid. "I've told the team to—"

Carston got up, grabbed a sheet of paper from his desk and walked straight past him into the squad room. Reid looked at Ross, who just gave a little shrug and followed him.

The briefing turned out to be short and brutal. First, Carston asked for their various reports and wasn't surprised when no-one came up with anything that clarified the picture at all. Next, he warned them that they'd be working through the weekend. The news made them all look at one another. Spurle said "Shit" loudly enough for Carston to hear.

"Yes, and if you don't pull your bloody finger out and start acting like a CID officer, we'll be here every other weekend, too," he said.

Spurle looked at him, his expression challenging.

"For the benefit of the rest of you, I'll explain," Carston went on. "Spurle and I were having a chat with Bole, who I think is guilty as hell. Maybe not of this, but certainly of something. So I get him talking about what he thinks of our gay friends. And before long, he's telling us that he'd kill any of them that messed with him."

There was a murmur around the room.

"Yes. Useful, eh? Except that good old, heterosexual Spurle tells him he feels the same way. Yes. He agrees with him. And it's all on tape."

"What a dickhead," said Fraser.

"It's not just Spurle. Here's another little bit of professionalism. Gallacher seems to be in a different league from the rest. Seems to be trying to remember, trying to give a clear picture. Could all be a smokescreen, of course. Doesn't matter if it is or not, though. Because we're going to have to throw his statement away."

He paused as they waited, frowning, to hear his reasons.

"Today, he suddenly remembers Bole getting out of a red Nissan outside the pub. Last night, he said Bole came into the pub. There was no Nissan. Never was."

"Bole's got one, sir," said Reid.

"Yes, but he didn't drive it. It was at home."

"Bit of a coincidence that Gallacher chose the right car and the right colour though, isn't it, sir?" asked Fraser.

"No, because someone fed him the information."

He held up the piece of paper he'd brought through with him.

"Last night, when Gallacher was still drunk, the way he was questioned put memories into his head which he didn't have."

"But he—" Reid began.

"No," snapped Carston, without even looking at him. "That's the way memory works. We all know that. Drop in a few words here and there and you can paint whatever bloody pictures you like in their minds. They remember the version you want them to, not the real one. It's basic interview technique. Put him on the stand, give the defence his statements and he'd be laughed out of court."

He stopped, but nobody tried to fill the silence. He was usually a reasonable enough boss to have. Not when he was in this mood, though.

"So, thanks to some really bloody abominable police work, we're going to have to let them go again."

"We could keep Bole, sir," said McNeil.

"How?" asked Carston.

"Suspicion. You know we asked them for the clothes they were wearing? To check for blood transference?"

"Yes."

"Well, they all produced stuff except Bole. He said his tee-shirt was so messed up he'd thrown it away. Said he was afraid of all the AIDS bugs it would have on it."

"Where did he throw it? Did you look?" asked Carston, glad that McNeil was still as sharp as ever.

"He says the bins were collected soon after he ditched it. If he's telling the truth, it'll be at the tip," she said. "I would have sent somebody but there wasn't time."

"There is now," said Carston. "Reid, Spurle, get onto it. You know what you're looking for. Talk to the bin men, the manager of the tip, go through the stuff if you have to. If we can find Baxter's DNA on any of them, we can start putting this together properly. Jim, you and Julie charge Bole. Talk to him again. See what you can get. It's about time he met somebody who knows what they're doing."

He stopped. The silence was now tinged with embarrassment. Everybody knew, including Carston himself, that sending Reid and Spurle to the tip was petty, a little act of vengeance to punish them for the mistakes they'd made. On the other hand, he was right. If samples of the blood taken from any of the clothes matched Baxter's DNA profile, it would give them a focus. The tee-shirt was important. Carston had just handled the whole thing badly. And it wasn't like him. He seemed to be losing it.

****

For a change, Vicky had been able to relax. Sex with McEwan had not taken very long. Not like the early days, when he went to lots of trouble, lingered over things, played with her and caressed her in ways that drove her crazy. Maybe it was her fault. Maybe the constant abuse of what had been erogenous areas had dulled them, made her insensitive to the gentler touches. That afternoon, neither of them had had an orgasm. In Vicky's case, that was normal. But he'd stopped deliberately, being more concerned, according to him, that she should enjoy what they were doing. Whatever the reason, she was at least happy that he still wanted her.

When he'd left, he'd more or less given her the evening off. Well, the first part of it. She'd agreed to meet the new punter at nine at her flat but, until then, her time was her own. It was a rare luxury and she used it to take Billy to the dark, dripping swings at the park and play at being a normal mother. She got back, cleaned up the flat and suddenly realised that it was past eight o'clock. She grabbed Billy and his things and was lucky enough to arrive at the bus stop just seconds before the number eleven, which took her almost to Mandy's door. The trip was so quick that she had time to sit for a while with her sister and drink a glass of white wine.

The television was on. Billy and Mandy's kids were watching it.

"Busy night tonight then?" asked Mandy, blowing her cigarette smoke in a fast column towards the ceiling.

Vicky shrugged.

"Dunno. There's a special at nine. After that, I s'pose I'd better get some time in down the canal."

Mandy coughed and put her cigarette in the ashtray beside her.

"I'd've thought you'd had enough o' specials. After last night."

Instinctively, Vicky's hand went to her back, where the weals were still tender.

"Aye, well, it's no' that kind of special. This one's a pal of Ally's."

Mandy looked at her.

"Sharin you round, is he?"

Vicky smiled.

"They all pay," she said.

The two sisters were very alike but the demands of Vicky's profession hid the fact. Mandy's growing roundness was draped in a loose orange sweater and a black skirt which she'd unzipped at the waist for comfort. Her hair was brown, she wore no make-up and the only aroma surrounding her was that of stale tobacco. Vicky's blonde hair shone like plastic, her red lurex dress hugged her like a sheath two sizes too small and, as she moved, her perfume wafted from her with the pungency of a fly spray.

"Dave was great about that guy with the whips," she said.

71

Mandy sniffed.

"Aye, but he's the one who sent him."

"He didn't know, though. He's never set me up for that sort o' thing."

"No. Just like a social worker to you, isn't he?"

"Social workers don't fuck you in the afternoons," said Vicky with a smile.

"They do round here," replied Mandy.

The two of them laughed and started to talk about Billy. He was still too engrossed in the telly and his Mars bar to notice them.

"Guess what I'm gettin for Christmas," said Vicky, when the talk had turned to holidays.

"What?"

"A car."

Mandy was lifting her cigarette again. She stopped, holding it still in front of her.

"What?" she said, managing to drag out the single syllable and fill it with several layers of disbelief.

"From Ally. He's comin into some sort of bonus or something. Asked me what I wanted. I said a car."

"And he said yes, did he?"

Vicky nodded. Mandy took a long drag at the cigarette and sent another column of smoke upwards.

"You're a sucker, Vick," she said. "Believe everything they tell you."

Vicky smiled, then told her the things that Baxter had said to her. He'd been so earnest that many of them had stuck with her almost word for word.

"They think he's queer, you know," she said.

"Who?" asked Mandy.

"His pals. Offshore. They play tricks, feel him up, write stuff on his cabin wall—all sorts of things."

"He's not, though, is he?"

Vicky didn't answer right away. When she did, her voice was thoughtful.

"Hard to say. He fucks me, but I've had better. Just wants to talk a lot of the time. He could be AC/DC."

Mandy shuddered. For her, sex was women on their backs, men on top of them and no variations.

"And he's had a lot of bother this trip," Vicky went on.

"What sort o' bother?" asked Mandy.

"Wi' safety an' that. That's what he does, you know? Sorts out stuff. There's something going on with the other guys… I'm not sure about it but he reckons they'll be gettin their P45s before too long."

"Why?"

Vicky shrugged again and told Mandy what he'd said. It didn't make much sense to either of them but it had obviously been very significant for him.

"That's why he said he'd get me the car," said Vicky, wanting to get back onto small talk. "He's in for some big bucks, Mand. Honest."

"If he fancies you that much," said Mandy, "why don't you borrow something from him? Pay off your bloody pimp."

Vicky preferred not to be reminded of the chains that locked her to McEwan. She shook her head.

"I don't think so," she said. "Dave wouldn't like that. He's got no time for Ally. Thinks I'm too soft on him, do him too many favours."

Mandy picked up the wine bottle and held it towards Vicky.

"Oh, no thanks, Mand. I'd better be goin. Got to clean up a bit more before the new guy comes."

Mandy poured wine into her own glass.

"I'm workin tomorrow mornin, remember," she said as Vicky stood up and dragged at her dress to ease it back down over her hips.

"Aye. Don't worry. I'll be here early to pick him up. How do I look?"

Mandy looked her up and down, taking the question seriously. She liked the colours that Vicky chose and often wished she herself had the nerve to wear the sort of sexy things Vicky's job demanded. With the dress back in place, there was no doubt that she looked good. OK, the effect was tarty and close up there'd be signs of wear and tear, but from across the room, she looked tasty enough to be in a soft porn movie. Mandy liked her a lot. Loved her even. And she was genuinely sorry that Vicky had to make her money the way she did. The thought of the whip marks beneath the red material of the dress took the smile out of her lips.

"Well?" asked Vicky, seeing the change of expression as Mandy's eyes still wandered over her outfit.

"Not bad for an old bag," said Mandy.

Chapter Six

Kath still preferred film to digital. She'd fitted her Canon EOS into its housing in the foam rubber lining of her camera bag and chosen two flash guns, her main one and a slave unit. She'd leaned her tripod against the side of the door jamb and was now picking out rolls of film and stuffing them into her pockets. Carston watched her movements, caught the changes in her face, the compressing of her lips, the little nods, as she ticked off the items on her mental list. They were all so familiar, so essential to his own living.

He'd never taken her for granted and, sometimes, he found himself looking at her and suddenly seeing her in a different way, noticing the smile in her eyes, the fullness of her lips, the softness of the dark hair that was always falling across her face. She was almost as tall as he was but had none of the skinniness that often goes with height. Her breasts were still full, her stomach had that soft, light convexity that was so much sexier than the taut, flat slabs of the catwalk brigade.

"What's the matter? What're you looking at?" she said, taking him by surprise.

"Unadulterated beauty," he replied.

"Well, if you're after sex, forget it," she smiled. "Dot's expecting me."

"Not sure I'm capable of it any more," he said.

"Not another mid-life crisis," said Kath, snapping shut the catches on her case.

"You've noticed, then," said Carston.

"What?"

"I'm menopausal."

"Rubbish. You're just feeling sorry for yourself again."

"Why should I do that?"

"I don't know. That's usually what brings it on, though. Anyway, it's not menopausal, it's andropausal for men."

"God, tits and intellect too."

Kath threw him a vee sign.

Carston smiled and thought for a moment.

"Seriously, love," he said at last. "D'you think I've changed recently?"

"How?"

"I don't know. Any way, really."

Kath stopped what she was doing, considered his question, then shook her head.

"Not that I've noticed. Why?"

Carston reached across for the bottle of Cahors they'd been drinking with their meal and poured himself another glass.

"I don't know. I've been losing it a bit at work. Letting that slimy little bugger Reid get to me. I find it hard to just ignore him."

"It's understandable. Well, it is if he's as bad as you keep saying," said Kath, going out to the hall to get her coat.

Carston waited until she came back in.

"He is," he said. "But I used to be able to handle it. Didn't let it affect me. It's not exactly important, is it?"

"It is if it gets in the way. In fact, rather than you acting differently, I'd say you were acting even more like yourself."

He got up and held her coat as she slipped her arms into it.

"How d'you make that out?" he asked.

She turned and kissed him lightly on the mouth.

"You've never suffered fools gladly," she said. "This particular fool's there all the time, so it's bound to build up."

"Yes. It's not just him, though. I'm not even sure I like the job any more."

"Ah, that is serious."

Carston nodded, then reached out and put his arms round her.

"But you reckon I'm OK?" he said.

Kath kissed him and rested her hands on his chest.

"Why not have a little chat with him? Clear the air. Find out if he's as bad as you think."

Carston shuddered.

"I might strangle him if he is."

"That's alright, he'll have deserved it."

"God, you're so wise."

"I know."

They were joking, of course, but once again Carston was glad for the balance that Kath gave him. She was right; he'd always been able to spot time wasters and ignore them. All the same, though, he shouldn't be losing his temper quite so easily, and he shouldn't be behaving in such an unprofessional way. He was glad that she saw no changes in him but he continued to feel them in himself.

They were still standing facing one another, his arms around her back.

"Will you be late back?" he asked. "I may want some sex and violence later."

She lifted her knee gently into his crotch.

"You can have the violence now if you like," she said.

He pretended to consider the offer.

"No. Later'll do," he said.

She kissed him again and picked up her camera bag and tripod.

"I won't be long. Dot wants the shots ready for tomorrow evening. I'll get some close-ups before they start, then a few as they rehearse. I'll need to get back to develop them."

"I'll be here," said Carston, sitting down again and picking up his glass.

Kath went to the door.

"Oh," said Carston, suddenly remembering. "See if you can choose a couple of gays who might help me out with this case, will you? You know, sensible ones." ·

"Any particular type?" asked Kath.

"Really butch ones," said Carston. "Like you."

Kath gave him another small vee sign and left.

****

Vicky was checking her lipstick in the mirror. She was wearing a dark red dress. It was tight around her hips and pushed her breasts higher. She looked good. Maybe she'd suggest to McEwan that a few more afternoons off like today's might make her more marketable. The flat, too, was tidier than it had been for months. She was still feeling relaxed, partly because of the wine she'd drunk at Mandy's and when she'd got home and partly because she'd had almost twenty-four hours without punters. She'd been thinking about Baxter and his promise of a car and she was really beginning to believe that he meant it and that, this time, she wouldn't be disappointed.

The doorbell rang. With a final flick at her hair, she smiled and winked at herself and went to let in her nine o'clock special.

****

Carston was in early again the following morning. He hadn't been able to switch off his thoughts about Baxter and he'd woken at six, showered, had breakfast and slipped out without waking Kath. He'd reread everything they had on Bole and the others and started trying to organise it into a coherent pattern. They wouldn't be able to keep Bole very long unless they could give his guilt a clearer focus.

He sat back, tapping his pen against his lower lip. The whole building, although it never stopped popping with distant noises, calls, conversations, movements, hadn't yet settled into the perpetual clamour of what other people called normal working hours. He enjoyed these quieter times in the office, when he could simply sit with whatever was on hand and think about it without too much fear of interruption. His problem this morning was that, as he tried to keep his concentration on Baxter and Bole, memories of how he'd treated Reid kept recurring and he felt annoyed and embarrassed at his actions.

Ross came in at eight-thirty, bleary-eyed from a night spent walking up and down cradling Mhairi, his younger daughter, who was teething. The thickness of the coffee Carston had made was exactly what he needed to speed up his reflexes. He shuddered as he tasted it.

"What'd you get yesterday?" asked Carston, sipping from his own cup of the treacly brew.

Ross shook his head and reached for his notebook.

"Not a lot," he said. "I'm away to type this in with the rest of the notes. I'll give you a print-out."

Carston nodded. Ross and McNeil had spent well over an hour with Bole the previous evening, trying to get more sense out of him about the whole affair. They'd treated him with as much sensitivity as they could manage in the face of his brutishness, certainly far more than he'd got from Fraser and Spurle, but there was no change to his story.

"I wish there was something. I'd like to keep him here till we get the reports from forensics and the lab," said Carston. "Might have managed it if it hadn't been for some of the daft buggers we've got here."

Ross didn't react. He was tapping away at his keyboard. When he did speak again, his voice was deliberately lower.

"They had no luck at the tip," he said, keeping his eyes on the screen.

Carston looked across at him. He knew him well enough to get the sub-text of what he was saying.

"I know," he said. "And I know I'm a prat for treating them like that."

"Aye," was all Ross managed.

"He pisses me off so badly," said Carston. "But it's no excuse. You'll have to give me a hand, Jim."

Ross stopped typing and looked at him. He said nothing.

"Stop me acting like a kid," insisted Carston. "Remind me now and again."

Ross grinned.

"I've tried to, but you're a thrawn bugger at times."

"Bloody good job I don't know what that means," said Carston.

The air had been cleared a little and the two of them got on with their work, Ross typing up his notes and Carston rushing impatiently through the pile of sundry papers, circulars and administrative junk that he'd so far managed to avoid seeing. McNeil and Reid arrived just before nine and Carston took this as his cue to stand up and go through to the squad room for the morning's briefing. Everyone was there, Bellman, Fraser and Thom sharing a copy of the Sun, Spurle reading the Daily Mail.

"Bonjour, patron," said Fraser.

Everybody ignored him. His Francophilia, developed during summer holidays with his wife, caused him to practise his appalling French at every opportunity and they'd almost stopped noticing it.

"Right, first thing on the agenda," said Carston, "is 'Apologies'."

It got their attention. They all looked at him.

"From me," he went on. "I was pissed off yesterday and I acted like a kid. I shouldn't have spoken the way I did, and the business about the tip was … unnecessary."

He noticed that Spurle was nodding and that the corner of his mouth was twitching into something like a smile. Carston looked away and suppressed the impulse to retract or attenuate the apology. He was grateful when the phone rang and Ross picked it up.

"Before you get any fancy ideas, though," Carston went on, "so was the shoddy work that provoked it. If you want me to treat you like professionals, start acting like them. Now then, let's get some work done. Fraser, you and Bellman get back to those houses around the dustbins. There are windows everywhere there. Somebody must have seen something. Take—"

He was interrupted by Ross.

"Sorry, sir, but you're wanted right away. Superintendent Ridley."

"Did he say why?"

"No, sir. Just that it was urgent."

For a change, Carston wasn't altogether sorry to be called up to the second floor. The smile at the corner of Spurle's mouth had spread like a virus across his face and was now a full-blown sneer.

Carston nodded to Ross.

"Promotion, I expect," he said.

"Bonne chance, patron," said Fraser.

"Oh, don't worry, Fraser. I won't accept it. Not if it means leaving you."

He left Ross in charge of the briefing and went up to Ridley's office. Its size was supposed to reflect the superintendent's importance but merely served to make him look even smaller than he was. The desk was huge and the walls were full of diplomas and certificates that had been sent by grateful companies and organisations in town in recognition of (police) services rendered.

Carston stood in front of the desk, waiting for Ridley to acknowledge him. Ridley signed two more sheets of paper before putting down his pen and looking up.

"I find it hard to imagine what sort of outfit you're running nowadays, Carston," were his opening words.

Carston thought of an answer but held it back. Ridley was obviously on a short fuse. Something was in the air.

"I mean, is it policy to send sergeants off to search through the town's garbage?"

So that was it. Reid again.

"No, sir," was all Carston said.

"So why did you?"

"Resource optimisation," said Carston. "Personnel deployment on the basis of structural competency."

"Don't give me your bloody dictionary act," said Ridley. "This is undermining discipline, respect, everything we expect from our officers."

Carston's anger at the fact that Reid had, once again, gone snivelling to Ridley blotted out the memory of his recent resolution to be mature.

"Respect has to be earned, sir," he said, managing to make it sound like an accusation aimed at Ridley as well as a comment on Reid and Spurle.

"And you're fast running out of it," snapped Ridley, bafflingly.

"So," he went on, "before you go any further with this case against the Anstey people, I want some ground rules made clear."

Carston picked up the expression "the Anstey people" and knew immediately that there was some sort of manipulation going on. The usual way of referring to an enquiry was by the name of the victim or the nature of the crime. Suddenly, here, the investigation no longer seemed to involve individuals; in the dock was an organisation.

"First, before you bring any charges or make any arrests, I want you to report directly to me."

It was worse than Carston had thought.

"But CID don't usually—"

"No. CID get away with murder most of the time," said Ridley. "So for this case, you report to me, right?"

"Sir," said Carston.

"All it needs is for you to go clod-hopping your way into Anstey's, giving them a bad press, and they'll have their lawyers crawling all over us. We rely on companies like that for all sorts of sponsorships and cooperation, you know. They could do us a lot of harm."

"Yes, I wouldn't want that, sir," said Carston.

"You're not getting it," said Ridley. "Because I'll make sure it doesn't happen. You think you're ahead of the game, Carston, but there are many, many things you know nothing about. And dealing with Anstey's is one of them."

"Maybe if you told me, I'd be better placed to—"

"I doubt it," said Ridley. "And anyway, you're going to be backing off on this one. Other things have come up."

Carston frowned, waiting for the explanation. Ridley picked up a single sheet of paper. It had just three lines of print on it. He handed it to Carston. It was a time, a name and an address.

"We've got another body. News came in while I was on my way in. I took it from Sergeant Dwyer and brought it up."

There was no sense of urgency about him. In his mind, the discovery of a body was obviously secondary to the need to reprimand Carston.

"Prostitute, apparently," said Ridley. "Her sister found her when she took her kid back. She'd been baby-sitting. The SOC team's on its way."

"How do we know she was a prostitute?" asked Carston.

Ridley picked up a second sheet. This time it was full and closely printed.

"Sergeant Dwyer knew the name. I got him to check it with Vice. They confirmed it. Vicky Bryant. Been on the streets for years." He gave the sheet to Carston. "Here's what we've got on her."

"I don't see how we can take it on, sir," said Carston, swallowing his disgust at Ridley's callousness. "The Baxter case is already—"

"Just for the moment. There's nobody else free. You've got three sergeants with you anyway. I think it'd make sense to give Reid a chance with Baxter. He's got to cut his teeth on something more—"

It was Carston's turn to interrupt.

"You're not suggesting putting him in charge?"

Ridley smiled.

"Of course not. He'll have to report to you. And to me. It'll still be your case. But I think he might handle Anstey's with a bit more sensitivity than—"

Again Carston interrupted him. This time it was a snort.

"He'll bugger it up. Simple as that. There won't be anything to 'handle Anstey's' with."

"Be careful, Carston," said Ridley. His tone was hard. He was delivering not advice but a warning. "Whatever you think, Reid's a very competent officer. He's more than capable of holding the reins while you start on this other case. It'll only be for a while, until I've changed some of the schedules. All you're doing is hanging around waiting for details on Baxter anyway."

"Yes. I'm just hanging around," said Carston. "Amazing they pay me really, isn't it?"

"Yes, it is sometimes," snapped Ridley. He pointed at the paper Carston was holding. "I've told you the score. Just get on with it. You can take one of your other sergeants with you."

Carston had one last try.

"Reid hasn't even been on the CID course."

"So what?"

"So he's not even clear on the basics. He's not qualified to handle an enquiry."

"He's not handling it. You are. And you're responsible for it. And you're also opening the file on that woman. I don't think there's anything else."

He stared straight at Carston. It was the first time he'd challenged him so openly. Carston felt a huge frustration, which overwhelmed all the logical arguments that he should have used to prove to Ridley that the whole issue was being badly mishandled.

"Is there?" asked Ridley, as the silence lasted.

Carston held his stare a little longer, then shook his head, turned and walked out of the office, not trusting himself to say a word. He walked straight downstairs and outside into the street. The late Autumn air was still full of moisture but, even though he was wearing only a jacket, he was unaware of any discomfort. He looked around, then walked very quickly along the pavement. At the end of Burns Road, he turned and continued along Estover Avenue. The buildings he passed were mainly offices. Outside some of them, smokers hung around in sad, guilty little groups. Carston hardly noticed them. His mind was racing and bubbling with anger at the latest meddling.

Ridley had always been a pain in his arse but to actually interfere with how Carston did his job was a new development. Reid was the catalyst but there was more to it than that. Maybe one of Anstey's people was a fellow mason. Or maybe he really was just afraid that Carston wouldn't show due respect to the captains of local industry who ran the company.

By the time he'd gone right round the block and arrived back at the station, his anger still hadn't lessened, but he'd remembered what Kath had said about his attitude to Reid. She was right; he had to talk to him. If he let the anger take over again, he'd end up saying and doing things that might get him suspended.

He slowed down and took his time climbing the stairs to the squad room. On the way, he read the notes on the second sheet of paper Ridley had given him. It was the usual pitiful catalogue.

Regular fines for soliciting, two early records of petty theft. No need for any psychological profiling. Carston had come across too many records almost identical to Vicky's. Victims before they knew it or could do anything about it, but villains in the eyes of the law and the respectable local tax-payers. Ridley and his ilk would prefer it if police time didn't have to be wasted on looking for those who had done the rest of the community a favour by disposing of her.

Fraser, Thom and Bellman had already left the squad room. Spurle was sitting at a table, underlining entries on a long computer print-out. Carston scribbled a name on a piece of paper and put it on top of the list.

"I want this guy brought in. We need to talk to him."

Spurle looked at the name.

"What about?" he asked.

"Never mind. A new case we've got. You'll get his address from Vice. Find him. Get him in. But tell him nothing, got it? Not a word. I want him here when I get back, right?"

"Right, sir," said Spurle.

Carston wondered why Spurle had called him 'sir'. Usually, it had to be dragged out of him. He must be taking the piss. If so, he was getting better at it. Carston turned away and went through to the office. Ross, McNeil and Reid were all at their respective computer terminals. They looked up as he came in, their faces expectant, wanting to hear what Ridley had wanted. Carston took a deep breath and blew it out in a long sigh.

"Right," he said. "Jim, Julie, we've got another body to look at. Vicky Bryant. Her sister found her in her flat in Chapel Lane this morning."

"We're running two investigations?" asked Ross, surprised.

"Seems like it," said Carston. "Never mind. Reid's going to look after Bole and Baxter while we're away."

The three sergeants looked at one another.

"Jim, Julie, go and get the car ready." He turned to Reid. "You and I need to have a chat."

Ross and McNeil grabbed their coats and left, aware that major things had happened but knowing better than to ask about them. Reid waited. Carston walked to the window, opened it, took a deep breath of damp air, and turned to face him.

"I expect you think I've been treating you a bit harshly," he said.

Reid shrugged.

"It's understandable, sir. I haven't been up to speed in some things."

"Not up to speed? You've buggered it up, that's how I'd put it."

"I've paid for it, though, sir," said Reid, risking a tiny complaint.

Carston waved a hand and nodded to acknowledge it.

"I know, I know, and I've already said I'm sorry for that. It was unfair on you and made me look a complete dickhead. So I'll try … I'll really try not to lose it like that again. But—" He stopped, emphasising the word to make sure he had Reid's full attention. "I've got to be sure that you're fully committed to what we're doing."

"I don't know why you doubt that, sir," said Reid. "What good would it do any of us, me included, if I didn't pull my weight?"

"Depends how you do it."

Reid paused, not clear of what Carston meant. Carston looked at him, noted the elegance of his jacket, the crispness of his shirt and the irritatingly fashionable glasses, a different pair yet again.

"OK, let's be completely upfront, shall we?" he said.

"Sir?"

"I'm going to say something which is just between you and me, because I think it needs bringing out into the open. Can I trust you?"

"Of course, sir," said Reid.

To Carston, the reply was suspiciously quick.

"You see, sometimes I get a nasty feeling that you don't really think I'm your boss."

Reid waited.

"I think you're still part of Superintendent Ridley's team."

"Well, I am, sir," said Reid.

It took Carston aback. Was he admitting that he was a spy?

"He's my Super," Reid continued. "He was the one who got me seconded to you. I still have to report to him."

"Every bloody thing?" said Carston, his determination to be calm slipping slightly.

"Everything relevant," said Reid.

They guy saw nothing wrong with what he was saying. He seemed to have no idea that he was Ridley's nark. Surely he couldn't be that naïve?

"This is still between us, right?" said Carston.

"Of course, sir."

"I think part of your brief is to report to Ridley about me."

Reid hesitated before replying. It was enough to confirm in Carston's mind that he was right.

"No, sir," said Reid. "Part of my brief is to report on any areas where I think our operations can be streamlined or made more efficient."

"And if I mess up, that gets reported, right?"

"It's not a blame culture, sir," Reid began.

Carston interrupted him.

"Don't give me bloody jargon," he said. "Look, we've obviously got different ideas on what police work's about. I'll just say this, if your reporting to Ridley interferes with our cases, or if any of this conversation gets to him, I'll give you a workload that'll make your visit to the tip start looking like a bloody tea party. I can be a really nasty bugger, OK?"

Reid didn't doubt it for a moment.

"Understood, sir," he said.

He'd given nothing away. He'd been completely upfront about his allegiance to Ridley. Carston was no further ahead. Either the man was an innocent pawn of Ridley's or he was a consummate con-man. Not knowing which increased Carston's frustration once more. He decided that he'd done what Kath had suggested and that it was time to restore the status quo.

"OK. Now, as I said, you're going to be taking a bit more responsibility in the Baxter case."

"Yes, sir," said Reid.

"But you don't do anything, you don't question anybody, you don't talk to anybody on the phone, you don't say anything to the press. If the forensic or path reports arrive while I'm away, you can look at them but you take no action, right?"

"Yes, sir," said Reid.

"And when the others get back, get them to type up what they've found and put it on my desk. You can look at it but that's all. Got it?"

"Yes, sir," said Reid again.

Their "chat" and Carston's treatment of him seemed to be having no effect. His responses were measured, his expression was serious.

"If anything—anything at all—comes up, get me on my mobile."

"Sir."

Carston wanted to say more but had no idea how to get through the blandness of the surface.

"Right," was all he managed, before picking up his coat and hurrying down to the car park where Ross and McNeil were waiting.

"I'll murder him," he said, shaking his head as he came up to them. "OK. Sorry about that. I'll fill you in on the way. You drive, Julie."

The three of them got into a black Mondeo and pulled out into the traffic. As they drove down towards the canal, Carston controlled his mood sufficiently to allow him to tell them what had happened in Ridley's office. Neither of the sergeants said anything. They'd seen Reid's dangerous inefficiency for themselves but they'd also seen how often Carston pushed his luck with Ridley. Their sympathies were with their boss but they weren't surprised that he was in trouble.

"What do we know about this woman we're going to see?" asked McNeil, to move the discussion away from the causes of Carston's continuing anger.

"Not much," said Carston. "Vice have had her in a few times. The usual stuff. She's been on the game for at least five years. Pimp's a guy called McEwan. I've told Spurle to bring him in. He should be there when we get back."

"Is he connected then?" asked Ross.

Carston shrugged.

"No idea. Always the first place to look, though, isn't it?"

They'd left the relative affluence of the streets around the town centre and were driving past rows of solid, respectable but shabby semis. Occasional splashes of colour from late flowering roses showed that some of the owners cared about their homes but the patches of earth outside most of them were either bare or clogged with weeds, newspapers, fast food cartons and no doubt even less savoury articles.

"Somebody'll have to talk to the sister," said Carston. "That's probably your job, Julie."

"Right, sir. Where is she now?"

"They took her and the kiddie home. Don't know the address. But you can drop Jim and me at Chapel Lane then give Sandy a ring to find out and go straight there. She'll still be in shock."

The streets lined with semis gave way to ravines between four storey granite tenements. Chapel Lane was one of them. The whites of the police cars outside Vicky's were stark, bright splashes in the gloom. McNeil dropped Carston and Ross at the end of the street.

"God, Jim, I hate this bit," said Carston, as they walked towards the house.

"Aye," said Ross.

"So few of the poor sods ever deserve it."

"Nobody does," replied Ross.

"I'd make an exception for Ridley."

"I wouldn't."

Carston shook his head.

"Christ," he said. "This is like having a conversation with Jesus."

"How would you know?" asked Ross.

They climbed the dark, narrow stairs to Vicky's flat where Carston, once again, felt his throat tighten at the sight of a corpse lying amongst the simple ordinary things that had been part of the patterns of its living days. There were no pictures on the walls and the only ornaments were some dolls in various national costumes on the mantelpiece, three Silk Cut ashtrays and a gilt carriage clock. Photographs of Billy were propped against the dolls and stuck into the frame of the mirror above the fireplace. Vicky's handbag was lying in one of the two maroon armchairs. On the dining table, which was pushed against a wall, was a neat pile of magazines and a plastic bowl with two apples in it.

Vicky herself was lying face down near the table. Her red dress had been split along the left side seam and the material lay rumpled around her. Her bra strap was still fastened but her pants had been pulled down as far as her knees and the flesh of her side and back was bruised and heavily marked. Her blonde hair looked surprisingly neat and, as Carston bent to look at her face, he saw that while her left eye had the glaze of death, the right, slightly shadowed by her brow and cheek, still seemed to sparkle. It gave the illusion that a tiny filament of life still burned in her.

Brian McIntosh had finished his examination and was standing back as the SOC cameraman took some more video footage of the body. The doctor's face was grim and Carston knew that he, too, was unable to take his job for granted and shrug off the little tragedies over which the two of them constantly met.

"Strangled," he said as Carston moved to stand beside him.

"Beaten about a bit, too," said Carston, pointing at the bruises.

McIntosh shook his head.

"Don't think so. They're not recent. They were done a while ago—the day before yesterday perhaps, maybe earlier than that. Not at the same time as the strangling anyway."

Carston nodded slowly as his eyes searched Vicky's body for more information.

"So was it just sex?" he asked, looking again at the torn dress.

McIntosh's head was shaking.

"Not sure, but I don't think so. The only recent marks on her are around her throat. Some sort of ligature. From what I can see, there's nothing around her vagina or anus."

"No signs of a struggle?"

"Not really. I've still got to confirm it, but it does just look like a simple asphyxiation. Probably didn't have time to resist."

The whole look of the room seemed to support McIntosh's reading of what had happened. Everything was in place, there were no scuff marks on the carpet, no overturned chairs. Apart from the strangulation, the only other sign of violence was the torn dress. Death had come quietly into all her normality and choked the life out of her. The small, pathetic truth was that, like the old bruises and the gel that held her hairstyle intact, murder was always likely to be part of Vicky's experience.

Carston and McIntosh talked some more about what the doctor's examination had revealed but there was very little detail to be had before the autopsy. The two of them, with Ross, went back down the gloomy staircase and out into the street. It would have been nice to be able to comfort themselves with the thought that Vicky was well out of a life lived in such surroundings doing the work she did, but none of them could. The thought of her silent, lonely death and the terrible panic that must have been with her as her throat was compressed weighed in all three of them.

"This is no job for a sane person," said Ross.

Neither of the others contradicted him.

****

Billy was watching the lunchtime news on ITV. His future would be decided in the next few days but, for the moment, it was as well for him to be with Mandy, for both their sakes. A uniformed policewoman, experienced in social work cases, had settled them in to Mandy's flat and stayed to help with all the little things that Mandy needed in order to start coping with the experience of being the one who found her sister's body.

McNeil knew that she wouldn't get much from this first session but, if there was any information to be had, it would be given more readily if she built some early confidence and trust and waited for catharsis to do its work. One of her strengths was an ability to sense the wavelength of the people she was dealing with and subtly match it with her own. With Nicholas at Anstey's, she'd been poised and professional. Now, with Mandy, she was more relaxed and her accent took on a rougher edge. It wasn't deliberate or condescending; just a product of her natural empathy.

And it was working. Mandy's faith in the police had been diluted over the years by their treatment of Vicky but McNeil's ease with her and the genuine understanding she seemed to have of Vicky's lifestyle and its dangers soon moved aside her resistance. Now and again, the memory of her sister's body would hit her and, in mid sentence, the tears and sobs would shake her into silence. Each time, McNeil waited, her hand around Mandy's shoulders, gently rubbing up and down to massage the pain away.

"She was always sayin she'd get out of it," said Mandy. "Competition was gettin tougher."

"Aye. I've seen 'em," said McNeil.

"Kids. Eighteen, nineteen, even seventeen, some o' them. Used to be twenty-eight, thirty-odd. Not now."

"Aye. It's the only way they can pay for the drugs," said McNeil.

"Not Vicky," said Mandy, fiercely. "She never touched 'em. She wanted out. She wanted Billy to—"

She stopped as the sobbing hit her again. McNeil waited. Surprisingly, as Mandy regained control, the sobs ended with a short laugh.

"She was doin it in Cairnburgh because she said it was safer than Aberdeen," she said. "Funny, eh?"

"What did she mean?" asked McNeil, knowing the answer but wanting to keep her talking.

"There's plenty o' punters here still—from the oil, students, businessmen. They're mostly just singles. In Aberdeen there was the ships. That bastard McEwan made her go on board. It was OK sometimes. Vicky had a laugh about it. It was like she was special, she said. Got food, chocolates, clothes, all sorts o' stuff. Stayed a couple o' days and nights once or twice. Other times, though, it was gang rape. The bastards got her on board and wouldna let her go. That's why she came back here."

"What about the McEwan guy? Did he mind?"

Mandy snorted.

"Course he did. Vicky owed him money. Lots. He wanted her workin day and night. What could she do? She said if he let her work here, she'd do more tricks. Give him a bigger cut. He said OK as long as she earned enough. Set her bloody targets."

Her anger at the thought of McEwan had pushed her tears right away. McNeil took the chance to ask some more direct questions.

"D'you think McEwan would know who Vicky was with last night?"

"Aye. He fixed it for her. It was a pal o' one of her regulars. Phoned him up, askin for her."

"She didn't know his name?"

Mandy shook her head.

"We'll ask McEwan," said McNeil.

"Aye. Ask Ally Baxter, too."

McNeil was immediately alert. She kept her tone even and gave nothing away as she asked, "Who's he?"

"One of her regulars. Works on the rigs. Sees her a couple of times when he comes ashore. He was the one who told this new guy about her. She was tellin me last night."

McNeil was desperate to push harder for information but disciplined enough to let Mandy make her own pace. Slowly, with frequent interruptions as the immediacy of her recollections of a sister who was so recently alive and happy forced more tears out of her, she went back over the conversation they'd had. Vicky hadn't told her everything Baxter had said but there was enough substance to it to pose some very interesting questions.

Chapter Seven

McIntosh was driving Carston and Ross back to Burns Road in his own car, a black Volvo whose back seat was spread with sweet wrappers, toys, broken bits of plastic, crumbs, and all the other debris generated by a young family. Carston, who never looked as tidy as Ross, had opted to sit amongst it. Ross was in the front and he and McIntosh were talking about the relative merits of the town's three main pre-school nurseries.

Carston marvelled at this evidence of New Men in Cairnburgh but was glad that he didn't have to contribute and looked idly out at the patterns of a normal Friday afternoon; an old man with what looked like an even older dog, two young mothers pushing prams with one hand and somehow eating chips and smoking fags with the other, a man eating a hamburger from a paper wrapper, which was crammed against his face, obscuring it totally, and, on one corner, as they waited to pull out into the traffic, a girl in a doorway crying. Carston wondered idly why he always seemed to see individuals rather than the crowds of which they were part.

The sound of his mobile startled him. Quite often, he kept it switched off, but his uneasiness at leaving Reid in charge of things and the instructions he'd given him to get in touch if anything happened left him no choice. As he hit the answer button, he was already hardening his mind in anticipation of more trouble. McNeil's voice gave him a pleasant surprise.

"I've just left Mandy Bryant," she said.

"Any joy?" asked Carston, immediately regretting the choice of words.

"Better than we could've dreamed," said McNeil. "One of her sister's regulars was Alistair Baxter."

"What?" said Carston, so loudly that Ross turned to look at him.

"Aye, sir. Not only that. She had a special last night. One of his pals. Baxter recommended her to him."

"Don't know his name I suppose?"

"No, sir. McEwan might, though. The guy phoned him to arrange it."

"Well done, Julie. Anything else?"

"Aye. I'm on my way back now. Better if I brief you when I get there. Thought you'd need to know about the Baxter connection right away, though."

"Yes, you're right. With any luck, McEwan's already been brought in. Get back as soon as you can. I won't talk to him till you've given me what you've got."

"Right, sir."

"See you soon."

As he punched another button to connect to the station, he said, "Bingo, Jim. Vicky Bryant was Baxter's woman. Mate of his visited her last night."

Ross whistled.

"Your job's so easy at times," said McIntosh.

Carston grinned as he listened to the ringing tone. When the desk sergeant answered, he confirmed that Spurle had brought McEwan in just five minutes before.

"Right. Make sure nobody says a word to him. Not even hello. I want to deal with him myself," said Carston. "And tell Superintendent Ridley that there's no need to allocate this new enquiry to another team. If he asks why, tell him I'll explain later."

Ross's head was shaking as Carston put the mobile back in his pocket.

"What?" said Carston.

"Haven't you got enough trouble with him already?" asked Ross.

"Trouble? I'm keeping him informed of everything. As it happens. Where's the problem?"

****

Hamer had joined Anstey Oil because he wanted some of the offshore wealth that was around the place. The problem was that, without a background in engineering, his options were limited. A degree in Psychology and a Masters in Business Administration led him inevitably to personnel management, or rather to the chillingly named discipline which had replaced it, Human Resources. His main skill had been in avoiding mistakes.

Through the various purges that Anstey's North American parent company had forced on them in the Eighties and Nineties, his low profile kept his name off the lists and he'd moved quietly up the hierarchy. In the end, he'd gathered so much information about how the company was run that he'd been able to start making positive contributions.

When he did eventually get noticed, it was because of his ability to pinpoint theoretically superfluous personnel for the periodic slimming exercises. Thanks to his perpetual squeeze on manning levels, the annual wages bill had not only met its targets, it had made them appear generous, an achievement greatly appreciated by his bosses in the States and their shareholders.

The off-duty antics of Bole, Gellatly and Milne, in theory at least, were none of his concern. But the adverse publicity they'd generated was creating negative associations with the name Anstey and Baxter's death would make sure they didn't go away. He was used to dealing with punters who'd had a night on the juice, but this particular episode threatened to set his credit back a long way.

Gellatly and Milne were on leave but he'd called them into his office. Nicholas was also there, invited in by Hamer as back-up for the line he was planning to take with the two men. They were sitting on the other side of his desk, looking down at the floor and around at things in the room, neither of them willing to catch his eye. They wore Anstey Oil jackets over sweatshirts and old jeans which sagged under their stomachs. Gellatly's face was even scalier than usual. The contrast between them and their two bosses was extreme. Hamer and Nicholas were in classic business suits, Hamer's black, Nicholas's a dark grey pinstripe.

"You know the rules," Hamer said. "Any trouble with the police, especially if it's related to booze, makes it an internal disciplinary matter."

"It was in our own time," protested Milne, without much conviction.

"Yes, but as soon as things got difficult, you started asking for the company lawyer."

"That was Rick," said Milne.

"Doesn't matter who it was. It got the company involved and we don't have any options. We can't pretend it's got nothing to do with us because it's all logged in the Cairnburgh nick."

His use of slang was awkward. He often adopted what he took to be hearer-friendly expressions but he was always conscious of using them and so, instead of dropping them seamlessly into his speech, he isolated them, gave them a special stress which served only to underline their artificiality.

"I don't think we can overlook this one," he went on. "The Yanks'll be on us like a ton of bricks when they hear about it."

"Why should they?" asked Gellatly.

"Because they always do. When their lawyers hear about queer-bashing, they'll … shit bricks," said Hamer. "And if we try just keeping quiet about it, our competitors'll have a field day. Not telling head office will make it worse."

"So what's the score?" said Gellatly.

Hamer shook his head and straightened the pad on his desk.

"There's nothing we can do until the police have finished with you, but you're suspended until we've had time to consider our options."

"Bloody hell," said Milne. "Just for gettin pissed?"

"More than that," said Nicholas. "Ally Baxter's dead."

"So what?" said Milne. "What's that got to do with us?"

"Oh, come on," said Nicholas. "You were out looking for gays. Ally was gay. Rick had already had a punch-up with him about it. We saw it, for God's sake."

"Rick's a bloody head-case, we all know that," said Gellatly. "Doesn't mean he'd kill anybody."

"No, and we're not accusing him," said Hamer. "But the three of you pulled in for assault and Baxter being beaten to death on the same night—what sort of a cock-up does that look like to head office?"

Gellatly and Milne had been with Anstey's long enough to know that arguing their case was futile. Once they'd got a mark on you, you were out.

"This … suspension," said Milne. "How long's it likely to be?"

"Hard to say," said Hamer. "Depends on the police to some extent."

"You could help yourselves, though," said Nicholas.

94

The others looked at him.

"Were the three of you together all the time?"

"From about nine, yeah," said Gellatly.

"So if one of you killed Baxter, the others'd know about it."

"None of us killed him," said Milne. His voice was angry.

Nicholas held out a hand to stop his protest.

"OK, then just cooperate with the police. Be completely straight with them. That's your best tactic."

"But don't get your hopes up as far as the company's concerned," said Hamer. "This sort of thing can't just be brushed aside."

It amounted to a dismissal notice. Both Milne and Gellatly felt the urge to grab Hamer and let their fists tell him what they thought of him and his company. But that really would be suicidal. They cast around for something to say. It was Milne who broke the silence.

"We weren't together all the time, Jim," he said to Gellatly.

"How?"

"Rick was a bit late gettin to Bell's, wasn't he?"

Gellatly frowned.

"Aye. So what?"

Milne shrugged. "Nothin. Just—"

"That's the sort of thing to tell the police. I don't think we want to be discussing it here," said Hamer. "I just wanted to let you know how things stand at the moment."

His manner told them that the interview was over.

"You'll need to clear out your lockers but you can't do it yet," he went on. "The police have sealed them."

"What the bloody hell for?" asked Gellatly, his aggression beginning to surface.

"Because they're dealing with a murder," said Hamer.

"Yeah, right," said Gellatly. He stood up. He'd had enough of being treated like a kid. "Won't be the only bloody one either if we get the boot for this."

The rest were quiet and Gellatly himself knew that he hadn't been very clever. Oppressed by the silence, Milne stood up but he had nothing to say. He tried smiling at Hamer but got no response. Nicholas nodded at him but again, there seemed little sympathy or support in the gesture. Milne's bitterness was as deep as Gellatly's but he was controlling it without difficulty. There was nothing new in being accused by people who had no idea what they were talking about. It all confirmed the gulf between the poor sods out on the rigs and platforms putting up with the dangers and the graft and the smooth buggers onshore who drew graphs and awarded themselves fat bonuses. Every so often, members of the management team would appear in one of the company's videos thanking everybody for their efforts and talking shite about teamwork. Nobody was impressed. The word most frequently chorused in response was "Bollocks".

"We'll let you know the decision after the police investigation's over and when the board's discussed it," said Hamer.

"Thanks for nothin," said Gellatly.

He and Milne went out, making sure they slammed the door behind them. Hamer heaved a long sigh and shook his head.

"It was the right thing to do," said Nicholas.

"Yes," said Hamer.

Nicholas went to the door, opened it and paused.

"Tell you what, though," he said with a smile, "You'd better hope the police find Bole guilty, or you'll have to do it all again. Won't be so easy with him, will it?"

Nicholas shuddered and reached into his desk drawer for a Bisodol tablet. It had been a stressful week.

****

The rest of the team arrived back at the station just after Carston and Ross. Their door-to-door interviews with the people whose houses overlooked the spot where Baxter's body had been found had produced nothing.

"I reckon the best idea's for you to take them up to Anstey's to clear out the lockers Julie got sealed," said Carston, as Ross poured him a cup of severely stewed coffee.

"Aye. Should've been done before now," replied Ross.

"I know. Don't think we'll have problems there, though. I got the impression from Julie that they're wanting to help us on this one."

"Savin their own arses, that's why."

"Cynic."

"How do you see it, then?" asked Ross, grimacing as the oily coffee coated his throat.

"Saving their own arses," said Carston.

"Wish I was a Chief Inspector," said Ross.

Carston smiled.

"See if you can talk to some of their people, too," he said. "Find out what you can about Baxter."

Ross looked at his watch.

"Better get going," he said, deciding against draining the coffee from his cup. "See you tonight. You can fill me in on Julie's stuff."

"Yeah, we'll have the briefing as soon as you get back."

Ross hesitated.

"D'you want me to take Andy with me?" he asked.

Carston gave a small shake of the head.

"It's tempting," he said, "but I'm supposed to be getting him involved. Find him something to do out in the squad room. I don't want him here when I'm talking to Julie."

"Sir—" Ross hesitated.

Carston looked up at him.

"Well?"

"Watch your temper," said Ross.

"Alright, I'll take him with me when I talk to McEwan. Maybe he'll learn something. Now goodbye, Sergeant."

Ross grinned and went to get the others.

Left alone, and with still no reports from forensics or pathology, Carston allowed himself the luxury of sitting back and speculating on the significance of the link between Baxter and Vicky. Establishing the identity of the friend who'd visited her on his recommendation was a clear priority but, if Baxter was gay, what was the nature of his relationship with her? And was he really in a position to know whether she was any good at sex or not? If he wasn't, what was the recommendation about? There were still too many unanswered questions about Baxter himself.

And then there was McEwan. The whole story of the recommendation came from him. Maybe it was a ploy, the old trick of introducing some untraceable stranger. But if so, why? Did he have something to hide, as well as his pimping? And there again, if he was involved, why would he invent something that would put his activities as a pimp in the frame?

The scenarios that Carston concocted became more and more complex. They absorbed him so much that he was surprised by McNeil's arrival. He looked at his watch. He'd been sitting at his desk for twenty-five minutes with McEwan and the rest of them flitting about on his mind's stage, more real than the objects around him.

"Right, Julie. What have you got, then?" he asked eagerly.

McNeil was at the coffee pot. She looked at its contents and changed her mind.

"Plenty," she said. "And I think there's more to come."

Carston waited for her to go on. She looked at her notebook, nodded and put it on the desk in front of her. Her fair skin was flushed and her own excitement about what she'd heard kept bringing her unique lop-sided smile to her lips. Carston often found himself letting his eyes wander down from her face. Her breasts were a disappointment, but her bum was as sexy as that of the barmaid in Carston's local. Whenever thoughts such as these came to him, he felt annoyed with himself. On the other hand, it would be hypocritical to pretend they weren't there. You get your pleasures where you can.

To Ross's disgust, McNeil shared Carston's liking for hunches and conjecture and it was obvious that Mandy's information about her sister and Baxter had had the same effect on her as it had on Carston.

"Vicky wanted out," she said. "She owed McEwan money, though. That's what he had on her. Why she had to stay on the game. He set her targets."

"Enterprise culture again."

"Aye. 'specially when you hear the cut he took."

Carston nodded grimly. Pimps were not far above paedophiles on his personal hate list.

"And it was McEwan who set her up with this mystery punter, was it?"

"Yes. Took the trouble to soften her up for it, too, according to Mandy."

"Oh?"

"Aye. Asked her if she minded. Let her have the afternoon off."

"So he was pretty keen for her to see the guy?"

"Looks like it. Mandy said Vicky was in a good mood for a change."

"But she had no idea who the guy was."

"No. There was stuff about Baxter, though." She checked her notes again. "He was going to buy Vicky a car."

"Is that what he said?"

"Aye. She believed him, too. Told Mandy about it. He was supposed to be coming into some money."

"How?"

McNeil shrugged.

"No idea. There was something going on with the other guys he worked with. He reckoned there were some of them who were getting the push."

"But not him."

"Don't know. Maybe that's where the money was supposed to be coming from. Severance pay."

Carston doubted it.

"Probably just another story to keep her sweet," he said. "Dreams are all they have to live on."

"Well, whatever it was, it convinced her," said McNeil. "Baxter was a bit anxious about something, though. Last time she saw him, he told her he was off to see a guy to sort something out with him."

"When was that?"

"Wednesday night. Must've been just before he was killed."

Carston nodded, absorbing the information. This wasn't straightforward. Something was going on which spread beyond Baxter's sexual habits. Homosexuals and prostitutes were perennial victims but Carston was sure that these two had died for very specific reasons, reasons not necessarily connected with their sexual orientation and function.

By the time McNeil had finished the report of her conversation with Mandy, Carston was more than ready for McEwan. With his pivotal role of organiser of the meeting between Vicky and her nine o'clock special, he'd been in direct contact with the person who had probably killed her. Unless he'd got rid of her himself and the whole thing had been dreamed up by him to cover up a totally different scenario. As Carston went down the stairs, followed by McNeil and Reid, his mind was crowded with possibilities and he was feeling good.

They stopped outside the door of the interview room.

"Right. If he says anything that seems odd, anything that contradicts what Mandy said, chip in, Julie. It's probably a good idea for you to get involved anyway. This guy has to have a pretty low opinion of women. Talking to you may lower his guard."

"Right, sir," said McNeil, resigned not only to McEwan's attitudes but also to the hint of sexism Carston's words had betrayed in him.

"And you," went on Carston, pointing to Reid, "keep quiet. Ridley wants you to have a higher profile in all this. Fine. Just make sure that it doesn't throw any shadows over what I'm doing."

Reid contented himself with a nod. He had so far made no signs that Carston's treatment of him was having any effect, but it was becoming progressively harder to swallow his pride. The long-term reward—his promotion and a move back into a branch far removed from Carston—was worth the effort but Carston was making it difficult. Reid knew that Ridley had moved him to CID to keep tabs on the DCI, but he suspected that it might also be a subtle test of his own ability to handle pressure. For that reason, he was never tempted to protest at being treated like a half-wit.

The room was well lit. McEwan was at the table looking relaxed and self-contained. It was by no means his first visit to them and he'd learned how to behave. Carston switched on the tape recorder and sat directly opposite him. McEwan's smile made Carston want to unsettle him right away.

"Comfortable?" he asked.

"Fine thanks," said McEwan.

"Must be well used to this, eh?"

"You could say that."

"Yes," said Carston. "Trouble is, this time it's murder."

McEwan's smile disappeared before he had time to control himself. Carston was sure that what flashed into his eyes was panic but it might just have been the shock value of the word and the unexpected direction of his attack. McEwan said nothing.

"Don't you want to know who?" asked Carston.

McEwan just looked at him, his mouth set tighter, straighter, the dark hollows of his eyes giving little away.

"It's one of your customers. Alistair Baxter."

"Never heard of him," said McEwan, too quickly.

"I see. So it's on record that you do have customers, but you don't know Alistair Baxter," said Carston, pointing to the machine on the table between them.

"Depends what you mean by customers. And Baxter, well, it's an ordinary sort of name. I might know somebody called that. But not that I can think of."

"Right. So he wasn't the man who was with Vicky Bryant on Wednesday night? He wasn't the one who thought she was so good that he sent one of his pals along to her?"

As he mentioned Vicky's name, Carston watched McEwan carefully, but his expression gave nothing away. The hesitation before he spoke might have been to allow him time to decide what line he'd take to avoid the possibility of incriminating himself in any way.

"No idea," said McEwan, backtracking. "I remember a guy phoning. Didn't know he was called Baxter."

"Not Baxter," said McNeil. "His pal."

McEwan flicked his eyes across to her. They stayed briefly on her face, then dropped to her breasts. She noticed the slight shake of his head before he looked back at Carston.

"There may not even have been a phone call," said Carston. "That may be a little porky you've put about."

"What for?"

Carston shrugged and raised his eyebrows.

"I don't know. You tell me."

"Dunno what you're on about," said McEwan.

"No, of course not," said Carston. "OK then, let's talk business. How many girls are you running nowadays?"

"Girls?"

"Oh Christ, you're not going to be tiresome, are you?" said Carston, injecting a little whine into his voice. "You're a pimp. You've been done for it before. We know all about you. Don't waste our time."

"I know some girls who like to put it about," protested McEwan. "If a pal wants a fuck, I try to fix him up, that's all. Nobody gets hurt. It's harmless. They're just having a good time."

"Where do they learn to 'put it about', though?" asked McNeil, her voice hard. "They start with you, then you con them into doing it with your brothers and cousins. Before long they're having to do it with your grandfather and anybody else who's got cash to spare."

"Some imagination your sergeant's got," said McEwan to Carston. "Isn't she getting enough at home?"

Carston banged his hand on the table, making them all jump. He pointed a finger at McEwan. There was no need to articulate the warning; McEwan could see it in his eyes, which were burning with rage.

"We've been through this with you before," said Carston, the control he was exercising obvious in the tightness of his throat.

"And it's the same story every time," said McEwan. "You don't listen. The girls, they want to do it. What else would they do? Stack shelves in Sainsbury's? This way, they make a bloody good living. On their backs, legs apart, easy money."

"Aye, and most of it goes to you," said McNeil.

McEwan shook his head.

"No. Sometimes they give me presents for finding a guy for them, that's all. The guys want sex, the girls want the money, what's the problem?"

"The problem is that prostitution is illegal," snapped Carston. "And it spawns too many parasites."

McEwan sat back in his chair.

"Be real," he said. "It's supply and demand. I don't make whores."

"No," said McNeil. "You let them make themselves. Get them dependent, get them sleeping around, then one day they wake up beside a stranger and that's it."

McEwan tutted and shook his head. Carston looked across at McNeil and gave a little flick of his head to tell her to back off. She sat back, tapping her pencil on the pad in front of her.

Carston stayed with generalities for a while, trying to assess how open or defensive McEwan wanted to be. The man was shifty. His past contacts with them had taught him how much he could safely admit and, as the interview went on, he obviously felt more and more comfortable with it. If he was hiding something, he was doing it well.

"I'm surprised you let Vicky work in Cairnburgh," said Carston, changing direction yet again. "More punters in Aberdeen, surely? Certainly more money."

Still, the name Vicky provoked no noticeable reaction in McEwan.

"This is crazy," he said. "Am I being charged with something? If so, I want a brief."

"No. There's no charge. Yet," said Carston. "But you can help us with our enquiries."

"Gladly," said McEwan, with another of his smiles.

"Tell us about Vicky."

"I've known her a long time. Good girl. Got a kiddy, you know."

"We know," said Carston. "Baxter was a regular of hers, wasn't he?"

"Yes, I think she mentioned him now and again," said McEwan, obviously forgetting his initial claim that he'd never heard of him.

"What was he like?"

"Complete twat as far as I could make out."

"How?"

"Just that. Twat. Wanted a mother more than a fuck."

"So you didn't like him?"

McEwan thought about it.

"No," he said. "Gets complicated."

"What d'you mean?"

"Look, men want a blow-job, a hand-job, a fuck. They don't want to hang around. He was a pain in the arse with Vicky. She couldn't get rid of him."

"Cuts down productivity, eh?" said McNeil.

"He was a pain in the arse," said McEwan again.

"Did he pay regularly? On time?" asked Carston.

"I don't know what you mean."

"Alright," said Carston. "What about his pal? The one who phoned for a special last night. Who was he?"

McEwan's head was shaking.

"No idea," he said. "Phoned me out of the blue. Asked if I knew Vicky."

"Just like that," said McNeil.

"Just like that," echoed McEwan.

"Lucky for him you did then, wasn't it?" said Carston.

"Aye. I suppose it was."

"Not for Vicky, though," said McNeil.

"Why not?" said McEwan. His expression was still giving nothing away.

"Because she's dead, too," said Carston.

There was silence. Carston looked at Reid in case he decided to break it. The sergeant was sitting with a blank face. Carston hoped he was learning from it all.

"Poor Vicky," said McEwan at last.

"You're not surprised by the news, then?" asked Carston.

"Course I'm bloody surprised," said McEwan. "I saw her yesterday. She was looking good."

103

"Yeah, well she's not looking so good now," said Carston. "So maybe you can understand why we asked to talk to you."

"No. What's it got to do with me?"

If the news of Vicky's death had been a shock, he'd recovered from it very quickly. The truculence was back.

"Well, we don't know where you were when she was killed, do we? And even if you come up with something, at the very, very least, you're probably an accessory to murder."

"What?"

"Well, you're the one who sent this guy along to her. Told her to be there at nine."

"No I didn't. What the hell makes you—" He stopped. "That bloody sister of hers, isn't it? She's been yakking to her again. Stupid cow. She was jealous. Nobody'd want a fat slag like her, so she was always on at Vicky to—" He stopped again, aware now that he was digging himself into things too deeply.

"So you're saying there was no phone call," insisted Carston.

"I'm saying nothing," said McEwan. "I'm in here to help and suddenly you're chucking two murders at me."

"Where were you at nine o'clock yesterday evening?" asked Carston.

McEwan stared at him, his lips set, his eyes defiant. Carston held his stare and tried to see beyond it. McEwan's face was ratty; that was the only word for it. How the hell was someone who looked like that so attractive to women that they went on the game for him?

"And how about the night before? Wednesday. Between, say, eight and twelve?"

McEwan's expression didn't waver.

"So that's it, is it? You're not playing any more."

McEwan's eyes dropped to his fingers, which were tapping on the table. Carston waited. The silence in the room thickened and felt heavier. At last, Carston recorded the time on the tape and switched it off.

"OK, Julie," he said. "Get that report of yours printed out. We'll come back to Mr McEwan a little later."

"You keeping me here, then?" asked McEwan. "If so, I'll need a brief."

Carston nodded at McNeil, who, with a final look of disgust at McEwan, got up and left the room.

"No tits," said McEwan, as the door closed behind her.

Unable to stop himself, Carston reached forward and grabbed him by the front of his blue jacket.

"You bloody scumbag," he hissed, his face only inches from McEwan's. "If I had my way, we'd lock this bloody door now and leave it shut until the smell got too bad and we had to scrape what was left of you away."

McEwan was pushing at Carston's hands to try to free himself.

"I don't know how deep you're into all this shit," said Carston, his grip even tighter, "but I'm going to get you for something, you bastard."

"That's it. I want a brief," shouted McEwan.

Carston flung him down into his chair. The wooden slats across its back dug hard into his kidney and the pain made him wince.

"What for? You can go," said Carston.

Reid couldn't keep up with it all.

McEwan was looking at Carston, not trusting him an inch.

"I mean it," said Carston. "We've got no reason to keep you. We just wanted information. You can go."

McEwan stood up slowly, still expecting to be grabbed again. He went to the door. As he got there, Carston spoke very quietly, all traces of anger gone.

"But don't go very far away. We'll need to talk to you again. Sooner rather than later."

There was a smile on his face.

"Oh, by the way," he continued, the smile still in place. "I do mean it, you know. I loathe and despise everything about you—the work you do, the way you use people. I'm going to have you."

McEwan didn't risk an answer. He left the room. Carston waved at Reid to leave as well and sat down in his chair again. The anger in him was directed as much against himself as against McEwan. He'd let his temper take over again. He'd acted like Spurle and he'd put McEwan even more on his guard than he must have been before. It was natural, normal, to despise him and the corruption in which he traded. But McEwan was right; sex was a commodity and there was a big market for it. Carston even believed that, if the whole sex industry was properly regulated and monitored, there'd be less not more crime. But why the hell had he been so bloody unprofessional again? He dragged himself to his feet and put his hand to his forehead.

"Must be some sort of death-wish," he muttered.

Chapter Eight

When Carston got back to the office, there was no sign of Reid but McNeil was standing at the window reading something in a dark grey folder.

"I let him go," said Carston.

McNeil nodded, her face clouding again.

"No choice, I guess," she said.

Carston shook his head.

"Sorry you had to put up with all that, Julie."

"Would you have been sorry if it was Jim? Or Fraser?" she asked.

"Good point," said Carston. "No. I'm as bad as the rest."

McNeil smiled.

"No, not quite," she said, coming across and handing him the folder. He caught a faint lemon smell. Perfume? Surely not. Maybe just an up-market deodorant.

"Pathologist's report on Baxter," she said. "Sandy gave it to me on my way up."

"Ah. Interesting?"

"I haven't read much of it but it's better than the average."

Carston sat down, looked briefly at some photographs in the folder, then skimmed quickly through the main report. He was familiar enough with the formatting to skip past the technical details that were there to confirm the pathologists' thoroughness. One of the main findings was that, in spite of the evidence of multiple blows to his head, Baxter had in fact died of asphyxiation. At least one of the blows had been delivered before he died, which suggested that he may have been unconscious when he was strangled. He'd been killed in another location and his body had been brought to the dustbins to be dumped. Most of the blows to his head and all the genital and rectal mutilations were post mortem.

It was the pattern of slight bruising around his neck that Carston found most interesting.

"Did you see this?" he asked. "The bit about the stuff wrapped round his neck."

McNeil came to stand beside him and look over his shoulder.

"No. What was it?"

"Some sort of polythene. Bit of a carrier bag maybe. They found a scrap of it in one of the folds of flesh. Didn't notice the marks at first because there were other bruises there. From a fight he had earlier."

"Aye. With Bole."

Carston looked up at her.

"With Bole? How d'you know that?"

Momentarily, McNeil was thrown.

"I thought you knew, sir. They told us at Anstey's. There was a fight when they got out of the bus bringing them from the heliport. It's in my report."

"Where is it? I haven't seen it," said Carston. "I was looking through all the case notes this morning, too."

"Ah, I did it when I got home last night. I've downloaded it into the network. It's there now."

Carston nodded. Linking Bole directly with Baxter was a bonus but the bruising the fight had produced clouded the interpretation of the rest of the evidence.

"That explains a lot, then," he said, flicking through the sheets of paper and pointing at paragraphs here and there. "Pre mortem bruising. Here. And here. Fighting for real, by the look of it."

"I canna see Bole fightin any other way."

"You're probably right. This is weird, though."

He'd pulled out a particularly gory photograph showing a close-up of Baxter's head. In fact, it was barely recognisable as such because it had been hit so many times that the skull had been crushed and its contents had spilled and oozed out of it.

"Why?" asked McNeil.

"That's not what killed him," said Carston. "Brian McIntosh reckons it was the polythene. It was pulled tightly round his neck while he was still alive. Strangled him. How do you see it, Julie?"

McNeil went back to her own desk and sat on the edge of it.

"Just one thing," she said. "If I was going to strangle somebody, I don't think I'd use a carrier bag."

"Maybe it's all there was."

"Aye, maybe."

Carston's mind was racing, freed into all sorts of possibilities by McIntosh's findings.

"Or maybe it was for something else," he added.

McNeil looked at him, waiting for his explanation. Carston tapped the photo.

"If you do this to somebody, there's going to be blood everywhere. But the report says that some of this was done after he was already dead."

McNeil still didn't see where Carston was heading.

"So, why do you carry on beating at a guy's head when he's dead?" he asked.

She thought about it.

"'cause you don't know what you're doing," she offered. "You're mad. Just hitting out."

"Or you want to hide something. Want us to think it was fury or passion or whatever."

McNeil's expression showed that she wasn't convinced.

"Remember the mutilations. All done long after he was dead. All the sort of thing queer-bashers might do. Somebody's trying to mislead us."

"He's no' doin a very good job of it," said McNeil.

"No. But think, if what you're doing is calculated, you're probably thinking about not leaving any evidence. So you won't be wanting Baxter's blood spread all over wherever you killed him, will you? Or over whatever transport you use to take him to the dustbins."

"No."

"So, if he's already bleeding because you've hit him on the head, you wrap something round it. Something the blood won't soak through."

"Like a carrier bag," said McNeil.

Carston spread his hands.

"I can't think of any other reason for putting plastic round somebody's throat. And if you make sure it's really tight, so that nothing'll drip out, chances are you'll cut off the air and—" He snapped his fingers to suggest the likely result of the action. "Then you take him to the bins, take off the bag, beat him about the head some more, cut him around the genitals, carve 'faggot' on his chest and leave him for us to find."

McNeil smiled.

"So you've solved it, then?" she said.

Carston smiled back. His enthusiasm had obviously been getting the better of him.

"Just about," he said. "All we need now is to pin it on somebody."

McNeil pointed to the folder.

"Well, we've got a DNA profile already."

"What?" said Carston, looking at the folder again.

"Last page. The summary. He had someone else's blood on him."

Carston looked quickly at the end of the last page. McNeil was right. He'd missed it as he'd skipped over what he'd taken to be the more formal parts of the report. He slammed the report shut and sat back.

"That's it then," he said. "We can both retire."

He knew that he'd already taken chances keeping Bole as long as he had. They had nothing concrete against him and, if a lawyer ever did get involved, they'd have to do some ducking and diving to hang on to him. The news of his fight with Baxter did offer a bit more leverage, though. It was enough to hold him for assault, and with Baxter's subsequent death, an extended period of questioning looked reasonable. It was tenuous stuff but he wasn't willing to give up on Bole yet.

He went back down to the holding cell and was let in by a uniformed constable. As the door opened, his nostrils caught the stale smell of smoke and armpits. Bole was lying on the bunk, lighting a cigarette from the stub of the one he'd just finished. The ashtray on the table beside him was full. His bald head was shining with sweat. His greyish tee-shirt was stretched over his stomach and had ridden up to reveal a crescent of hairy flab.

"That'll stunt your growth," said Carston, pointing at the cigarette.

"Fuck off," said Bole.

"Yes. In a minute. Wanted another word, though, first. Just a couple of things."

"I'm not sayin anythin else without a lawyer."

"Pity, because we've found some marks on your mate Baxter's body. And guess who made them? You."

Bole sat up in the bunk. His scorn and his determination to wait for a lawyer both vanished.

"That's shite," he said.

Carston pursed his lips and shook his head.

"Nope. Finger marks round his throat, bruises round his back and on his chest and face. Punches, some of them look like."

Bole dragged deeply on his cigarette, then, to Carston's surprise, laughed. The laugh became a cough, which simply shifted around several litres of mucus.

"That was when we came back," he said, when he could breathe again.

"What was?"

"The marks. We had an argument. Bit of a punch-up. Well, not really. The bastard's not capable of fightin."

"What was it about?"

"Got a bit uppitty, didn't he? Shootin his mouth off. Bloody shirt-lifter."

"So you … what, you taught him a lesson?"

Bole's hand went up to his nose, which was still swollen from Baxter's head butt.

"It was nothin. I gave him a couple of taps. Bastard tried to nut me. It was nothin."

"Had any fights with him before?"

Bole snorted and lay back on the bunk again.

"I told you. He's a bloody fairy. He wouldna fight to save his life."

"Bit late for that," said Carston.

"Good riddance," growled Bole.

"Didn't like him much, did you?" said Carston.

"Nobody did. Waste of space offshore. Bloody girl."

"Oh yes," said Carston, as if he'd just remembered something. "I meant to ask you about offshore. Is everything OK there? On the platform, I mean."

Bole looked at him and dragged on his cigarette again.

"Why?" he asked.

Carston shrugged.

"Dunno really. I wondered if everything was normal."

"You been offshore?" asked Bole.

Carston shook his head.

"What would you know about normal, then?" sneered Bole.

Carston smiled.

"Plenty of job security, is there?"

Bole was wary.

"What's all this about?" he asked.

"I just wondered. There was some talk of people being paid off. Redundancies. That sort of thing."

"Not on Falcon Alpha," said Bole.

"And you'd know, would you?"

Bole snorted again. It produced another fit of viscous coughing.

"If they laid off any more, they wouldn't be able to run the bloody thing," he said, as the last bubbles settled in his chest. "The only ones to get rid of are girly Baxter and his lot."

"You may be wrong about him, you know."

"How?"

"He had a girl-friend."

Bole laughed again.

"Aye, so he kept tellin us. S'posed to be shaggin her Wednesday night. Crap. If he's a stud, how come he's always in the Swan?"

"Is that who you were looking for when you went there?"

"No."

"When did you last see him?"

Bole shook his head and held up a dirty hand.

"That's it," he said. "We've done all this. You want more questions, you charge me. An' get a bloody lawyer in here."

Carston was quiet for a moment.

"You know, I think we might," he said at last. "We've got the evidence of your fists on him. I think we could probably match up the marks on his throat with your fingers—"

"Course you could. An' I'd've strangled the bastard that afternoon if they hadn't pulled me off him."

"Oh, you know he was strangled, do you?" said Carston.

Bole stopped, thrown by Carston's words.

"No. I... How would—? Aw, fuck off. I want a lawyer."

"You're a bit repetitive, you know," said Carston, tapping on the cell door for it to be opened. "Tell you what, though; it's going to be a pleasure putting you away."

111

His voice was quiet, confident, authoritative. It sounded to Bole as if he knew something which he wasn't revealing. As Carston went gratefully out into the corridor, away from the stale air, he was wishing he did. Next time he talked to Bole, he'd better have something more specific or there'd be no choice; he'd have to let him go.

As he went into the upstairs office, McNeil, who was sitting at her computer, turned and said, "Ah."

Carston stopped and looked at her.

"'Ah?'" he echoed. "What's that? Appreciation? Disappointment?"

"No. More like, 'Ah, I'm sorry you've come in because you won't like the message I've got and it would've been better if I hadn't seen you again this afternoon.'"

Carston smiled.

"That's a lot of 'Ah'. What's it all about?"

"Message from Superintendent Ridley, sir. He wants to see you."

"Ah," said Carston, the smile disappearing. "What did you tell him?"

"That you were following a new lead we'd got and that I wasn't sure where you were."

"You're going to get very quick promotion at this rate."

Carston went to the window and looked out. The late afternoon had already thickened into a slate grey evening. One of the few things he disliked about living so far north was being subjected to early darkness. He never understood the arguments for banging the clocks back and forward and resented being dictated to by the farming lobby. He looked at his watch and decided that he could do the rest of his paperwork just as easily at home. He turned to look at McNeil again. She was typing more notes. Pity about her breasts. One of Carston's fantasies involved having on his team a woman sergeant with ash blonde hair, hazel eyes, a 36D bra and a Swedish accent. As with most of his fantasies, he was ashamed of it.

"Right, Julie," he said, taking his coat from its hook and grabbing a pile of folders from his desk. "Now I'm going to follow up a new lead we've got. I'd rather not tell you where."

"I understand," said McNeil.

"Can I leave the briefing to you and Jim? Perhaps if he's got anything new from Anstey's, he could give me a ring at home later."

"Right."

"And you can fill him in on the stuff about Vicky Bryant."

McNeil nodded.

At the door, Carston had another thought.

"And, if anybody other than you or Jim wants to get me on my mobile, it'll be switched off. I don't want it going off in the middle of a new lead, do I?"

"Certainly not, sir."

He winked at McNeil and left. Avoiding Ridley and joking about it with a sergeant wasn't very clever or very mature, however much McNeil appreciated his reasons for doing so. It set an example of disrespect for rank and the formal processes of the force which might some day come back to plague him. But with a working weekend ahead and lots of ammunition for a bit of creative sleuthing, he wasn't prepared to subject himself to Ridley's carping and procedural moans.

One of his concessions to fitness was his determination, whenever the weather allowed, to walk between home and work. The air wasn't sharp enough to suggest frost, but instead the dankness of late October tried to get into his pores. He rubbed at his cheeks and almost stopped at the window of a travel agent where special offers invited him to go to India and Thailand for a fourteen day tour. The photograph of the smiling couple standing in front of the Taj Mahal reminded him of the sort of people who were likely to be his fellow-travellers, however, and the idea was discarded before it had even had time to form. He hurried on, much more tempted by the thought of spending a warm evening with Kath and curling his hand around a mug of lemon, honey, cinnamon, hot water and rum. Yet more evidence that he was already middle aged, he thought.

****

On Saturday morning, he was already regretting that he'd promised to spend that evening at the theatre with Kath. He'd had two calls, one from Ross, the other from Gallacher. Ross had sketched in what they'd found at Anstey's and it was more

113

intriguing than even Carston could have hoped for. The other call had also hinted at some new information. It was from Gallacher but he seemed unwilling to say anything on the phone. Instead, he asked Carston to come to his house. Carston had no choice but to agree and he arranged to stop by on his way to Burns Road.

He pulled up outside the neat granite semi at eight-forty and rang the bell. Through the velvet curtains of the front room he saw the statue of the naked woman and was irritated to catch himself being surprised that it wasn't a man. Gallacher opened the door and waved him along a narrow hallway, hung with small tapestries, through the red, gold and black dining room with its exotic statues and ornaments and on into the kitchen. The smell of fresh coffee was delicious but Carston decided not to accept Gallacher's offer of a cup. He was anxious to get to the station.

"Nice place," he said, looking round the kitchen with its gleaming pans and coloured utensils.

Gallacher was pouring coffee for himself.

"Thanks," he said. "It's part of the reason why I asked you to come here."

"Oh?"

Gallacher turned and leaned back against the cooker as he took a sip of coffee. In his lean, tanned face there was tension. He looked as if he hadn't had much sleep.

"What sort of progress are you making?" he asked.

Carston made a non-committal gesture.

"Bit of a surprising question," he said. "Coming from somebody who's part of the enquiry."

Gallacher looked at him and Carston saw anger flash in his eyes.

"You say this is a nice place," he said.

Carston nodded.

"All Darren's work," said Gallacher. "In the back bedroom there's faded, peach-coloured paper. He's going to replace it with gold, cream, clay, or burgundy. He hasn't made up his mind yet. And in the utility room at the back, he's painting the doors and windows hunter green. Not the jambs, just the doors and window frames. And he'll use the same colour for the enamelled pulls and handles on the cabinets."

"Mr Gallacher," said Carston, irritated by what seemed a deliberately frivolous attempt to rile him.

"No, listen," snapped Gallacher. It was an order and his anger was pushing behind it. "There's a taupe colour on the sofa in the spare room. He's been looking for ages for wallpaper which'll pick it out and he's already found various sizes of fringed pillows to make the room richer. It's going to look great."

Carston wondered if these little asides on interior design were all another attempt to stir up his own unease about homosexuals. He said nothing, letting Gallacher make whatever point was on his mind.

"It's maybe not to your taste," Gallacher continued, "but it's individual. Darren went to a lot of trouble choosing it all and he's very proud of it." He paused and looked round the room. When he spoke again, there was a break in his voice. "So am I."

He turned, took two steps to the window and looked out at the back garden.

"Same out there," he said. "The displays. Spring, summer, they're all his."

He turned and looked directly at Carston.

"And now, he won't be able to see them," he said.

Carston waited, guessing what was coming.

"I was there last night. His right eye's completely useless and the optic nerve's been damaged. They don't think his left will last long."

"I'm sorry," said Carston, feeling once again the inadequacy of the words.

"So 'm I," said Gallacher, with a bitter little laugh. "But that's why I wanted you to come. That's why I wanted you to see this. For Darren, losing his sight is like dying. He lives for these colours, these shapes, all this … stuff."

Carston felt uncomfortable. His sympathy was with Baigrie and Gallacher but they were both still part of the investigation. He understood why Gallacher had gone for the dramatic or, rather, melodramatic revelation, but it made no difference to anything.

"I really am very sorry," he said, "and I'm doing what I can to find out the truth of what happened, but since I last spoke to you, there've been other things."

"Things more important than Darren going blind?" shouted Gallacher, suddenly losing his temper.

"Things like murder," said Carston.

115

Gallacher turned away. There was no way of Carston knowing what was going through his mind. When he turned back again, he looked once more at the garden.

"I don't care," he said. "D'you want to know why? 'cause I'm wrapped up in us. Darren and me. If you knew… If you understood half of it, you'd see why. Christ, maybe you'd even agree."

The image of Vicky lying on the floor of her flat amongst the cheap shapes of her unconsidered life came to Carston and his sympathy for Gallacher's sense of loss ebbed a little. She'd have given plenty to have just some of the choices open to Gallacher and Baigrie.

"Living here. Amongst this lot," said Gallacher, waving a hand at the window to encompass all their neighbours. "It's bloody awful."

He turned to look straight at Carston again.

"You married?" he asked.

Carston nodded.

"Happily?"

Carston said nothing. It was none of Gallacher's business and he didn't like the idea of Kath being brought into anything connected with his work.

"Just think for a minute, then," said Gallacher, "what it'd be like to pretend you and your wife were just friends. Think you could do that? Hide your love in public, even in the car? That's what we have to do. We're big, back-slapping mates, Darren and I. Not lovers. Not a couple. Mates. Lads."

For the last two words, he'd made his voice fierce and rasping, a parody of masculinity. When he spoke again, it was back to its normal, measured register.

"Know what we want to do most? Hold hands. Yep. Walking in Macaulay Park or on Glasgow Road, I want to grab him, yell out that I love him. But I don't. And if I look at him, he knows. And we have to just smile at each other. And keep this distance between us. So if you think you're a liberal sort of cop, just let your imagination loose on that sort of thing for a while. I don't think you've any idea, have you?"

Carston looked at him, keeping his expression deliberately neutral, and shook his head. It was true; he couldn't conceive of the deprivation involved in their sort of love.

"Does … Darren know? About his eyes?" he asked.

116

Gallacher shook his head. "Not yet. I'll be up there again today. I'll probably tell him then. Depends what the doctors say."

Carston made a quick decision.

"I don't think we'll need to bother him again," he said. "Except to confirm a few things. When we make charges."

His hesitations betrayed the fact that charges were still a long way away.

"You may have to," said Gallacher. "He thinks he saw a car. Wednesday night."

Carston remembered Gallacher's own confusion about the red Nissan but Gallacher's next words drove that memory out.

"A four by four. With Anstey's logo on the side."

This was new. Bole and the others had claimed that there was no car. They said they knew they were too pissed to drive—an admirable display of social conscience from a trio bent on assaulting homosexuals. Had they been lying? Was there somebody else? If so, why use a car with a bloody great label on it? Or was this all a ploy by Gallacher and Baigrie?

"When did he tell you that?" Carston asked.

"Last night. He's got nothing else to do there. Can't read. Can't watch telly. All he does is think about it."

"Where did he see it?"

"He can't remember. Late, that's all he said."

Carston couldn't get very enthusiastic about the evidence. Even if there had been a car, so what? It added nothing to what they knew about the fight. And there were so many of them around that you could almost bet on seeing one every time you went into town. All the same, it had to be noted.

"Did he remember anything else?" he asked.

Gallacher shook his head right away.

"That's it. I thought you'd like to know."

"Yes. Thank you. We'll get along and have a word with him."

Gallacher nodded and suddenly seemed to be as eager for Carston to leave as Carston was himself. They walked back through the colours and decorations that, in the light of what Gallacher had told him, Carston looked at with new eyes. When they got to the door, he said, "I mean it. It is a very nice place. Very impressive."

Gallacher nodded.

"When you talk to him," he said, "don't tell him. About his eyes, I mean."

"We won't," said Carston.

As he drove away, he saw the correct, well-tended villas of the neighbours and knew that, amongst that sort of deadly respectability, Gallacher and Baigrie's love would always have to remain hidden. The anger that Gallacher had shown and the depth of his passion for Baigrie were in part fuelled by the permanent state of rejection in which they lived. Carston couldn't help thinking that, together, they could add up to a very strong motive for striking out against anyone who threatened them in any way.

****

When he got to his office, he found Ross standing at the window.

"Coffee's just made," said Ross.

"Very thoughtful."

"I made it for me."

"Well, you can bloody well pour one for your superior officer," said Carston, throwing his coat onto a chair and going round to flop in the seat behind his desk.

"Tired?" said Ross.

"No. Just trying to work out whether I've been wasting my time."

Ross poured him a coffee as he described his visit to Gallacher.

"Bit airy-fairy, isn't it?" he said when Carston had finished.

"Yeah, but we can't ignore it. I just can't make up my mind about him at all."

"Well," said Ross, "there's plenty of other things in the stuff we brought back from Anstey's to keep you going."

"Yes, so you said on the phone," said Carston. He pointed to a print-out on Ross's desk. "Is that it?"

"Aye, most of it," said Ross, handing it across.

Carston sipped some coffee and started reading the report. This time, there was no skipping through it. He had all day.

Predictably, before long the telephone rang. Ross answered and, almost immediately, switched the call through to Carston.

"Guy called Nicholas at Anstey's," he said. "About a trip to the platform."

Carston nodded and picked up his own receiver.

"Mr Nicholas? Carston here," he said.

"Yes. Short notice, I'm afraid, but I've got a seat on a helicopter doing a special delivery for us tomorrow. Any good?

Carston didn't hesitate. He'd always wanted a trip offshore anyway and Sunday was as good a day as any to make it.

"Yes, yes. The sooner the better."

"Good. The flight's scheduled for nine. Not too bad, is it? If you could check in here around eight?"

"No problem," said Carston. "What do I need to bring?"

"Just work clothes. Something warm. Have you got boots?"

"Not your sort, no."

"OK. We'll issue you with a pair at the base before you leave. What size d'you take?"

"Ten."

"Right. Eight o'clock at reception here tomorrow then."

"Fine. Thanks."

As he put the phone back, Ross saw the smile on his face.

"Having a day out?" he asked.

"It's work, Sergeant. Somebody has to do it."

He finished reading the report, resisting the occasional temptation to stop and talk about the things Ross had found. Only when he'd finished did he sit back, nodding his head in appreciation.

"Good job, Jim. Plenty to think about there, eh?"

"Aye, except his workmates. Nobody was wanting to give much away."

"D'you think there was more to be said, though?"

"Hard to say. Some of them were sympathetic. Not many, though. The guy didn't have many friends there. Same as with Bole and the others. Thought he was gay and got pissed off with him interferin with their work."

"How about the other safety guys?"

"Same, really. Not about the interferin with work; they get that all the time themselves. But none of them had much time for him. Reckoned he was a boss's man."

Carston got up and went to pour himself some more coffee.

"Think we'll get much from their lockers? I mean, I know Baxter's was good, but how about the rest?"

Ross shook his head.

"We bagged it up and sent it to the lab but it just looks like what you'd expect—some hard core Dutch magazines, working clothes, newspapers."

Carston was nodding.

"You never know," he said.

"What struck me about it was how similar the buggers are," said Ross.

"How d'you mean?"

"Well, you'd have thought there'd be some differences, some personal bits and pieces, but the lockers were all the same—same porn, same newspapers, same overalls, same boots. Except Baxter, of course."

Carston went back to his desk and pulled the report towards him again.

"Yes, what about his stuff?"

"Well, same boots and overalls but none of the rest. No magazines or papers, just a couple of safety pamphlets and manuals, two fire extinguishers and a gas-testing kit."

"And his survival suit," said Carston, still looking at the report.

"Aye. Lots of blood on it. All round the neck."

"This business of the wrist seals being cut. What's that all about?"

"Couldn't tell you. I got the stores guy to look at it. He couldn't believe it. He said Baxter wouldn't be allowed in the helicopter with that sort of damage to his suit."

"So it was done after he came back," said Carston.

"Must've been. The storeman checked them all in. He was surprised that it was in Baxter's locker at all. He hangs them all up on a rack in his store."

"Is he sure he took Baxter's from him on Wednesday?"

"Positive. It's the routine. He has to account for every one. They're double checked."

"Good," said Carston. "We'll see what the lab gets off it."

He looked back at the report and tapped his fingers on it.

"This is the thing that gets me, though. This stuff in the bottle of oil, what's that?"

Ross shrugged.

"Not sure yet. It was stuck inside one of his boots. One guy there reckoned it might be sodium."

"Sodium? That's dangerous, isn't it?"

Ross nodded.

"Aye. This guy said he had no idea why it was there. It goes berserk in water, oxidises very fast in air—it's no' the sort of stuff you want lying about the place."

"Was it something to do with his safety work?"

"They didn't think so. There's all sorts of weird things that safety guys are allowed to take offshore—smoke bombs for line testing and stuff like that—but sodium's something else."

One of Carston's neighbours, Alex Crombie, was a safety engineer. They played golf together and had seen more of one another since Crombie and his wife had split up a few months before. Carston decided to try to pick his brains at some point. Crombie wouldn't mind; he was used to it.

Carston pushed the pages of the report back together and slid them back across the desk.

"Looks as if it's more than just queer-bashing, doesn't it?" he said.

Ross took the report and put it in a red folder.

"How do we know?" he said, guardedly. "It's the only motive we've got so far, and Bole and his pals had had a row with him already."

"Yeah, but how about Vicky? What's it got to do with her?"

"Maybe it hasn't. She was on the game. Strangled by one of her punters. It's not exactly unusual, is it?"

Carston smiled at Ross's dogged determination to avoid speculation.

"Even when her last punter was sent to her by Baxter?" he said.

"Where's your proof?" asked Ross, who was as intrigued as Carston by the apparent links but unwilling to go chasing after theories without some positive, corroborated reason to do so.

"Her sister," replied Carston.

"Oh aye. Cast iron, that, isn't it?" said Ross.

"OK, you tell me, then. What exactly have we got?"

They talked about and around the evidence they'd so far accumulated, Ross reining Carston in regularly and playing devil's advocate at each of his suggestions. By lunchtime, they'd covered all of the evidence they'd gathered, some of it more than once, from different perspectives, and their talk had brought together all the threads to make the patterns clearer in their minds.

Carston was persuaded that the most interesting enquiries would be into Baxter's relationships at work and that the queer-bashing was a separate issue. Ross preferred to keep them all in the same focus since the work relationships seemed influenced by the general perception of Baxter as a homosexual. In effect, there was more than the usual level of agreement between them. In addition, they both knew that McNeil should be closely involved with the enquiry into Vicky's death, which would mean talking to some of the women who worked the same beat as her and certainly involve some sensitive questioning of her sister.

At one o'clock, Carston checked his watch and stretched.

"OK, Jim," he said. "There's no need for you to hang around. You've been putting in plenty of extra hours. Why don't you get back home?"

"Aye, might as well," said Ross, switching off his computer. "I mean, it's always a pleasure spending time with you, but Jean did want me to fix a cupboard in the kids' room."

"So many talents," said Carston.

Ross grinned, stood up and pulled on his coat.

"Have a good trip," he said around the door as it closed behind him.

Almost immediately the phone rang. Carston ignored it. He wanted more time to reflect on what they'd been talking about. If it was some new crime being reported it could be passed on to another team. If the call was personal or genuinely important, Sandy Dwyer would send a man up to tell him. If it was just Ridley or one of his lot, Carston wasn't in the mood to have his weekend spoiled.

Chapter Nine

The steel was cold against Carston's neck. As he flinched instinctively away from it, knowing the pain that would quickly follow, a hand came up to his forehead and pulled his head back upright. A command was rapped out.

"Keep still!"

"But you're going to—" he began.

Kath knew what was coming.

"You never change, do you. You're just a baby."

Carston submitted to her scissors without trying further explanations. She was right. He was always the same when the monthly haircut on the yellow stool in the kitchen came round. She did a good job. Saved him God knew how much nowadays but he always paid when she got to the hairs around the side of his neck. The points of the scissors always managed to catch in them and uproot as many as they severed.

There. As anticipated, the hot little pains began. His jump was involuntary. She tapped him on the back of the head.

"If your men could see you acting like this, you'd never ever get any respect from them again."

"I don't now."

"I'm not surprised."

The lack of logic in the exchange went unnoticed. They'd been married so long that there was lots of comfort in the patterns of sounds they made together. Very frequently, they didn't hear the words that were being said, feeling themselves fall instead into a conversational loop that they'd travelled together many times before. It was a cosiness that was sometimes worrying.

She stood back, looked critically at his head, moved in to make a few more tidying snips, and released him with a "There". He brushed the little clumps of bristles off his chest and legs, and began clearing up the debris around the stool.

Kath looked at the kitchen clock.

"Right. Get showered. We're leaving in an hour," she said.

"Yes, Adolf," he replied. "Just got to make a quick call."

Kath suspected that he'd try to wriggle out of the trip to the theatre and wondered whether the call was part of a plan. She was reassured, though, when she heard that it was Alex Crombie.

"Yes. Just wanted to ask you about some safety stuff. One of your colleagues has been killed. Guy called Baxter."

"Ally Baxter?" asked Crombie.

"Yes. D'you know him?"

"A bit. Know of him anyway."

"Great. How about a drink, then?"

"Tonight?" asked Crombie.

Carston looked at Kath. She was still watching and listening carefully.

"No. Can't tonight. And I'm due offshore tomorrow. How about Monday?"

"Aye, OK."

"Great. I'll give you a shout Monday afternoon."

He rang off and went obediently to the bathroom for a shower, trying to compose himself for the rigours of the evening ahead.

****

Dot's theatre was a professional organisation which relied very heavily on the goodwill of actors, directors and playwrights to keep going. The Scottish Arts Council had resolutely refused to subsidise it, and only the willingness of those involved to produce entertainments for pennies kept it from being converted to a MacDonald's or a wine bar. It seated just over a hundred and Kath had made sure that they got seats near the front so that there was no question of Carston slipping out when the thing was under way. Only fifteen minutes into the action, she knew that she had been both wise and cruel.

The writer started from the premise that pneumoconiosis was a virtue. His characters spoke in long paragraphs, full of adjectives, most of which either rhymed with one another or set up dynamic oppositions or cadences. Since there was no escape, Carston tried hard to follow it all. His first attempts were sustained by the apparent parallels that the hero was establishing between the Brecon Beacons and his girl-friend's breasts, but he got lost when the image evolved to incorporate his father's lungs as well.

From the point at which the hero began a long exploration of the affinities between the "dripping ebony shaft that plunges perpendicular into the black, slack body of the lost hills" and the "moist mysteries of that shy and secret sliding into the warm wet womb-way of my lover's self", Carston's suspension of disbelief was less and less willing. Only Kath's fingers digging hard into his thigh kept reminding him to keep still and enjoy the aesthetic experience.

By the time the hero staggered onto the stage for the final time, stared at his white skin in disgust and then started to smile as he began to be racked by a wheezing cough, Carston felt that he'd done his duty and that it was time to get the rewards in the form of inside information on the gay scene from the cast.

Dot was waiting for them when they left the hall.

"Well?" she said.

"Bit heavy," said Kath.

"How's your warm, wet womb-way?" said Carston.

"God, he was actually listening," said Dot with a smile.

"Well, how is it?" insisted Carston.

"Go on, show him," said Kath. "You're in no danger. He wouldn't know what to do with it."

They went into the crush bar where members of the audience were braying at each other and already beginning to talk about the show as if it were significant. Before long, the actors began to appear and Dot went to fetch the one she thought would probably be most helpful. She brought him across and introduced him as Pill. There was no need for Carston to ask how he got the name. His face was white, small and round, with the features bunched in the middle of it like a pharmaceutical logo. He looked to be about forty and, to Carston's relief, wasn't one of the show's principals.

Dot took Kath away with her and Carston and Pill were left at a corner table. Dot had obviously primed Pill and there was no need for any preliminaries in their chat. Plenty of Pill's friends had had experiences of queer-bashing and he spoke about it with a combination of bitterness and resignation.

"What can you do?" he said, after they'd talked at length about the various forms homophobia took. "It's respectable. It's the norm. Defence lawyers exploit it. Juries are always on the side of anybody who says he's been approached by a poof."

Carston wished he could disagree, but he couldn't. Even with the most violent killings, a quarter of the people accused managed to get a verdict of manslaughter, not murder. All because they pleaded they'd been assaulted in some way.

"Yes," he said. "But God knows what the answer is."

"Yes. No use waiting around for Him to help, though," said Pill.

"Does it depress you?"

Pill shook his head. His fair, thinning hair fell across his forehead. He pushed it back.

"No point. Tell you what does, though. It was well into the nineties before the TUC set up a lesbian and gay workers' conference with democratic powers. Even then, the general council opposed it. Black workers had their conference years before that."

Carston could only nod. He was uncomfortably aware of the fact that he had no answers.

"D'you use the Swan at all?" he asked, trying to get away from generalities.

"Now and again. Sometimes go round after the show."

"That's where the problem started last Wednesday."

Pill nodded.

"Aye, I heard about it. Heard about Darren Baigrie's eyes too."

"How d'you know about that?"

Pill shrugged.

"You hear. Some of the guys were talking about it this afternoon. It's a bugger. I mean, he's a bit of a queen but he wouldn't hurt a soul. If it'd been Paul, I'd've understood."

"Why?"

Pill smiled.

"He gets angry. Won't put up with any crap. I've seen him wade in to sort stuff out before it started. And he's fierce about Darren. Protects him like a daddy."

A woman pushed through the crowd to the table, smiled at Carston and kissed Pill expansively on both cheeks.

"Wonderful, wonderful show," she said. "Lots of balls."

"Thanks, love," said Pill, with a smile.

The woman left as quickly as she'd arrived. Pill's train of thought didn't seem to have been interrupted.

"Paul's had to put up with a lot of shit at work. Had to show them he was a bastard to shut them up."

"Is Dillinger's as bad as the rest, then?" asked Carston.

"It's not so much there. It's the people he comes across from the offshore crowd. The ones who had a go at them the other night—he knew them before apparently."

"Oh?" said Carston.

"Yes. The fat guy. Paul had to go to Falcon about some contracts or something. He was talking to Ally Baxter out there and the guy started mouthing off at them. The usual crap."

"First I've heard of it. What happened?"

Pill made a "don't know" face.

"Paul told him to piss off I think. Ask him. It's no secret."

It wasn't an opinion that Carston shared. Gallacher and his pals seemed to have been a bit selective in what they'd revealed to the police. He'd told them that he didn't know Baxter, Bole or their workmates. Behind all his pleas for sympathy and understanding lay something which had led him to withhold information that might be significant. Maybe it was just his natural mistrust of others, learned over years of constant, unsubtle oppression, but maybe there was something else, something more specific. Between the brutishness of Bole and the fragile sensibility of Gallacher lay as yet unglimpsed areas of dissent. Motives were even more elusive than Carston had thought.

"Look, Dot's told me you're OK," said Pill. "That's why I don't mind talking to you. But you seem a bit surprised by some of the things I'm saying."

"I am," said Carston. "To tell you the truth, I'm having a helluva job sorting out the difference between what I think, what I know and what I feel about all this."

"Ah, the liberal dilemma, eh?" said Pill, with a smile and a wag of the finger. "Know what you should do?"

"What?"

"Come and have a drink in the Swan. Get the broader perspective. Face up to your prejudices."

Carston was ready to protest at this but he realised that there was some truth in it. The pub and its landlord and customers had already been checked out by some of his team but Pill was right. If he really wanted to understand some of the undercurrents, he ought to see for himself.

"OK. I'll need a guide, though."

Pill's smile was still in place. He seemed to enjoy Carston's little discomfitures.

"Tomorrow?" he said.

"Can't make it tomorrow. I'm going offshore. I'm meeting a pal on Monday for a drink, though. I suppose we could make it then."

"Safety in numbers, eh?" said Pill, with a smile. "OK. I'll be through here by nine-thirty. See you there."

The two of them stood up. Pill was as tall as Carston but much thinner. He held out his hand. Carston shook it.

"Thanks," he said. "I appreciate your talking to me. You must still be worked up from the show."

"No," said Pill. "I'm been doing it too long for that. Anyway—" He looked round before continuing. "It's rubbish, isn't it?"

Carston didn't know if he was being teased. He hesitated.

"It's OK. I know it's a load of bollocks. You've only sat through it once. I've had three weeks of rehearsals."

They both laughed and Pill made his way back through the crowd. Carston found Kath and Dot talking to the man who'd played the hero and had to smile, congratulate him and make positive, intelligent noises for ten minutes before he could suggest they leave. At several points during the ordeal, he caught Pill's eye. Each time, Pill's fingers went to his open mouth and he made the familiar retching mime. Although he'd only just met him, Carston liked him.

He took Dot and Kath to eat at Salvo's, a cheap Italian restaurant where they knew they could rely on the pasta but that they shouldn't risk anything else. At the same time, in the decorous surroundings of L'Estaminet, which was so much further up-market as to be invisible from Salvo's, McEwan was ordering a third Armagnac for his new girl-friend, Catherine. She was a French student who'd come across to be an assistant at a school in Elgin and liked the north east so much that she'd decided to stay. Her problem was that her contract couldn't be renewed. She'd been working as a waitress but the wages were almost as insulting as the tips she got. She was just beginning to think that it might be better to go back to La Rochelle after all when she met McEwan and life became an altogether more luxurious experience.

She'd already drunk three gin and tonics and most of the bottle of Merlot he'd ordered with the meal. He'd promised her that this would be a special evening. They were going on to a party at his place afterwards. He'd told her that some of his friends were coming round and that they'd be playing games. Catherine liked games.

Chapter Ten

Carston's early morning drive to Aberdeen was in darkness on empty roads. He knew that, on the early stretches of the trip, the lower hills on the edge of the Cairngorms pushed the road into long curves beside the Dee and, in the spring, he sometimes made the drive just for the pleasure of being in amongst them. Today, though, it was just the headlights, surprising plenty of rabbits and even a couple of pheasants. He pulled into Anstey's car park at ten to eight and was met by Nicholas at reception. His survival suit was already laid out and, as he pulled it on, Nicholas explained the procedures. At the heliport, there'd be safety videos to watch, then they'd fly to Falcon Alpha, where he'd watch another video, be given overalls, boots, hard hat and gloves and do whatever he needed to do.

"Any idea what you're looking for?" asked Nicholas.

"Whatever's there," said Carston, pushing his feet down hard into the survival suit. "Just want to talk with the others out there, find out what I can about Mr Baxter. Try to learn something about what it's like living offshore."

Nicholas shook his head.

"It's not for the likes of you and me," he said.

Carston wasn't sure that he appreciated the bracketing but he supposed it was meant as flattery. He bent to tie his laces. The feet of the survival suit felt lumpy inside his shoes.

"We've tried," Nicholas went on. "But there's not much in the way of refinement. It's not a place for people. In fact, nowadays there are more and more unmanned platforms. Remotely operated. The two Falcons are second generation but even that's long outdated."

Carston listened and nodded as he forced his hands down the sleeves and through the rubber wrist seals. He remembered the way Baxter's had been cut and it dawned on him why it had been necessary. The seals, as their name suggested, were designed to be tight around his wrists. They dragged at the skin of his hands as he pushed through them. Trying to force loose, uncooperative limbs to do the same thing would be almost impossible. It would be much easier just to cut them. It suggested that Baxter was already dead, or maybe unconscious, when someone put the suit on him.

Nicholas was still giving his mini-lecture on offshore platform design as Carston zipped up his suit.

"Floating production vessels, that's the preferred option now," he was saying. "Moor a boat over the well, pump up the reserves and, when it's finished, sail on to the next one. Makes much more sense."

Rather than enlighten him, it made Carston even more aware of the extent of his ignorance about the mystical things that were happening on all those steel islands out there in the North Sea. At five past eight, he said his goodbyes to Nicholas and left for the heliport with the other seven passengers in an Anstey minibus. After watching two safety videos, they were led through security and out to the Bristows S-41. Carston strapped himself in and freed the top of his zip slightly. His hope that that might ease the tightness of the survival suit around his crotch was forlorn. The one-piece orange outfits were designed to keep you alive for longer in cold water and also, it seemed, to make sure you never had any children.

As the helicopter lifted off, though, and dipped its nose before peeling away over the fields around Aberdeen, he got used to the tightness and began to enjoy the ride. Within minutes, they were crossing the long line of bright sand that marked the coast from Aberdeen all the way to Peterhead and heading north east across dark grey water. Overnight, the clouds and mist had vanished but the blue of the early sky was too pale to feed much of its colour into the sea. Boats were only visible because of the small vee of their wake and, with the land far behind, Carston soon had the impression that their drumming aircraft was hanging motionless over the featureless water.

After about an hour, he saw the first flares and the black dots of the platforms to which they belonged. Thirty minutes later, they were dropping towards one of a pair of flames which marked the two Falcon installations. Although the flare became more and more distinct, its boom and the platform still looked impossibly small in the vastness of the sea around it. Even as they dropped to a height from where they could clearly see the helideck crew, it seemed outrageous that anyone should dare stick a few square boxes and some bits of metal on top of some spindly legs well over a hundred miles from land and expect people to live and work on it.

As soon as they'd touched down, however, and been given the order to disembark, the deck onto which they stepped seemed huge, solid and completely natural. The wind grabbed at them as they stumbled across the rope mesh covering it and were directed down some stairs into a reception area that could have been the interior of a modern motel. Carston was met by a big, grey-haired man in dark blue trousers and a green tartan shirt. Despite the colour of his hair, he was only just forty and there were plenty of laughter lines around his blue eyes. It was the Offshore Installation Manager, who introduced himself simply as "Steve, the OIM". He shook hands with Carston and handed him the gear he'd need to wear outside the accommodation area. After a five minute video designed to tell visitors the basics of safety procedures, emergency signals and muster points, Steve took him to his office via the canteen, where they picked up two cups of coffee. The impression that they were simply in a normal suite of offices was only offset by the fact that there were no windows anywhere.

"First trip?" asked Steve, as they settled in his office.

"Yes. Fascinating," said Carston.

"I've been offshore seventeen years. It's not the word I'd use. Anyway, what can we do for you today?"

It was a directness Carston appreciated.

"I take it you know the background?" he asked.

Steve nodded.

"Poor old Ally," he said. "Good LPO. Conscientious."

"LPO?" said Carston.

"Loss Prevention Officer. That's what they call them nowadays." He smiled but without humour. "Started calling them that and taking them seriously after Piper Alpha. Once they realised that unsafe acts could wipe out profits. Anyway, you were saying."

"Yes. Really, what I'd like is to talk to your people here, the ones who worked with him, and just have a look round. Get the feel of the platform and the sort of things he did."

"God knows what he did," said Steve, his smile taking on a bit of warmth. "Law unto themselves, LPOs, most of the time. Can over-rule me if they fancy it, and I'm supposed to be in charge. We'll see what we can do, though. What have you got, about four hours before you have to start getting ready to go back?"

Carston looked at his watch and shrugged. He had no idea. Steve picked up his polystyrene cup.

"OK, we'll finish these and I'll take you down to Jamie. He's Ally's opposite number on this shift. He'll put you right."

As they drank the coffee, Steve filled Carston in on the story of Falcon Alpha. They were pumping oil, condensate, water and gas up through four production wells from a reservoir 11,000 feet down.

"Changed days, though," said Steve. "There's just 110 on board today. We've got a derrick maintenance shutdown scheduled for next month; there'll only be fifty or sixty then."

"Somebody was saying something about redundancies," said Carston.

Steve shook his head.

"Here? First I've heard. Wouldn't surprise me, though."

"Oh?"

"Aye. The well's getting marginal. Not producing like it used to. Don't need as many men."

"Would Ally Baxter know anything about that?"

"What, redundancies?"

"Yes."

Steve shook his head.

"Not before I would. If Dick Hamer decided we needed any, I'd be the first to know."

The telephone beside him rang. He picked it up, said "yes" and listened. After a couple more questions which made no sense to Carston, Steve put the phone back and stood up.

"Sorry. Got to go and look at one of the risers. You finished with that?"

Carston stood up, drained his coffee and threw the cup into the waste bin. Steve picked up a radio from his desk and spoke into it. When he eventually got a reply, he told whoever was at the other end that they were on their way.

"That was Jamie," he said. "He's down in module C. I'll take you there. Better get kitted up."

As he was speaking, he started pulling on his coveralls. Carston did the same, then put on boots and gloves and picked up his hard hat and safety glasses.

"All set?"

"Yep," said Carston and they left the office, went back along the corridors and finally out through a pressure door onto an exterior walkway.

To Carston, it was like the set for a James Bond movie. They were walking along steel grids some two metres wide. Everywhere he looked there were other steel structures—pillars, stairways, containers, machinery, pipes—and the air was full of clangs and a persistent driving of machinery and turbines. Men were working here and there or climbing stairways which led to the upper levels and through which they could look down well over a hundred feet to the sea washing in long, regular waves against the legs of the jacket. As they turned one corner, they found themselves at the foot of the flare boom. It stretched out high over the water and Carston could feel the heat of the flames even though they were well clear of the platform. It was a dramatic sight and Carston would like to have stopped and just stared at it. Steve, though, was striding ahead and they were soon outside a very noisy section. Steve motioned for Carston to wait while he went inside and fetched Jamie.

When they came out, Jamie took off his ear defenders and shook hands. He was a small, red-haired man with streaks of oil down the right hand side of his face and neck. He was holding a small black box with two gauges on the front of it.

Steve left them together and Jamie led Carston away from the noise before either of them tried to say anything. As they wove their way back through bewildering tangles of steel, Jamie pointed out the different parts of the drilling and production processes and made Carston even more aware of just how ignorant he was about the whole thing.

"The separators," said Jamie, pointing at a line of what looked like long steel boilers. "They separate the stuff comin up from the formation into gas, oil and water." He turned and pointed to another line of machinery. "It's heavy gas that comes out so it gets compressed over there. Up to about 180 bar."

Carston whistled.

"That's some pressure."

"Tell me about it," said Jamie, with a smile. "That's what we need, though, compressin an' coolin, to get out the butane and propane. They're liquids when they come out, so we put them back into the oil stream that goes ashore. We take out any water that's still in it, too, so that what you've got left is basically methane, the stuff your missis uses to cook with."

Carston smiled to himself at the sexism of the remark. The problem was that, in his case, it was true. He could boil an egg or make a sandwich but hadn't had to think about cooking for years.

Jamie talked easily about the work they were doing but, as Carston listened to him and heard the power of the machines and the substances flowing through them, he was uneasily aware of their enormous destructive potential and the fact that he was walking within a few feet of them. He thought, as he had many times before, of the terrifying tragedy of Piper Alpha, when men had sat quietly waiting to be evacuated as the inferno beyond the walls was fed by the gushing reservoir and exploded into immense, greedy fireballs. One hundred and sixty-seven people had been killed that night and God knew through how many lives the explosion still echoed. No-one who lived in the north east would ever forget the pain it sent through the community. It was a devastating price to pay for a barrel of oil.

He was grateful to get inside again and sit with Jamie in his office. In the accommodation module, you could push away the vastness of the threat outside. Jamie's room was small and stuffed with manuals, videos and various items of safety equipment. It could easily have been chaotic but Jamie managed to keep it tidy.

"You have to," he answered, when Carston commented on it. "Every time I come here there seems to be more stuff. And there's always somebody wantin to check some bloody procedure or other, so you have to know where to look."

"Is this where Ally Baxter worked, too?" asked Carston.

Jamie nodded.

"Loss Prevention Centre," he said.

"Is there anything here belonging to him?"

"Shouldn't think so. All safety stuff here." Jamie waved at the shelves around them. "Gas testers, fire extinguishers, spare lifejackets, breathing sets."

"Was he as tidy as you are?"

"Aye. Always stowed stuff away. Left labels on things he'd tested, notes on anything outstandin, anything he didn't have time to do."

Carston pointed to the computer console on the desk.

"Did he use this?" he asked.

"Aye, we all do."

"And would there be stuff of his in there?"

"Might be." Jamie tapped at the keyboard and looked at the screen. "You won't get at it, though. We all use our own passwords. Ally—" He stopped. "Ah, you're too late. His files have been downloaded and deleted. None of his stuff left."

"Who could delete it?"

"Dunno. Maybe he did. Wonder if he's taken his memory sticks too."

He got up and reached into a locker behind him. After shuffling the contents around for a while, he brought out a single stick and looked at it.

"Aye, this is his. It'll be the same as the stuff that was on the hard disc, though. Protected."

"Can I take it?" asked Carston.

"Aye," said Jamie, handing it over.

Carston thanked him, got him to initial it and confirm the time and date and put it into a clear plastic wrapper before slipping it into his pocket.

"Did you get on alright with him?" he asked, when Jamie had sat down again.

Jamie flashed him a quick, amused look. He had the pale, slightly reddish skin of the true Celt but none of the presumed dourness. He seemed easy-going and looked as if he laughed a lot.

"Been hearin about him, have you?" he said.

Carston shrugged, then waited.

"He did his job," Jamie went on. "Helped me to do mine. I didn't give a shit whether he was a poof or not. He didn't go out of his way to make friends, though. I know he had a bird he shafted every time he went ashore but he didn't bother tellin folk about it when they took the piss."

"Why was he so unpopular?"

Jamie thought for a while before speaking.

"It was just who he was. I don't think it'd have made any difference if he'd tried to get along. He was a natural for bullying. Looked like a poof. What could he do?"

"It didn't affect his work, though?"

"No. In fact, that last shift he hardly stopped. Did a full inspection on all the pipework around the separators and compressors."

"Isn't that normal?"

"Not as often as he's been doin it. It's scheduled as a quarterly process but he's been doin it bit by bit every time he's been out here this last few times."

"And you've no idea why?"

"Nope." Jamie thought again. "An idea he had in his head. We haven't had any instructions from the beach to do anythin special. I suppose it could be to do with next month's derrick shut-down. Production's gonna be shut down at the same time. But I think I'd've known about that. He'd've told me. No, there's somethin else. He's been testin gear an' settin it aside."

"What sort of gear?"

"Safety gear. The usual, extinguishers, gas sniffers, smokehoods."

"What for?"

Jamie spread his hands to indicate that he had no idea.

"He's even put some of it aside. Locked it up in the store and took it out of commission."

"Why?"

Jamie repeated the gesture.

"Probably being extra careful. Must've found something wrong with it."

"What sort of stuff was it?"

"Dunno. Like I said, it's locked away."

"Could I see?"

Jamie gave a deep sigh.

"Difficult," he said. "It'll take a while."

Carston thought for a moment. It might be nothing but it had to be checked.

"D'you think you could have a look at it for me?" he asked. "Give me an idea of what it is?"

"Sure. No bother."

"And if there's anything … personal. Can you just leave it. Don't handle it or anything. I'll come out again myself. Or send a team."

"Christ," said Jamie. "Just like bein on telly."

Carston smiled. He was beginning to feel warm in his overalls. He pulled the zip down and loosened his collar a little more.

"Could he have been up to something," he said.

"Like what?" asked Jamie, sitting forward and leaning his short fat arms on the desk.

"I don't know. Maybe just trying to make more work for other people. Getting his own back on them for … you know, taking the piss and things."

"Doubt it. It's all been goin on too long. I reckon the poor bastard had got used to it. Accepted it, if you like. Nobody liked him and he thought they were all shitheads. Work took his mind off it. End of story."

Carston was flicking through a thick book which he'd taken from a shelf beside him. It listed hazardous materials and gave details of how to handle them.

"We found some stuff in a bottle in his locker onshore," he said. "Looked like sodium. Why would he have that?"

"Sodium," said Jamie, his voice rising sharply. "What the hell's he want that for? Bloody lethal, that is."

"So it's not something you use for your safety work in any way?"

Jamie laughed and sat back.

"If you brought any of that out here, there wouldn't be any safety work to do before long. The place'd be—"

He made a gesture with his arms to signify an explosion and the disappearance of the platform and everything on it.

"Ever seen it in water?" he asked.

Carston shook his head. Jamie's face was serious.

"Gets white hot in no time. Talk about a source of ignition. With the gases here it'd just—" This time there was no need for the gesture. "Ally was a gambler, but he'd never take risks out here."

"A gambler?" said Carston.

"Didn't you know?" said Jamie. "Yeah. Horses, dogs, football. Silly bugger was up to the balls in debt. Used to phone his bets ashore every day."

Carston shook his head.

"He was a fascinating character, wasn't he?" he said, sounding as if he meant it. "Workaholic, homosexual, heterosexual, and now a gambler. Who did he owe money to?"

Jamie shrugged.

"Bookies. He had accounts with 'em. Ladbroke's, I think. You can find out from the radio room. All the numbers he called'll be listed there."

Carston thanked him and turned the conversation back to Baxter's relationship with his workmates. Everything Jamie said simply confirmed the information he already had. In a way, Baxter could be categorised so easily as far as his work and his sexuality were concerned that he seemed two-dimensional, and yet there was much about his moods and motives that made him very elusive.

When he'd exhausted the ever-willing Jamie's store of answers, Carston asked him to take him on a tour of all the places Baxter had worked. They started in the cabin he'd used during his shift, which was now occupied by Jamie, then went to various stores and locations on most of the platform's four main levels. All the time, the PA system was echoing messages over the background din and Carston found the noise as tiring as the effort of climbing up and down stairways and dragging himself along walkways with the wind hitting him from different directions as he went. Everywhere, there were warning notices, caches of emergency equipment, guard rails and reminders that this was no place to take chances. By the time the tour was over, Carston was ready to get back ashore. He'd had his adventure but the enigma of Ally Baxter, far from being solved, had developed even greater complexity.

He checked in at reception, said his goodbyes to Steve and Jamie and pulled on his ball-crushing survival suit again. After watching the statutory video, he and the other passengers were shepherded into the aircraft by the helideck crew. He looked out of the window as the rotors spun faster, the engine noise screamed higher and they lifted off and swooped away from Falcon Alpha. Very quickly, the platform became a small, dark shadow flickering its flame into the gathering gloom and Carston already found it difficult to associate it with the massive webs of steel among which he'd so recently been moving. The trip back to the heliport was a long drone but Carston's mind was buzzing with the experience and his tiredness made him just sit back and enjoy being carried through

139

the air knowing that there was nothing to do until they touched down.

Back at Anstey's, he handed his gear to the man at the counter, who checked it in and asked if he'd enjoyed his trip.

"Definitely," he replied with enthusiasm.

"Fancy working out there, then?" asked the man.

"Definitely not," said Carston.

They both smiled. Carston thanked him and went out to his car. As he drove back towards the Cairngorms, he was aware that the day had passed very quickly and that he'd been fortunate to experience, if only briefly, life offshore. By now, darkness was well established and his thoughts went back out to the black waters, the platform, whose lights and flare kept it permanently lit, and the little group of men walking around in their closed, dangerous world. It gave an extra edge to his pleasure at the thought of an evening at home with Kath.

He stopped briefly at the station to give Sandy Dwyer the list of telephone numbers he'd got from the radio room and ask him to get them checked. His own brief look at them showed that almost all were to an 0800 number, which he assumed would be the bookmaker, and Anstey's head office. Sprinkled elsewhere, though, were one or two in Aberdeen and Cairnburgh. Given Baxter's ability to surprise them, Carston didn't pin many hopes on them revealing anything.

He'd rung Kath from the platform to tell her that he'd eaten copiously in the dining hall there and that he wouldn't need an evening meal. By the time he got home, she'd finished the light supper she'd made for herself and was sitting with a glass of Chablis watching television. She turned and raised her glass to him as he came into the room.

"Pissed again?" asked Carston.

"Yep."

"Good."

Her lips lifted into a bigger smile than the one which always seemed to be waiting in them. He leaned over and kissed her, feeling the wetness of the wine on her lips.

"Good day?" she asked.

"Fascinating," he replied, going through to the kitchen to pour himself a glass.

"You going to tell me about it?" she asked, when he came back in a flopped onto the sofa beside her.

"Only if we can have outrageous sex tonight."

"Forget it," said Kath. "I'll watch telly."

He kissed her again and told her about the trip, forcing himself to think of the generalities of the experience rather than the bits of it relating to Baxter and the case. His curiosity about the extremes of the location and the processes going on there was infectious and Kath's questions helped him to look more closely at his reactions and relive the trip's fascination. Their talk, lubricated by the wine, ranged over the demands of jobs of which separation was an integral part, the rhythms, routines and essential alienation of offshore schedules and the effect of extreme environments on the male psyche. Nothing happened to disturb their evening. When they did eventually go to bed, the sex they had wasn't outrageous, but it was very good.

Chapter Eleven

McNeil's fiancé had been giving her a hard time about the amount of work she'd been doing. When she came in on Monday morning, she was in no mood to put up with the comments that Spurle, Fraser and the others usually felt obliged to keep making. The fact that she outranked them hadn't stopped the elephantine gibes and, unaccountably, they still seemed to find them funny.

She was in the squad room cross-checking some statements. Spurle, Fraser, Bellman and Thom were all there and the way she'd reacted to their cracks had already flagged her mood and drawn from them the inevitable asides about the time of the month. Naturally enough, it was Spurle who was pushing hardest.

"See that programme about lions last night?" he asked.

Bellman and Thom shook their heads. Fraser was reading a paper and said nothing.

"They're on heat every three months," said Spurle.

"So?" said Bellman.

"Guess how often they fuck?"

Bellman shook his head.

"Every twenty minutes," said Spurle. "That's seventy-two shags a day. I worked it out."

"Bloody sore," said Fraser, without looking up.

"Aye," said Spurle. "OK for the females. They just have to stand there. But gettin it up every twenty minutes, day in, day out, that's somethin else."

"I should think once is hard enough for you," said McNeil, drawn in despite herself.

"Yeah. Well," said Spurle.

It was all he could manage. Any reference to the size or effectiveness of his penis immediately triggered all his inadequacies. The arrival of Carston and Ross saved both of them, her from her anger and Spurle from its barbs.

Carston had been looking through the lab's notes on Baxter's survival suit, which had arrived in the first bag. He and Ross had talked through them and were anxious to follow them up.

"Anybody seen Sergeant Reid?" asked Carston.

Nobody had.

"OK, we'll have to try to manage without him somehow," said Carston, drawing a look from Ross. "Time we sorted out where we are with all this. We're dealing with a double killing. There's nothing definite to say they're linked but it'd be a helluva coincidence if they're not. We haven't got enough on the woman yet but there's plenty on Baxter to keep us occupied."

"It's that fat bastard in the cells, then, is it, sir?" asked Fraser.

"Careful, that fat bastard's taxes pay your wages," said Carston, incongruously. "No. We can't pin him down. I don't necessarily think this was anything to do with the queer-bashing, anyway. We're just supposed to think it was."

Carston's own experience of putting on a survival suit had more or less convinced him that Baxter was already dead before he was wrapped up in his.

"And there were no bloodstains anywhere else except around the neck, so all the cuts around his crotch were done after the suit was off again. And to me, that means he was brought to the dustbins in the suit, it was taken off him and then he was slashed. It's all too deliberate to be simple queer-bashing."

"Aye," said Ross. "And why put the suit back in the locker? Why not just ditch it? It was bound to have contact traces of some sort on it."

"Right," said Carston. "Anyway, apart from all that, the timing's wrong. Bole and his mates were here from about eleven. Unless one of them killed him later, after they'd been released by Sergeant Reid."

"'scuse me, sir," said McNeil.

Her cheeks were slightly flushed from the anger produced by Spurle's earlier goading. It made her eyes seem clearer. Carston wished he'd stop noticing such things.

"You think we're looking for a single perpetrator, do you?" she asked.

"Your guess is as good as mine," said Carston. "Why?"

"Well, it's another thing that lets Bole off the hook. He was in the cells the night Vicky was killed."

"Yes, I know. I'd love the fat tax-payer to be in the frame but it's hard. I still want him for the queer-bashing, though."

McNeil nodded and made a note in her book.

"We'll stick with Baxter for the time being," Carston went on. "Out there on the platform, there was something going on. Why was he telling the guys he worked with they'd soon be on the dole? He told Vicky he was coming into money. Why? Just gambler's optimism?"

"Gambler?" said McNeil.

"Yes," said Carston. "Used to phone bets in from the platform. I got a list of his calls. There was one to Vicky, one to McEwan, two to video shops, but the bulk of them were to Anstey's office, the Tote and Ladbroke's."

He handed McNeil a piece of paper.

"These are their numbers," he said. "The one at the bottom's his account number. Have a word with them. See what they say."

"Right," said McNeil.

"One way and another, there are plenty of reasons for him to be involved in something dodgy," Carston said. "And nobody could tell us why he had sodium in his locker. And one other little gem; one of the survival suits had spots of blood on it. Don't know whose suit it was. Don't know whose blood either. Not yet anyway. So we need another look at Anstey's. I'm going back there this afternoon to poke around a bit more."

"What about us, patron?" asked Fraser.

"You and Spurle are coming with me," replied Carston. "And Julie, I want you to have another word with Vicky's sister, too. We need a bit more on what he talked to Vicky about. See if you can get any idea about the guy he recommended to her."

"Right, sir," said McNeil.

Bellman and Thom were sitting patiently, fully expecting to be relegated to whatever dogsbody work was left when all the rest had been handed out. Carston was aware that that happened too often.

"You two," he said. "First, I want you to get me contact numbers for everybody involved here—Bole and his lot, the gays, the witnesses—all of them. Mobiles would be best. I want to be sure we can get hold of them if we need to."

Both the men nodded, accepting that they'd be stuck with routine paperwork yet again. Carston pointed at Thom.

"Then, after that, you link up with Sergeant McNeil. And Bellman, you'll be with Sergeant Ross."

"Where, sir?" asked Ross.

"First, see if you can get Bole to agree to give us a DNA sample. We've got the other blood on Baxter to identify, remember. If he won't agree, get one of his fag ends and we'll do it on the quiet, just to see."

Ross nodded.

"There are the fibres on his survival suit to cross-check, too. And some of the prints they found there were Bole's. Let's build up as much as we can. Then you'll need to talk to Baigrie and Gallacher again. See if you can get a bit more about this 4 x 4 Baigrie thinks he saw. Oh, and Gallacher conveniently forgot to mention that he'd already had a set-to with Bole."

The news came as a surprise to all of them.

"When?" asked Ross.

"Some time ago. He was out on the platform on a job. Talking to Baxter."

"He said he didn't know him."

"Yes, that's another thing. He did, though. Bole tried to wind them up. Check it out. Find out what all the bloody lies are about."

"Right," said Ross.

The door opened and Reid, looking good in a pale grey suit and dark blue tie, came in.

"Evening, Sergeant," said Carston. "Good of you to join us."

"Sorry I'm late, sir," said Reid, pushing his gold-rimmed glasses higher on his nose. "Superintendent Ridley called me up to his office when I came in."

"Of course," said Carston. "And how is he?"

"Er … very well, I think. He … er … he wants a word with you. Asked me to—"

Carston interrupted him.

"Didn't you point out that we're a bit busy at the moment? I mean, a double murder does tend to eat up the time."

Reid's face was impassive.

145

"He did say that it was important, sir. Needs to see you before you leave this morning."

Carston bit back the other sarcasms that came to him. The thought of Reid and Ridley already into their little tête-à-têtes right at the beginning of another week needled into him.

"I wonder whether it occurs to you," he said, "that investigating a murder isn't the same as writing out lists and keeping up appearances. Maybe you and the superin—"

He was interrupted by a bang. Unaccountably, a box file had slipped off the table against which Ross was leaning.

"Sorry, sir," said Ross.

It was enough. Carston turned back to Reid.

"You'll find a copy of the lab report on Baxter's survival suit and the others on my desk. Read it, then go through everything else we've got in the computer so far. Maybe you've got ways of seeing parallels and link-ups which escape tiny minds like mine."

"Yes, sir," said Reid.

Carston glared at him. It was the first time he'd actually risked insolence. It didn't augur well for the meeting with Ridley.

He picked up the memory stick he'd brought back from the platform and handed it to Ross.

"That's Baxter's personal stuff. From the platform. No idea what's on it but we'll need to crack the password. Get it down to I.T., will you?"

"Right, sir," said Ross.

There was nothing else to help Carston postpone the visit upstairs. With lots of apprehension, he went up to the superintendent's office, where his suspicions were immediately confirmed. There was no pretence at greeting and he was told to sit in the chair in front of the desk in a tone that would have better suited a headmaster speaking to a very young pupil. Ridley even dispensed with the usual charade of making him wait while he did some theoretically crucial paper signing. Instead, he opened a black file that was ominously thick and lifted the top sheet from it.

"How come it's taken me three days to get hold of you," he asked.

"Sorry," said Carston. "I've been a bit tied up. Two murders, you see. I know it's a nuisance the way it keeps me out of the office but—"

146

Ridley was looking at the paper, seemingly ignoring his reply. He spoke over Carston's voice.

"It's costing us a fortune in forensic services," he said.

Carston was thrown. Even people like Spurle and Reid knew that forensic reports were essential. Ridley pressed on.

"I thought I made it clear, too, that I wanted Sergeant Reid more fully involved."

"Yes, sir. I've taken that on board. He's—"

"I've told you what I thought about sending him to search through garbage. You're supposed to be training him in CID techniques."

"I'm trying. It's not easy."

"No. Especially with the sort of example you're setting."

"Sir?"

"Manhandling the people you're interviewing. Threatening them."

That little prick Reid had been telling him about McEwan. Carston said nothing. It was too dangerous given the mood that was building in him. And at the same time, he was puzzled by Ridley's strange self-assurance. He was usually a bit more wary than this, a bit defensive. This morning, he seemed to have an agenda and a sort of edgy confidence. He turned to the next sheet of paper.

"Another thing. I don't take to being instructed by a desk sergeant not to assign a murder case to another squad. Without explanation or clarification. Just a message from you."

He was referring to the call Carston had made from McIntosh's car.

"It was late on Friday. I'd only just got the news myse—"

"Where were you yesterday?"

What was going on? This was like an interrogation.

"I went out to Falcon Alpha. In connection with the Baxter case. Last minute arrangement."

"Did you clear it with Grampian?"

All platforms came under the jurisdiction of the Grampian force in Aberdeen. Ridley was right; any investigations had to be cleared with them. There just hadn't been time.

"As I said, it was a last minute arrangement," began Carston, surprised to find himself on the defensive. "My report—"

"And I thought I made it clear that I wanted you to be a bit more circumspect in your dealings with Anstey Oil."

Carston decided to shut up. Ridley was going somewhere specific with all this. The sooner he got there, the sooner Carston would know the line to take.

Ridley was leafing through more sheets.

"Nearly two years' worth of evidence," he said, holding up a handful of them.

Carston had no idea what he was talking about.

"Time after time after time. And always excuses, manipulations, irregularities."

Eventually, Ridley got fed up with looking at the papers. It was obviously a pretence anyway.

"It's come to a head, Carston," he said, tapping the papers on the desk to straighten their edges and putting them carefully on top of the folder. "I've had a word with the DCC. Put in an official complaint. He's agreed to appoint an Investigating Officer."

The news took Carston completely by surprise. He knew that he'd been sailing close to the wind with Ridley for years but never thought the man would have the balls, or the occasion, to face up to him. He still didn't. Unless there were some other evidence he hadn't revealed, none of the things he'd mentioned added up to a real charge. They were just lots of irritants that, together, had pushed Ridley to uncharacteristic action. On the other hand, if the DCC had agreed to appoint an Investigating Officer, Ridley must have convinced him that there was justification for his complaints.

"May I ask the charge, sir?" he said, his voice slow and even.

"Indiscipline to a senior officer," said Ridley, his tone smug but his eyes still unwilling to meet Carston's directly.

Carston just nodded.

"Right, sir," he said, injecting a brightness into his tone which he didn't feel. "Is that it, then? Because there are still these two murders."

Ridley shut the folder and let out a short sigh of frustration. He'd hoped to puncture Carston's inflated opinion of himself for once but there was no outward sign that his words had had any effect.

"Disciplinary papers will be served on you, with the allegation and the name of the Investigating Officer."

"I know, sir," said Carston.

He'd regained all his composure and sat still, his face showing nothing. Ridley waved an impatient hand to dismiss him.

"Thank you, sir," said Carston. He got up, pushed the chair silently back into its position and went slowly out of the office, closing the door quietly behind him.

Ridley sat, his fingers tapping nervously on the file. He'd been sure that, for once, he'd reduce Carston to silence, unsettle his arrogance, stifle the wisecracks. And yet the man had seemed entirely comfortable and left the office as if they'd been talking about some minor administrative adjustment. He began to wonder whether he'd misjudged the situation, whether Carston had another of his Houdini tricks at the ready. But he didn't think so. This time, there was a big enough accumulation of misdemeanours to convince the DCC. Carston was about to be reminded of exactly where he stood in the hierarchy.

Downstairs, Carston had forced all his fury back into himself. The way things were, venting it through some broadside at Reid would fit nicely into Ridley's scenario. The iron control he'd tried to keep on his contempt before would have to be even greater now that Ridley had mobilised the suits against him.

It had only been possible because of Reid's diligent reporting of his departures from protocol and Carston was sure that Ridley had told him what he was planning. Reid was at one of the desks in the inner office. He looked up when Carston came in, fully expecting a bollocking. Carston smiled at him, a warm, broad, friendly smile, worthy of an advert.

"Carry on, lad," he said.

****

McNeil had never been on a job with Thom on his own before. He was a tall, fresh-faced twenty-four year old, with dark hair, a ready smile and a manner so young that it made her feel old enough to be his mother, even though there were just seven years between them. For his part, the ambivalence of having to partner a woman who was senior to him and still maintain his assumed status in the eyes of Spurle and the others was disturbing. But the assignment implied a new trust on the part of Carston and was a lot more interesting than the usual trudging around.

As they drove up Mandy's street, McNeil repeated the warning she'd already given him more than once.

"Remember. Softly, softly. The stories her sister told her have turned her right off men. No that that's hard."

Without the support and encouragement of the others, Thom's sexism was impotent. He made no protest.

"And she's maybe still in shock. So leave most of it to me, right?"

"Right," said Thom.

As soon as Mandy opened the door to them, the appropriateness of McNeil's warnings was clear. She'd not only been crying a lot; the tears were still in her eyes. There was no change in her expression when she saw McNeil, but her face closed when she noticed Thom behind her. McNeil said hello, introduced Thom and asked if they could have another talk. As Mandy stepped back to let them in, they saw that she'd been sorting through a pile of clothes. They were far too flashy to be her own and McNeil knew at once that they must have belonged to Vicky. The scene of crime people had told Mandy that it was OK to clear her sister's flat and she'd reluctantly gone over and emptied it. Most of the contents had gone to the rubbish tip or the Oxfam shop on Stirling Street but she'd brought the more personal things home with her.

"Tea?" she asked.

"I'll do it," said McNeil, but Mandy shook her head and went into the kitchen.

Billy was in a playpen in front of the television. He held up his hand to them. To McNeil's surprise, Thom squatted beside him, held his sticky fingers and baby-talked a bit. It didn't last long. Pretty soon, it was obvious to Billy that Thom had nothing to give him, so he turned his attention back to the American chat show. Thom picked up a skirt from the pile on the floor. It was a red silk-effect number with a mark on the front where some stain or other had resisted the efforts of whoever had tried to clean it. He laid it back with the others and trailed his fingers through a little heap of ear-rings, bracelets and necklaces beside the clothes. Billy heard the clinking and his head came round to look for his mother. When he didn't see her, he went back to his show.

Mandy had used her time in the kitchen to dry her eyes and shake off the recent crying. She brought in three cups on a tray with the teapot, milk and sugar.

"DC Thom'll pour," said McNeil.

Thom looked quickly at her but a flick of her head told him to get on with it. It had the effect she was looking for. Mandy sat down, surprised, slightly disorientated and secretly pleased that a man was waiting on her for a change. As they started talking, McNeil was careful to stay on general topics, asking how she was, what arrangements she was making for Billy, how he'd been, and the sort of smallish talk that simply fills gaps in the silence and reassures people that there's nothing threatening around. Mandy asked how their investigations were going and McNeil found the sort of formulae that sounded encouraging without actually saying much.

It was Mandy who brought up Baxter's name first. She asked if they'd found out about the money he was supposed to be coming into.

"Not yet," said McNeil. "It sounded as if it was going to be quite a bit from the way he was talking to Vicky, didn't it?"

Mandy nodded.

"He didn't say it was redundancy money, did he?" asked McNeil.

"No," said Mandy. "And if it was, you dinna get much these days, do you?"

McNeil tossed her head and gave a little chuckle.

"You're right there."

"No, it wasna that," said Mandy. "He said he was into somethin big."

"Something illegal?"

Mandy shrugged.

"No idea. Might've been. Vicky said he was a bit afraid of it."

"Afraid?"

"Aye. That's what he told her. Said there was big bucks on the way but he'd need to be careful."

"What of?"

"Dunno. But he said that she'd be OK. Whatever happened."

The irony of what she was saying suddenly hit her and the tears came back to her eyes. She grabbed a tissue from a box beside her and dabbed at her face, talking more quickly as she did so to force the misery away again.

"He was goin to look after her. Not just the car. Other things, too. She believed him."

"Did she say what sort of things?" asked McNeil. Her voice was gentle.

Mandy shook her head and blew her nose.

"Best thing he could've done was get her away from that bastard McEwan," she said, her contempt helping her to recover. "He got her so tied up wi' money and things, she couldna see her way out."

"Aye, you said," said McNeil.

"Has he told you who she was with yet?"

McNeil was aware that they hadn't got nearly enough from McEwan and didn't want Mandy to lose faith in them.

"Not yet," she said. "We're working on it. Did Vicky say anything else about the man? Did she know him?"

"Don't think so. Just a new punter. McEwan's the one to ask."

"Aye. We will. How about the money in the flat? Could that have been from him? From the punter, I mean."

"What, the eighty quid?"

"Yes."

"No. McEwan left her that. That afternoon. Bein nice to her for a change."

"How d'you mean?"

"He spent the afternoon with her. Took the money she'd earned that week but left her eighty quid. To make up for some guy he'd fixed her up with."

She paused to light a cigarette.

"Bloody sadist," she said, blowing out a cloud of smoke and picking a fleck of something off her lower lip. "Whipped her."

"When was this?"

"Wednesday night. She told McEwan and he was all sweetness and light. Said he was sorry. Treated her like a human bloody bein for a change. That's why he left her the cash. Bonus, he called it." She snorted her disgust and took another hard drag. "Poor Vicky was grateful for it, too. Over four hundred quid she'd made that week and he leaves her eighty. Christ, that Baxter guy was a weirdo but at least he used to look after her. Usually paid her over the odds."

"Did you know his mates offshore thought he was gay?"

Mandy coughed and nodded at the same time.

"Vicky talked about it once or twice. He wasna great on sex. Liked it, like, but sometimes didna even bother. Just lay there wi' her. Talkin. Suited her. She reckoned he was AC/DC."

Thom had been listening patiently enough. There'd never been a moment for him to say anything and anyway, he recognised the relationship McNeil had created with Mandy and knew better than to interfere with it.

"He didna have much time for his mates," Mandy said. He was screwin them somehow. Dunno how. Told Vicky they'd be gettin the push because o' him."

"How?"

Mandy shook her head.

"That's all he said. Started talkin about contracts. Vicky switched off. She hardly listened to him half the time anyway."

It was tantalising. They were two steps removed from a conversation that might have enabled them to target people or, at least, areas of investigation. Mandy's memory was clouded by the sorrows that kept welling up in her, and the information she was giving was only fragments of what Vicky had originally remembered anyway. McNeil tried, gently and without apparent insistence, to get more details, but there were none to be had. The only other snippet they got before Billy started crying and demanding attention was the fact that, when he left her, Baxter had said that he was going to look for a guy. To sort something out with him.

"And he didn't say who?" asked McNeil.

"No," said Mandy, picking Billy up and jogging him up and down on her shoulder to stop his girning. "He just gave her a hundred quid, an extra twenty for herself, and left."

McNeil stood up. Thom followed suit and went to the door. McNeil rubbed her forefinger across Billy's damp cheek and regretted it at once.

"We'll leave you to it, then," she said. "Sorry to have bothered you again but you know why we have to, don't you?"

"Aye," said Mandy. "It's no bother. Just get the bastard, eh?"

McNeil nodded, projecting a confidence she didn't yet feel.

As Thom opened the door, McNeil and Mandy walked over to it.

"Tell you what, though," said Mandy.

"What?" said McNeil.

Mandy nodded at Thom.

"You've got him well trained."

McNeil laughed.

"Girl power," she said.

Chapter Twelve

Carston was having difficulty concentrating. Images of Ridley kept burning into his head as he ran over the conversation they'd had and worked out the things he should have said to him. He had no real fear of being investigated but he knew that the sort of rectitude he could demonstrate might be at odds with the one Ridley and his ilk preferred. He was managing to retain his almost avuncular attitude towards Reid but knew that it would take very little to unleash his contempt for the young man in comments that would add significantly to the dossier Ridley was compiling so gleefully.

When he rang Anstey's, he was glad to hear that Hamer wouldn't be there until the afternoon. It meant that he could use the morning to settle himself. He arranged to visit at around three and, his tone friendly and his face impassive, gave Reid his tasks for the morning. It was convenient that the details of what the lab had found on Baxter's survival suit needed to be added to the material they'd already gathered. It would keep Reid occupied. Carston told him to enter the data and then, with the help of Fraser and Spurle, collate it under a series of headings that would allow them to analyse it from different perspectives; those of Baxter himself, Bole, Gallacher and any others who had made a statement or been involved, however peripherally. Reassured by Reid that that represented a full morning's work, he took his own notes on the two cases and went home.

Kath was reorganising her darkroom, a converted cupboard under the stairs. When Carston walked in, there were small square black bottles with white tops lined across the hall, packets of papers and stacks of grey, red and white trays on the telephone table and the sounds of Gerry Rafferty's Baker Street echoing from the radio she'd set up on one of the cupboard walls. She smiled when she saw him but the hug he gave her was warmer and lasted longer than usual and, as they drew apart, she saw in his face that he had something on his mind. She turned off the radio and the cupboard light and went through to the kitchen with him. Together they brewed fresh coffee as Carston told her all about his meeting with Ridley.

"Is it serious, Jack?" she asked, when he'd finished.

He shrugged, then shook his head.

"No. I've been niggling him for years."

"So why's he suddenly doing this?"

"Reid, I suppose. He's a bloody liability. But that's not a problem either. I can show them the cock-ups he's made. Nobody'll blame me for the way I've been treating him."

She kissed him on the forehead and sat at the table beside him.

"What's the worst that can happen?" she asked.

"Reprimand," said Carston. "Loss of increments. Could cost us two or three thousand."

"Not the sack, though?"

"Unlikely."

"That's alright then. From what you say, every day with Ridley's like a reprimand anyway."

Carston smiled and nodded his head slowly.

"Maybe I ought to just get out," he said.

Kath waited, giving him time to speak the thoughts as they came to him.

"I'm OK at the job, get on fine with Jim, Julie and the rest. Even that retard Spurle. But I don't really belong there. Seeing what folks do to one another. It's depressing. And anyway, I'm not sure who's right and who's wrong any more."

"What d'you mean?" asked Kath.

Carston shook his head.

"Not sure, love. I've had too many cases where the people doing the killing had every right to do something. It's bad enough dealing with innocent victims; it's worse when they're guilty."

"You've lost me."

"It's nothing. I'm just … I just don't know if I'm doing any good. And if I'm not, is it worth putting up with all the hassle from the brotherhood upstairs?"

He stopped. Kath waited again, then asked, "Well, is it?"

"What do you think?" he said.

"How do I know?"

"No, seriously," he insisted.

Kath leaned forward on her elbows, her right hand playing with the spoon in her saucer.

"You're too good at the job to leave it," she said. "For all their stupid disciplinary nonsense, I bet they'd have a fit if you asked to go."

Carston shook his head.

"Yes they would," she went on, picking up the spoon and, unnecessarily, stirring her coffee again. "Look at your clear-up rate. It'd make a huge hole in Ridley's statistics if you went. Anyway, where would you go? Dog-handling? Traffic control? You'd be lethal."

Her words brought another smile to his lips and, as they talked on, the therapy he'd known she would provide helped him to force Ridley's threat and his doubts about himself back into a proper perspective. Carston had never been a worrier. He'd always managed to stay in the present and leave regrets and anticipations to others. If a thing was going to happen, it would; worrying about it only made it last longer. If it didn't happen after all, you'd wasted bloody good time and energy on it. And, once it was over, what was the point of dwelling on it? Ridley was a constant irritant in Carston's daily routines. But he was external, as unimportant as spilt coffee or a creaky hinge. If Carston let him inside his head, it gave Ridley a power he didn't actually possess.

"Ever thought of taking up counselling?" he asked.

"No," said Kath, firmly. "Living with someone who's psychologically inadequate is bad enough. I wouldn't want to work with them, too."

The distant warble of his mobile saved Carston from having to find an answer. He went out into the hall and picked it up from the table where he'd left it when he came in. It was Brian McIntosh.

"Jack?" he said. "I've got the preliminary results of the autopsy on Vicky Bryant. Not the sort of reading you like, I'm afraid."

"What d'you mean?" asked Carston, taking out his notebook and picking up the pen from the phone table.

"Like I told you at her flat. Absolutely straightforward case of strangulation. No semen, no sex, no extras."

"What about the marks on her sides and back?"

"Old ones, as I said. Well, not old old, but they weren't made at the same time as the killing. Maybe one of her clients."

"Not like you to speculate, Brian. What makes you say that?"

"They look like whip marks to me. Straight weals. Blood vessels broken in lines. A few slaps, maybe. Not the sort of thing normal people get up to. Occupational hazard."

"You're probably right," said Carston. "Any contact traces? DNA?"

"Not that we've identified yet. From the marks of the ligature, I'd say whoever it was just came up behind her, looped a tie or something round her neck and throttled her. She probably lost consciousness quite quickly."

"Somebody pretty strong, then?"

"Probably."

"Male, d'you think?"

"Or a beefy female."

"What the hell did he do it for? No sex. Didn't take her money. Just got rid of her."

"That's where you come in, Jack. Now, there's more on the Baxter chap, too."

"Wow. Bonus time, eh? What is it?"

"I've had time to take a few X-rays, do a bit of reconstruction. The mutilations were an afterthought, we know that. So were most of the head wounds. But it looks as if there was one blow that started it all. Deep enough to cause unconsciousness right away and then cranial bleeding did the rest; kept him out while he choked."

"Interesting."

"Yes. More than that, though. I'd say that that first attack was made with something curved."

"Like the head of a hammer," said Carston.

"No. The post mortem blows, the ones that made all the splinters, they were made with a hammer. But the first depression was semi-circular. Something bigger. A sort of crescent. Edge of something circular, about six inches across."

"Bloody hell," said Carston. "That's a helluva hammer."

"No. It's more likely to be the rim of something. Some sort of container. I've done some drawings. I could talk you through them. How about lunch?"

"When?"

"Today."

157

The news of fresh complications for Baxter enlivened Carston. If he needed any other proof that he'd miss the job, the excitement he now felt supplied it. Ridley's interference was irrelevant. If he only knew a little more about real CID work, he'd understand why Reid was light years away from the level of experience needed to handle such investigations.

****

Lunch in hospitals is always served at a ludicrously early hour. By the time Gallacher arrived to visit Baigrie, the last of the stewed apples and custard had been removed and the staff had left for their own meals. It was just past noon. Much to the disgust of the red-faced man in the next bed, Gallacher kissed Baigrie full on the lips and the two of them stayed locked together for a long time, with Baigrie's arms flung greedily around his partner's shoulders. When they separated, Gallacher unloaded the goodies he'd brought—fruit, sweets and an iPod full of movie themes—and sat on the edge of the bed, holding Baigrie's hand as he told more tales of the nurses and patients who shared his world.

The words tumbled out as Baigrie constructed more elaborate theories about the dubiousness of doctors' motives for choosing such a profession, the latent fascism of nursing staff and the domestic circumstances of the men in the other beds. He obviously needed to talk and was happy to say anything that came into his head.

At last, he asked how the investigation was developing.

"Nothing. Absolute silence," said Gallacher. "Haven't they been to see you yet?"

"No, why should they?"

"I told them you'd seen that Anstey's four by four."

Baigrie's finger started tracing little patterns at the base of Gallacher's thumb.

"I've thought some more about that, Paul," he said, his voice very quiet. "You know, I'm not so sure I did."

"What?"

"See that car. I thought I did, but then I might just have wanted to so much that—"

Gallacher patted his hand.

"I know," he said. "Don't worry. It won't make any difference. I get the feeling the buggers aren't over-exerting themselves."

They fell silent. Gallacher was searching around for something light to lift their mood again when Baigrie asked the question he least wanted to hear.

"You've got to tell me, Paul. I know you've talked to them. What did the doctors say?"

Gallacher looked at him. His face was still pathetic under the bandages, the dark blue iris of his left eye surrounded by broken blood vessels and looking away across the ward, not wanting to make contact with Gallacher's.

"Nothing's definite," Gallacher began. "They—"

"Don't give me bullshit, Paul," said Baigrie, recognising the hesitation and guessing what it was trying to hide.

Gallacher gripped his hand tighter.

"It's not good, pet," he said softly.

"Tell me," said Baigrie, after a pause.

Gallacher took a deep breath.

"They think there's too much damage to your right eye," he said.

A shudder went through Baigrie and Gallacher saw his jaw clench tight.

"What about the other one?" asked Baigrie, his voice just above a whisper.

Gallacher felt a lump in his throat and could only shake his head and mutter, "Same. The nerve—"

Immediately, he saw the tears well in Baigrie's eye and start to run down his cheek.

"Oh Christ, no," said Baigrie, and his voice broke with the words and was choked off by sobs and whimpers.

Gallacher leaned forward and cradled his head, careful not to touch the bandages.

"I'll get them," he said fiercely. "I'll make the bastards pay."

Baigrie shook his head.

"No, no. I've had enough of all that," he sobbed. "Let's just … There's no need. Look at Ally. He's… We've done enough already. I'm sick of it."

As Gallacher rocked him to and fro, he looked up and saw the man in the next bed staring at them. When he caught Gallacher's eye, the man shook his head and tutted, making it very clear to Gallacher what he thought of the display.

"What?" said Gallacher.

"Disgusting," said the man. "In public, too."

Gallacher released Baigrie and stepped over to him. The man shrank back as Gallacher reached towards him and dragged off the earphones he was wearing. Before the man could react, he'd looped their cable around his neck and pulled it tighter.

"You wanna watch your mouth, granddad," he hissed. "Patients have fallen out of bed with these things on and hung themselves."

The man's face was even redder. Only Baigrie's voice cut through Gallacher's anger.

"Paul, stop it. Leave him. Don't make it worse."

Gallacher pushed the man back into his pillows.

"One more word out of you," he said, his face close to him, "one more opinion, and you're dead, you self-righteous bastard."

The man was too shocked to say anything. With a final warning point of the finger, Gallacher went back to Baigrie's bed.

"Sorry," he said, gruffly. "Make me so bloody mad, they do."

"I noticed," said Baigrie. He was still crying but, paradoxically, it was he who was trying to calm Gallacher. He needed his support and love. The anger would only get in the way again, as it had so often before. Instead of abating, Gallacher's fury flared more as he looked at his partner. The ravages of the fight were now made much worse by the knowledge he had that, before long, he'd be unable to see. The quality of their life together was going to be altered in ways that neither of them could guess at. The arbitrariness of it made Gallacher mad.

It was difficult to talk or think of anything other than the blindness waiting for Baigrie and, in a way, the arrival of Ross and Bellman was almost a relief. Ross had spent the morning organising things at the station. He'd got Bole to agree to give a blood sample and arranged for Reid, Spurle and Fraser to take samples of fibres from his clothes and get them analysed with a view to adding them to the data they were entering. Even as he did so, though, he knew that it was really overkill. They'd already found Bole's prints on Baxter's survival suit and, anyway, establishing proof of contact between the two men was almost superfluous because they knew they'd had a fight on Wednesday evening. Unlike Carston, however, Ross set great store by accumulating facts.

"How are you Mr Baigrie?" he asked.

"Not great," said Gallacher before Baigrie could answer.

"Mr Gallacher," said Ross. "Glad to find you here, too. Couple of things I'd like to ask you."

He signalled to Bellman to bring across two chairs. They sat on them. Gallacher sat on the bed again, taking Baigrie's hand as he did so.

"We were wondering if you could be a bit more precise about the car you saw on the evening of the assault," said Ross.

"I didn't see any car," said Gallacher.

"I meant Mr Baigrie."

Baigrie looked first at Gallacher then at Ross.

"I'm not even sure I did," he said.

"Sorry?"

"See a car. In fact, I don't see how I could have. One minute we were in the pub, the next, I was being battered by the fat guy."

"You told Mr Gallacher that you'd seen a four by four with a logo on the side."

"I know, but I was probably imagining it."

"What makes you say that?"

To Ross's embarrassment, Baigrie started crying.

"Think about it," he said, with a sniff. "When could I have seen it? I couldn't see a thing. Look what he's done to me. There was blood. I was—"

He stopped as the sobs got in the way. Gallacher gave him a tissue from the box on the bedside cabinet.

"Look, I misled you," said Baigrie, dabbing at his eye and cheek. "I'm sorry. There wasn't any car. It was imagination. I suppose I just … wanted there to be a car."

"Why an Anstey's car, though?" Ross persisted.

"Because that's who they were," said Gallacher.

"Who?" asked Ross, sticking doggedly to basics.

"The guys who attacked us."

"You knew them before then?"

Baigrie looked at Gallacher.

"I knew them," said Gallacher. "Knew of them."

"Yes," said Ross. "You worked with them, didn't you?"

Gallacher flashed him a look.

"No," he said.

"You did according to them," said Bellman, wanting to get in on the act.

Gallacher turned slowly to look at him.

"Being on the same platform doesn't mean you're working with somebody," he said.

"Tell us about it, then," said Ross. "When you were on the platform with them. Mr Baxter was there, too, wasn't he?"

Gallacher sighed, lifted his hand and scratched his forehead. He took a tissue for himself and blew his nose.

"Wasn't he?" said Ross again.

"Yes," said Gallacher. It was a reluctant admission. "I was working on a contract to supply catering services. They were changing their suppliers."

"What did that have to do with Mr Baxter? I thought he was safety."

"He was. I saw him while I was out there. I knew him onshore. I was chatting to him when whatsisname, the fat one, started shouting things."

"Bole."

"Is that what he's called? Well, whatever." He turned again to Bellman. "Does that sound like we were working together?"

"What was he shouting?" asked Ross.

"The usual witty repartee—about boy scouts, arse bandits, vicars. You don't need me to script it for you."

Gallacher was making no effort to hide his aggression. Ross was glad; it made people say more than they should.

"Did you react at all?"

"I blew him a kiss."

"And what did—?"

Gallacher didn't let him finish.

"Oh, Christ, don't ask daft bloody questions. There was a minor punch-up. Nothing serious. Not even thickos like him are going to risk getting the shove by fighting offshore."

"Paul. Easy," warned Baigrie.

Gallacher nodded and patted his hand again.

Ross pressed on, teasing away at what had happened on the platform and eventually getting Gallacher to admit that there was probably a connection between that incident and the assaults at the Swan. Apparently, Bole's real target was Baxter. The fact that Gallacher was talking to him was just an excuse but he'd linked the two of them and, when he saw Gallacher in the pub, he was a handy substitute.

The nurses were coming back from their lunch by the time Ross had finished his questions. As he and Bellman stood up to leave, it occurred to him that he hadn't asked Gallacher the most obvious question.

"How well did you know Mr Baxter?"

Gallacher and Baigrie looked at each other.

"Paul," said Baigrie. It was another warning. Gallacher ignored him. The anger was still there.

"I fucked him once," he said.

****

The Dolphin was a strange name for a pub which was so far from the water, but Carston knew that it had more to do with French royalty than fishermen. In the old days, it had had a public bar, a lounge bar, and even what they called a snug, but the changing demands of drinkers and the appalling vagaries of interior design had progressively demolished the several partitions so that the whole place was now a vast barn of a pub, scalloped around its edges by little alcoves that failed to recreate the intimacy that had been so natural to the grubby little snug. But there were a few tables in the big bay window which had a good view of the garden and the barmaid remained a reassuring and titillating constant.

At the counter, Carston turned to McIntosh and said, "What'll it be?"

"Gin and tonic, I think."

The barmaid heard him and turned to pick up a glass. Automatically, Carston's eyes dropped to her bum. It was everything he could have wished for. He gave a little shake of the head and looked to see what sort of food was available. Under a plastic cover on the bar there were several types of rolls, pies and sandwiches. They got two ham rolls and took them to a table near the door. Once there, McIntosh opened his briefcase, took out a folder, slapped it on the table and lifted his glass. After a good slug, he opened the folder and took out a sheaf of photographs and drawings. Some of the photographs showed, in glorious colour, very close-up shots of the interior of Baxter's head. Red and white slime mingled with black and white fragments of some solid

163

material. There was greyish foam oozing from splits in the larger pieces of bone and wriggly tissues that looked like small lengths of electrical wiring threaded from the base of the smashed skull down into the neck.

"What about this circular depression you mentioned?" asked Carston.

"Ah yes," said McIntosh, pulling some drawings from underneath the photos. "Here's the sequence as I see it."

He took him through the events that had led from Baxter's skull being transformed from a solid container to the mess he'd seen in the photos. His drawing of the first impact did indeed show a crescent-shaped mark which angled up from the base of the skull at the back to a point just above the left ear. As they moved on through the sequence, it was gradually obscured by the small circles caused by the hammer. In the end, the sketch might have been of a little gaggle of moon craters.

"And you're sure that's the order in which they happened," said Carston.

"No doubt about it. That first hit bled profusely. When whoever it was started using the hammer, there was no blood flowing any more. He was long dead."

"Any thoughts about the weapon?"

McIntosh teased out the first drawing again.

"Well, there it is. What do you think?"

Carston looked again and shook his head. It was just a dark crescent, deeper at the centre and getting shallower towards the ends.

"Small bucket? End of a tube of some sort? A pipe?"

"Yes. Anybody's guess, isn't it?" said McIntosh. "But we do have some flecks of paint from it. I sent them to the lab for analysis. They'll help."

"Christ, you make my job so much easier, Brian."

"Yes, I do, don't I? Might be worth another gin and tonic. What do you think?"

Chapter Thirteen

Fraser was driving, Spurle was beside him and Carston was in the back seat. That way, they could have their conversations if they wanted to and he could just dream his way into Aberdeen. Fraser and Spurle had kept up an intermittent dialogue most of the way and, as they drove up North Anderson Drive, Spurle checked the time on the new clock which Fraser had velcroed to the dashboard.

"We'll be there by quarter to," he said.

Fraser looked at the clock and nodded.

"Where d'you get that thing?" asked Spurle, knowing that, like most of Fraser's possessions, it would be from one of his catalogues. He was a sucker for gadgets.

"Mail order," said Fraser, proudly. "It's radio controlled from the European time signal transmitted from Frankfurt."

"Frankfurt? What's up wi' Greenwich?" asked Spurle, who was violently Anglophobic in all matters except those involving the European Union, when he felt an imperial solidarity with folk south of the border.

"Nothin. That's just where the signal comes from," said Fraser patiently. "It's guaranteed accurate to plus or minus one second for the next million years."

"How old are you now, then?" said Spurle, unimpressed.

Carston listened, amused, as the exchange developed into an argument about cryogenics. Fraser was adamant that it was possible to be frozen and wake up in a million years time, "just in time to buy a new clock". Spurle called Fraser a sad bastard and the two of them spent the rest of the trip trying to prove who was the sadder. It began to get repetitive and Carston was glad when they pulled into the car park at the side of Anstey's headquarters in Dyce.

They were early for their appointment and had a ten minute wait in reception. Carston used it to get a feel of the place. The previous day, he'd only seen the store and the changing area. On the surface, it looked like every other oil company interior—plaques on the walls boasting of some achievement or another, awards for production targets being met, export records, and the usual model of a platform in a glass case. But it was all sterile, functional. The only pictures featured platforms silhouetted against North Sea sunsets and pseudo-abstract close-ups of pipework and machinery. The receptionist sat in a little well behind her curved desk and Carston noticed that she'd hung her coat on a hook which had been positioned over a poster giving details of how to evacuate the building in an emergency. He wondered how often Baxter had passed through the area and whether he'd noticed such a classic "deliberate mistake".

Just after three, they were shown into Hamer's office. He stood up, shook hands with Carston (but, pointedly, not with the others) and motioned them to sit down. He asked if they wanted coffee and, when they declined, sat back in his chair and waited for their questions.

Carston had already spent more time than he liked in the offices of self-important people today. Hamer's greeting had been cordial enough but his position behind his long desk, the instruction he gave his secretary to "hold all my calls" and the discomfort of the chairs in which he'd put them combined to stress their relative insignificance and his unquestioned status. Whenever Carston was confronted with pomposity, his first reflex was to puncture it, but the shadow of Ridley's complaint and the warnings he'd had about not rocking the Anstey boat forced him into circumspection.

"Maybe we should put you on the payroll, Chief Inspector," said Hamer. "You seem to be spending more and more time with us."

Carston smiled.

"I thought the payroll was being cut," he said, grateful to get straight down to business.

Hamer brushed at some specks on the lapel of his dark blue jacket. Once again, it was too wide and too well cut for him.

"Is that relevant to your investigation?" he asked.

"Don't know yet."

"Where did you hear it?"

166

Carston shrugged.

"It was in connection with the Falcon platforms. Isn't it true, then?"

Hamer brought his hands together and interlocked his fingers.

"It's under discussion," he said. "The platforms' output has been slowing. We're due for a derrick and production shutdown on Alpha next month. Part of a feasibility study on further extraction to decide which way we go."

"And that'll involve redundancies, will it?"

"No, no," said Hamer quickly. "Well, not necessarily. During the assessment, we'll just keep essential personnel out there. The rest'll be re-assigned or take some leave."

Carston nodded. "It certainly seemed busy enough when I was there yesterday," he said. "Why the study?"

Hamer was glad of a rare opportunity to air some of his very restricted engineering knowledge.

"The Falcon reservoir's been producing for several years now. We've tried all the fractionation techniques but the sad fact is that the wells are just running down. It's a mature asset. Dipping down off its plateau. There's not all that much left down there."

"So there will be redundancies?" Carston persisted.

"You're rather dogged about that, aren't you?"

"Seems logical to me. If the wells aren't producing, you don't need people out there working them."

Hamer smiled. It was smug and superior.

"Anstey does have other assets. The North Sea's just a fraction of our overall operation. We value our personnel. As one door closes, another frequently opens. Look at Baku, for instance."

Carston knew that many of the oil-related companies in north east Scotland were already involved in projects in the Caspian Sea. Baku had taken over from Houston as the foreign city whose name recurred most frequently in the offices and workshops of Aberdeen.

"And is everybody happy at the idea of having to leave Scotland for Azerbaijan?" he asked.

"The choice is theirs. If they're worth keeping, they'll be offered the chance to relocate."

It was hardly the total job security he'd implied in his earlier answers.

"What about Alistair Baxter? Is that what he was being offered?"

167

Hamer frowned.

"No-one's being offered anything yet. I told you, we're still looking at options."

"So he wouldn't know any of the things you're talking about?"

"Of course not. He was an LPO."

"Yes. So he was," said Carston. "You know we found some sodium in his locker. Does that surprise you?"

"I'm sure he had a good reason for having it," said Hamer, defensively, having no real idea of the significance of the find. "He was a first class LPO. Very conscientious."

"All the same, seems a strange thing for him to be keeping."

"Are you familiar with the job of an LPO, then?" asked Hamer, in an attempt at sarcasm.

"No, but the one who's out there now—Jamie Kemp—he is. And he was surprised to hear about it."

"Really, Chief Inspector," said Hamer, with a flash of irritation. "I'd rather you were a little less expansive with the material you hand out."

It was a strange remark, implying that any information Carston had which related directly to Anstey's was somehow copyright.

"I would have thought you'd welcome a full enquiry into anything that might compromise safety," he said.

"Of course we do," said Hamer, quickly, covering his tracks. "We're very proud of our record. No lost time incidents for the past seven months."

"Very gratifying," said Carston, the image of the receptionist's coat obscuring the safety poster still with him.

"What about that guy that fell off the monkey board?" asked Spurle.

It took them all by surprise. He felt all their eyes on him.

"July," he said. "Falcon Bravo. Got tangled up in the tag lines. Fell off. Broke his ankle. My bird's a nurse. He was in her ward."

Carston was grateful for the interruption; not only had it unsettled Hamer, it had been spoken with Spurle's usual rawness. It sounded aggressive, made Carston's questions seem ultra-polite.

"He was employed by the drilling contractor," said Hamer, as if that were an explanation.

"Still broke his ankle," insisted Spurle. "That's an LTI, isn't it?"

"Reporting procedures make it the responsibility of the contractor," said Hamer. "They have separate records."

It sounded to Carston like a convenient way to manipulate figures and reminded him of his neighbour, Alex Crombie, who worked offshore and frequently spoke of the way lip service was still paid to some aspects of safety out there. Suddenly, Hamer leaned forward and tapped at the keys of the computer on his desk.

"Anstey's have the most sophisticated Loss Prevention procedures in the whole of the North Sea," he said. "This may interest you."

He waited, then turned his monitor so that they could see it. On it was a graphic display of what looked to Fraser and Spurle like well arranged spaghetti. Carston had seen the same image on a screen in the control room on the platform. Hamer tapped the monitor and was again pleased to air a little more of his limited engineering expertise.

"A mimic of Falcon Alpha's systems. That tells us exactly what's going on out there as we speak—all the flow rates, the active separators and hydrocyclones, which valves are shut and open, the condition of pipes and risers. Computer link, you see. A picture of the current state of the platform. If we spot any hazards, we can over-ride local systems and close the emergency shut-down valves from here. So there's not only the platform people keeping an eye on things—we're backing them up."

Carston nodded his appreciation. It seemed impressive enough.

"Has every company got these?" he asked.

Hamer smiled and shook his head.

"Some," he replied. "But none of them with the full over-ride facility. It's a recent innovation. The others haven't caught up with us yet." He pulled the monitor back to its original position. "But, forgive me for saying so, isn't this rather a strange line of enquiry? I mean, are you assuming that the element of—" He hesitated, preparing himself for the colloquialism. "queer-bashing is no longer a factor in Alistair Baxter's death?"

"Why should you assume that?" asked Carston.

"Well, this concentration on safety, LTIs and things. I wouldn't want the press digging around in the company's affairs just because one of its employees has dubious sexual preferences."

Carston couldn't resist it.

"Something to hide, sir?" he said, with a smile intended to make it sound like a joke.

Hamer's smile sensors were clearly switched off.

"Certainly not," he said, sharply.

For someone whose specialisation was human resources and who, therefore, should be used to interacting with others, he was strangely uneasy. He had a habit of running his hand back across his bald head. It dulled the shine briefly but, each time, the pink sheen crept quickly back. It was obvious to Carston that the need to speak to them was more than just a chore. Hamer was being defensive.

"Have any of your people been in trouble with the police before?" asked Carston, looking to cover his own failed attempt at lightness.

"Not to my knowledge," said Hamer. "They know better."

"Oh?"

"Company policy. Any illegal activities mean instant dismissal. No recall."

"Bit Draconian, isn't it?" said Carston. Fraser looked at Spurle, who shrugged his shoulders to indicate that he didn't know what it meant either.

"I would have thought you'd welcome it," said Hamer. "Moral support for you. Milne and Gellatly, for instance."

"What about them?"

"They've been suspended."

"What for?"

"Really, Chief Inspector. It's your investigation. You know what they did."

"No, we don't," said Carston. "I've got a pretty shrewd idea myself, but we've got no proof of anything yet."

"Their involvement was enough," said Hamer, seeming quite pleased with himself. "I don't think Anstey's will be bothered with their misdemeanours again."

"You said they were only suspended."

Hamer's smile was a tight, unpleasant twitch of the lips.

"A euphemism. Technically, that's true, but they won't be invited back."

At the beginning of the interview, it had been easy for Carston to make concessions for Hamer. His skinny frame, his bald head and his twitchy manner made him look misplaced, even vulnerable, in an expensively appointed office. Now, though, his casual dismissal of Gellatly and Milne and his unquestioning loyalty to Anstey's had revealed something like vindictiveness. It was as if exercising power over others compensated for his own deficiencies. As the interview went on, the occasional interjections by Fraser and Spurle showed that they shared Carston's opinion.

Another ten minutes was enough for them to get everything he had to offer. He phoned Nicholas to tell him they were on their way and, as he stood up to show them out, Carston took the chance to unsettle him again.

"What sort of mood was Mr Baxter in last Wednesday?" he asked.

Hamer looked at him, surprised by the question.

"How should I know?"

"Did he seem troubled, preoccupied?"

"I have absolutely no idea. There was the fight but otherwise..." He shrugged. "I think he was on his way to see his confidante. He probably didn't want to waste time with us here."

"Confidante?" asked Carston, interested both by the choice of word and the sudden, unexpected indication that Hamer did, after all, know his subordinates as individuals and not just ledger entries.

"It's something everybody says ... said about him. You must have formed an impression of him by now."

"I'd rather you told me."

"He was different. A loner. Never said much about himself to anybody. His workmates say that's why he goes ... went to see a prostitute."

"I'm not sure I—" Carston left the sentence unfinished, inviting Hamer to continue.

Hamer sighed. The subject seemed to make him feel uncomfortable.

"They say he's the sort who doesn't like women. He only goes ... went to her to talk, tell her his problems. That's what they say, anyway."

"I see. Did he say that's where he was going? Last Wednesday, I mean."

"I don't remember."

You did talk to him?"

"Briefly."

"And he seemed normal?"

"I don't know. I suppose so," said Hamer.

"And where did you go when you left that evening?" asked Carston.

Again, the question surprised Hamer.

"Home," he said.

"Right away?"

"Yes."

"And you didn't go out again?"

Hamer's eyes flicked to Spurle and Fraser before coming back to Carston.

"No," he said.

"Was there anyone else at home?" asked Carston.

Hamer's scalp shone redder. He shook his head.

"I live alone. Why are you asking?"

"Just filling all the gaps," said Carston. "Thank you for your time."

They left him to sort out the implications of Carston's words and went along the corridor towards Nicholas's office. In the rooms leading off it, designers were working at screens snaking with more multi-coloured spaghetti and other individuals were absorbed in their particular little contribution to Anstey's advance. At the end of the corridor, four big cardboard boxes were stacked in a corner, partially blocking an emergency exit, and a shiny sign saying FIRE POINT had an arrow on it angled down towards an empty fire extinguisher holder on the wall. It was like a set-piece for a "how not to" video and contrasted very strongly with the rigid adherence to safety regulations he'd seen with Jamie Kemp out on the platform. It simply confirmed that the truths about the company lay far behind the veils of PR he'd been seeing since the start.

Nicholas' office was as large and well appointed as Hamer's but he seemed to fill it. He greeted them as warmly as Hamer had done and there was an ease and naturalness about him that seemed sincere. Paradoxically, it made Carston wary of being drawn into some sort of alliance with him. Nicholas' manner, as well as his appearance, fitted too perfectly into the PR mould to be reassuring. Carston started with the question that had unsettled Hamer.

"Wednesday night. Where did you go between the time you left here and the time Sergeant Reid called you?"

Nicholas was as surprised as Hamer had been but there was no hesitation before he replied.

"Home."

172

"Anybody else there?"

"Nope. I'm a bachelor gay." He stopped, then added, "Ooops, not the most tactful word to choose. Sorry."

"Just like Mr Hamer, eh?" said Carston.

Nicholas smiled.

"Not really," he said. "With me, it's from choice."

"Meaning?"

Nicholas shook his head.

"Come on, now, Chief Inspector. You're not here just to chat about our domestic arrangements. Can we get on with things? I've got a lot to get through before I leave tonight."

As he spoke, he waved a hand across the documents which littered his desk.

"Yes, I heard," said Carston.

Nicholas looked at him, a raised eyebrow betraying his surprise at the comment.

"Oh?"

"Yes. The Falcon field being re-appraised. Must make balancing the books a bit tricky."

Nicholas laughed. It was a forced, unnatural sound.

"Please. You make me sound like a back street accountant."

His ease of manner surprised Carston. The North Sea's oilfields had been like golden geese since the late sixties; godsends to finance directors. The news that Anstey's main one was drying up ought to be causing Nicholas some concern.

"Surely it'll have some sort of effect, though?" said Carston.

Nicholas's expression changed. The smile vanished, the tone became brisk, efficient. He was suddenly in boardroom mode.

"Good and bad revenue. Simple as that. Good revenue's a solid deal, dependable, signed and sealed. Bad revenue may be promised, may even be written in a contract but, if it depends on other things, like government backing or industrial grants, forget it. There are no guarantees. And you have to treat costs the same way."

Already, Carston was out of his depth.

"I'm sorry, I don't see how that relates to what's going on with Falcon," he said.

"Falcon's only part of a big picture," said Nicholas, with something like impatience. "When my boss in the States gets on to me, he doesn't want to hear about staffing levels or single source outputs. What he wants is profit. And I have to deliver."

"The famous American work ethic, eh?" said Carston.

Nicholas fixed him with a stare that wasn't friendly.

"It's not a myth. When you're having to cope with it, it's very real."

"Stressful, then."

The stare didn't waver. It was almost a challenge.

"If you let it get to you."

"Never mind. Looks like you'll be making a few shillings in Azerbaijan. Mr Hamer was telling us about it."

The stare eased. The new direction was obviously to Nicholas's liking.

"It's still speculative. Hasn't become good revenue yet. But, yes, we're hoping. Lower investment profile for higher potential gains."

"That's good, is it?" asked Carston, content to play the ignoramus that, financially, he was.

"It's a more relaxed location altogether. Heard of the hundred year, hundred foot wave?"

Carston nodded. It was an expression used by oil people to describe an extreme event which might come along only once in a hundred years but which platforms had to be built to withstand. It meant, at least theoretically, that most of the time they were operating well within their safety limits, at least as far as the weather was concerned.

"Well," Nicholas went on, "none of that nonsense in the Caspian. The waves just don't get that big."

"So you can cut corners," Carston thought to himself. Everyone suspected that operations in Nigeria, the Gulf of Mexico, Venezuela and all the other frontier locations where oil was produced made fewer demands in terms of safety provision and protecting the workforce. It sounded as if Anstey's were planning to grab some early profits before legislation forced them to tighten their operation.

"I must say, though," said Nicholas, in the pause that Carston had allowed, "I don't really see how our expansion plans relate to your investigation."

"They don't," said Carston. "Curiosity on my part, that's all."

Spurle and Fraser both hoped that he'd curb it and get on with some questioning they could understand and maybe be part of.

"Can I ask you about Alistair Baxter?" asked Carston.

A slight frown dipped momentarily into Nicholas's brow.

"Of course," he said. "Although I told the sergeant who was here the other day—"

"Sergeant McNeil," prompted Carston.

"Yes. She asked about Wednesday night."

"Yes," said Carston, looking at his notebook. "You told her he left at half past six, but came back in to do some paperwork."

"That's right. Didn't take long. He had a date."

"Yes. With a prostitute, you said."

Nicholas nodded his head slowly. He lifted his hand and pushed his hair back. He seemed to be considering what he was about to say.

"If you want an opinion," he said, "I don't think Baxter was gay."

Spurle gave a little snort. Carston looked at him to shut him up.

"What makes you say that?" he asked.

"I think he cared about her. Really cared. Even if she was a prostitute," said Nicholas. "The talk was that she was more like his wife. The only person he ever really talked to. And he was furious with some man who'd beaten her up or something. Taken a whip to her. It upset Baxter. He said he was going to go looking for him." He stopped, his head shaking, still deep in thought, then looked straight at Carston. "It's another world, isn't it?" he said.

Carston looked up from the notes he was taking and shrugged. To him, it was familiar territory. The delicacy of Nicholas's sensitivity was unimpressive.

"I'm not sure I should tell you this," Nicholas went on, "I didn't say anything to your sergeant but, on reflection, I think it's important. I think Baxter would have wanted it. He phoned me from here on Wednesday night. When he came back to finish his forms."

Carston waited. He was getting used to things spinning off at tangents.

"He was asking about her. The woman. It makes no difference to Anstey's but it might to her. He wanted her named as his next of kin."

"Why?"

"So that she'd get his pension."

"So he gave you her name."

"No. He was just asking if it was possible. He meant it, though. That's why I don't think he was gay."

"They could have just been friends."

"I don't think so. He was pretty definite about it. When you trace her, it might be an idea for her to get in touch with us. Maybe Dick Hamer can arrange the paperwork so that she can get the money anyway. Somebody's got to. Baxter wanted it to be her."

"Was there anything more than a pension involved?" asked Carston. "Only, Mr Baxter seemed to suggest that he was due for some sort of bonus."

"He must have been dreaming," said Nicholas. "You talked earlier about Falcon running down. Not exactly the context for bonuses, is it?"

"How about redundancies?"

Nicholas smiled.

"I wouldn't know about that. Downsizing's Dick Hamer's game. Better ask him."

Now that they were back onto matters relating to business, he relaxed again. The charm and ease of manner which had struck Carston at the start returned and, as they talked of Bole's chances of keeping his job (which looked slim) and Gellatly and Milne's dismissal, he was once more in total control of his responses. There was not necessarily anything suspicious in the way he reacted to matters external to Anstey's; it was just that the company and its finances were his true medium. Carston felt sure that he was good at his job but might be a little lost away from the security of profit and loss accounts.

By half past three, they'd asked everything they needed to. Carston sent Fraser and Spurle to have a brief word with Taggart, the storeman, while he looked round the locker room again. It was a wide, tidy space lined with grey metal doors. At one end, a door with a frosted glass panel led into a shower room fitted with ten individual cubicles. Everything was spotless and all of the doors were locked.

Fraser and Spurle learned little that was new from Taggart. He shared the general opinion about Baxter and even blamed him for the mess that had been made of his survival suit. Apart from that, though, his comments remained guarded, unhelpful and were designed to keep him well out of any of the investigations that were going on. Taggart just wanted a quiet life, issuing and taking back survival suits, tools and all the other pieces of equipment that shuttled back and forth to the Falcon platforms.

They left for Cairnburgh just after four. Spurle was at the wheel and, reminded by Carston that speed limits applied to policemen as well as the general public, he drove them home through the mist in a silence only broken by Fraser's occasional bursts of French as they passed objects or scenes for which he'd learned the vocabulary.

****

The mood in his office was strange. Ross, McNeil and Reid were all there, each at a computer terminal. When he came in, they all looked up briefly, then bent back to their work without a word.

"Good afternoon to you, too," said Carston.

"Sorry," mumbled Ross. He pointed at his monitor. "Need to get this done."

Carston nodded, uselessly since Ross hadn't looked up. He looked at his watch and remembered that he'd promised to telephone Alex Crombie to arrange to meet him. He threw his coat over the back of his chair and picked up the phone. Crombie answered almost immediately.

"Still on for tonight?" asked Carston.

"Sure. The usual?" said Crombie.

"No. I thought maybe the Swan."

"What? You're joking."

"No. I've already arranged to see somebody there. About this case I'm on. We could leave it till later if you like."

"No, it's OK. I'm not afraid," said Crombie. "What time?"

"I'll come by your place around nine. That OK?"

"Aye. Lucky for you I'm such a piss artist," said Crombie.

"You took the words out of my mouth," said Carston.

He put the receiver back and was struck again by the silence in the room. It was like a bloody library.

"D'you think one of you could drag yourself away for a minute just to fill me in on what you've been at this afternoon?"

McNeil kept hammering away at her keyboard. Ross tapped at a few more keys then sat back. He still didn't catch Carston's eye, using the excuse of consulting his notebook to avoid doing so.

"Baigrie's changed his mind about the car," he said. "Claims now that he wasn't sure that he saw one after all."

"Great," said Carston. "Is that it?"

"No. Gallacher and Baxter. They were—"

He stopped.

"Well?" said Carston, sharply. The atmosphere was getting to him.

"He admits he knew him. Worked with him one time on the platform. They've been out together, too."

"What d'you mean, been out together?"

"Sex," said Ross, his discomfort obvious.

McNeil looked up from her keyboard for the first time.

"Sex?" she said.

"Aye," said Ross. "Just the once."

"When?" asked Carston.

"Last Hogmanay. There was a party. They met up at the Swan, went on to it about two in the morning."

"Where was Baigrie?"

"He was there. Says it was his fault. Says Gallacher only had it off with Baxter because he was messing around with a couple of marines from Arbroath."

"So why did Gallacher tell us he didn't know Baxter?"

Ross shrugged.

"It probably still causes trouble with Baigrie," said McNeil. "From what you've said about the two of them, they don't exactly sound secure. I bet they're jealous as hell of one another."

"And what's the link with Bole?" asked Carston.

"He saw the two of them on the platform," said Ross. "Made some comments. Gallacher played up to him. There was a bit of a scuffle."

Carston shook his head. This wasn't the accidental encounter it had seemed to be at first. All these seemingly independent individuals had met before. And in the case of Gallacher and Baxter, not just met but … well, was copulated the right word? It was time to talk to Bole again. They couldn't get any more extensions to keep him.

"OK, Reid," he said. "You're supposed to be keeping tabs on all this. Go and get things set up in room two. We're going to have another chat with Bole."

"Right, sir," said Reid, switching off his screen so quickly that Carston suspected that he hadn't been doing any real work with it.

As soon as he'd left, Carston was once more aware of the tension that was still there. His relationship with Ross had always been open and McNeil had quickly fitted into their ways. A silence like this between the three of them was a clear sign that something was irregular.

"OK, you two," he said. "What's going on?"

The way they looked at one another confirmed his suspicion. It was Ross who took the lead.

"We've had a visit," he said. "Just before you came back. Superintendent Murray."

Jim Murray was a local man who'd inched his way up the promotion ladder over many painful, time-serving years. Carston had always thought he was too intelligent to be stuck in the administrative branch but he seemed to like it and it gave him regular hours and time off to spend with his racing pigeons. He'd once told Carston that, as a boy, he'd advertised for friends in the Press and Journal. Carston wasn't sure whether it was a joke or not and it certainly belied the fact that, everywhere he went in and around Cairnburgh nowadays, there were always people who greeted him as if he were a relative. Nonetheless, it was a surprise to hear that he'd appeared in the CID rooms. He hated everything to do with cutting edge police work.

"What did he want?" asked Carston.

Ross tapped his fingers on the desk and thought for a moment before replying.

"He's the I. O.," he said.

Christ, that was quick! Ridley had only told Carston about the indiscipline charge that morning and already the Investigating Officer was at work. Ridley must have been getting it set up for a while.

"Ah," said Carston. "I see."

He paused, uncertain as to how much he should say.

"He talked to all of us, Jim, me, Andy," said McNeil.

Carston nodded. With a charge of indiscipline, it was standard practice to question every member of the team. Unfortunately, as both Ross and McNeil knew and as Murray had reminded them, what he wanted was facts, not character references.

"They're going way back, sir," said Ross, his tone serious.

Carston nodded.

"Yes. Ridley told me. But it's best for you to say nothing to me about it. Keep your nose clean. You, too, Julie."

"I don't think they've got anything," said McNeil. "The sort of things he was asking about… Scraping the barrel."

"We'll see," said Carston. "Reid and Spurle will probably be able to find something for them."

He became brisk, partly to shake off the memory of Ridley's charges and partly to hide a slight embarrassment at the degree of concern that was obvious in both sergeants.

"Now. Let's see what Bole's got to say for himself. I reckon I may charge him. See how I feel."

"Sir," said Ross.

"Yes?"

"Be careful with Andy. You know what he's like."

Carston smiled.

"He's only a sergeant. What power has he got?"

"True," said Ross.

At the door, Carston paused briefly. Ross and McNeil were both looking at him.

"Thanks," he said.

Chapter Fourteen

Bole started protesting as soon as he walked through the door. Reid was already there, sitting at the table. Carston sat beside him and looked steadily at Bole as he ranted on. Eventually, Bole realised that he was getting nowhere and slumped back in his chair. Carston switched on the tape recorder, spoke the necessary identification details into it and leaned forward on his elbows.

"Have you heard? Your mates have been sacked."

Bole scowled at him but said nothing.

"Gellatly and Milne. Well, suspended rather than sacked."

"Same thing," said Bole.

"Yes, so I believe. What d'you think'll happen to you?"

Bole shrugged and looked away. Carston pretended to consult a note in the folder on the desk.

"You're a supervisor, aren't you?"

"So?"

"Well, they'll deal with you differently, surely?"

Bole flicked a glance at Carston.

"Why'd they sack them?" he asked.

"Their involvement with us, apparently," said Carston, carelessly. "Seems Anstey's prefer their employees to stay out of trouble."

Bole snorted. It expressed what he thought of both Anstey's and Carston.

"That's why you held back on the platform, isn't it?" said Carston.

Bole looked at him, his jowls dark and spongy.

"That time Gallacher was there. With Baxter. You know, when Dillinger's were negotiating the new suppliers' contracts."

"What's that got to do with me?" asked Bole, saliva spraying from his thin lips.

"Mr Bole," said Carston, patiently, "did you ever meet Mr Gallacher before Wednesday night?"

"No."

"Are you sure?"

"I said no, didn't I?"

"You didn't see him on Falcon Alpha with Mr Baxter?"

"No. How would I know a bunch of poofs?"

The refrain was very wearing but Carston was pleased enough to hear it. For once, he'd be able to prove that Bole was lying. Gallacher would confirm it. So would Gellatly and Milne. And maybe other people from the platform. He leaned back and, before Bole could change his mind about knowing Gallacher, he moved to another subject.

"I was at Anstey's this afternoon. Talking to Mr Hamer and Mr Nicholas."

"So?"

"Nothing. They were telling me about Baku and things."

"Aye. The bastards want us all to up sticks and go out there to work with a bunch of wogs," said Bole.

"You don't like the idea then?"

"Would you?"

"What's the option?"

In his disdain for the company's policies, Bole was forgetting his original uncooperative role.

"Huh, what option d'you think they give you? Out in the wilds or on your bike. And they'll still be sittin here."

"I thought you said the jobs on the rig were secure," said Carston.

"So they should be, but with Hamer and that lot—"

"What?"

"Huh, some bloody detective, you are," said Bole. "You've been there, seen them. They're enough to frighten the shit out of you."

This took Carston by surprise. Hard man Bole, admitting to fear?

"Why?" he asked.

182

"Look at what they've done to Mike and Jim. Don't give a fuck if they're married or not. Out, just like that. Never know where you are with the bastards."

"They said it's company policy."

Bole snorted again. It triggered a bout of coughing and hawking.

"Company policy," he spluttered. "Aye, but it's they bastards that applies it. They love it. If the company told them to eat dogshit they'd ask for more."

Carston had obviously dug at a sore spot in him. He forgot to be surly, forgot that the machine was running, and gave a comprehensive put-down of Anstey's and every single line manager. As he spoke, Carston noted the fear inside his anger. The threat of redundancies that everybody except Baxter had denied so strenuously was very real. But none of it hung over the higher office personnel; it was the offshore staff who were expendable. And, beyond them, in even more remote echelons of the corporate structure, sat other string-pullers, shadowy figures, all Americans, all hiring and firing to please their shareholders.

"Bloody Mafia, it is," Bole was saying. "We've got to deliver or it's a goodbye job."

Suddenly he laughed. As with all other functions of his throat, this produced the Niagara sound of loosening phlegm.

"Same for them, though."

"Who?" asked Carston.

"Hamer, that lot. If they dinna hit their famous bloody performance figures, they're out the door. Goodnight, sweetheart."

"Doesn't sound like much of a place to work," said Carston.

"Beats this hole."

Reid's voice made them both turn to look at him.

"Would you say that there was a lot of friction between the staff at Anstey's?" he asked.

Bole didn't answer. He was staring at Reid.

"On a person to person level, I mean," Reid added.

Carston wasn't sure where he was heading and was ready to interrupt if he committed one of his usual blunders.

Bole was shaking his head.

"Dunno what you're on about," he said.

"I was just wondering if all this tension you're talking about, all these threats, well, if they caused problems, fights, disagreements," said Reid.

"Where you been hidin, pal?" said Bole.

"Mr Bole," said Reid, his voice surprisingly firm, "you're here for serious reasons. If there was animosity between you and your workmates, it might well be germane to the issues on hand here. There was blood on more than one survival suit—"

Carston was about to cut across him and prevent him revealing anything else but Bole beat him to it.

"Fuck off," he said. "Right. That's it. I've had it. You're gettin nothin else. I want a lawyer."

Reid looked at Carston, who was tempted to let him wriggle for a while. Luckily, though, he remembered Ross's warning.

"OK," he said, standing up. "Sergeant Reid, charge him."

"What with, sir?"

"The charges already on the sheet. Then he can talk to a lawyer."

His sudden decisiveness threw Bole. His blustering stopped as he looked from one to the other of them. Carston recorded that the interview was over and switched off the machine.

"What's the charge?" was all Bole could manage in the silence that followed. Carston was already at the door.

"In words you'd understand, it's queer-bashing," he said. "I only wish there was a law against being a complete dickhead. I'd have you on that, too."

He went out, closed the door and left Reid to his moment of glory. There was every possibility that he'd somehow foul up the charge sheet. On this occasion, Carston didn't care. His own credibility was now being measured against Reid's. It was no contest.

****

The door and exterior woodwork of the Swan was painted a strange plum colour but, in every other way, it was like any standard pub. There were more customers than you'd expect for a Monday evening and nearly all of them were men. Some wore shirts and pants in colours and materials rarely found in the traditional male spectrum, but the rest were identikit drinkers, between twenty and sixty years old, most of them disappointingly normal. Only one man, a sallow, brooding individual, strutted in the leathers and accoutrements Carston had expected to find. And yet, despite all this evidence that they were not in some alien environment, the body language of Carston and Crombie was awkward, stiff and self-aware. There was rather more eye contact than they were used to in a gathering of males and, despite the fact that nobody seemed very interested in them, they were themselves anxious to make it clear that they weren't an item.

Pill arrived just after nine-thirty with a tall man with a shaven head called Geoff, another of the actors from the theatre. After the introductions, Carston bought the beers and they took their drinks to a corner table. As they sat down, Carston suddenly wondered why they were there. Basically, he was supposed to be getting a sense of the place and the people in it to give him a better insight into what had happened to Gellatly and Baigrie, but his offshore visit and the time spent at Anstey's made him more interested in what Crombie might have to say about some of the things they'd found. After some faltering conversation, though, a remark by Pill brought his attention sharply back to the Swan.

"Geoff was here, you know. Last Wednesday."

"Really?" said Carston. "What, at the time it happened?"

Geoff nodded.

"It was a tech rehearsal. I was finished by half eight."

"Why didn't you come and tell us before?" asked Carston, curious rather than accusing.

Geoff waved a hand to indicate the other drinkers.

"Same reason they didn't. Been there before. No point."

His dismissal of the option of helping police enquiries was too easy and natural for Carston to take offence at it.

"So you reckon there were plenty of witnesses?" he said.

"Enough. But don't expect a stampede."

"No. We've already put out an appeal through the media. Didn't get any results. What made you change your mind?"

"Heard about Darren," said Geoff, simply. He tilted his head towards Pill. "And Pill said you seemed OK."

"Thanks for the reference," said Carston.

Pill raised his glass to him and drank.

"What happened, then?" asked Carston.

"Bog standard pub fracas," said Geoff. He pointed to the end of the bar nearest the door. "Darren and Paul were sitting over there, having a drink with Robbie Findlay. The door opens and these three guys come in, pissed out of their skulls."

"Did you know them?"

Geoff shook his head.

"Did … Paul or Darren?"

"No idea. They just stood there, looking around. It was obvious they were trouble. In the end, the fat one just went over, poured Robbie's beer in his lap and punched him in the face. Simple as that."

"So the fight started inside?"

"No. Paul grabbed the fat bloke by the shirt and shoved him back out the door. All the others went with him. That's where it started."

"And nobody tried to stop it?"

Geoff's eyes dropped to his drink and he gave a shake of his head.

"Were Paul and Darren drunk, too?" asked Carston.

"Darren had had a few. He can hold it, though. Not easy to tell with him. Paul hadn't had as many. He came in after Darren."

Carston made a mental note to check Baigrie and Gallacher's statements again. He didn't remember any mention of them going separately to the Swan.

"Would you recognise the men who came in? The ones who started it?" he asked.

Geoff nodded.

"And would you be willing to come into the station to make a statement?"

"Shit, I knew this'd happen," said Geoff, turning to Pill.

Pill shrugged.

"It's Darren's eyes," he said.

Geoff heaved a deep sigh.

"Yeah. OK," he said.

Carston arranged for him to come to the Burns Road headquarters the following morning and explained the procedures he'd have to go through. When he'd finished and Geoff had nodded his understanding of it all, Crombie, who'd been a passive and slightly irritated observer throughout, said, "I don't understand why you didn't go in before. I mean, your mates get beat up, one of them's in hospital—"

Pill and Geoff looked at each other and smiled. Geoff turned back to Crombie.

"Married man, are you?" he asked.

186

"Not any more," said Crombie. Geoff couldn't know that his separation from his wife, after many good years of marriage, had been traumatic, painful and relatively recent. Carston had helped him through it and neither of them wanted to be reminded of it.

"Ah," said Geoff, aware that he'd touched on something sensitive. "It's just that … it's sometimes difficult to explain things to … ordinary people."

"I'm as ordinary as they get," said Crombie.

Geoff grinned, grateful to be forgiven his indiscretion so easily. He looked around the bar and pointed to an old man standing beside a fruit machine.

"See Max over there? He was married once. Down in South Queensferry. He tried to be ordinary, too. Didn't make it, though. Had to admit it in the end. Bent as a corkscrew."

"So what?" said Crombie.

Carston thought that he could guess the sort of thing that was coming. He was wrong.

"Left his wife. Moved in with a gay couple in their sixties. Ben and Jerry, people called them. They helped him to … well, come to terms with it, I suppose. Being gay, I mean. Bit hard at his age."

Crombie nodded. He'd read plenty about that sort of thing. It was nothing new.

"Came back from work one afternoon and found them spread all over the kitchen floor. Faces all mashed up. Tongues and pricks in a jar on top of the fridge."

He was using all his acting skills to give his delivery maximum impact. His tone was light, matter of fact but touched frost into the air between them.

"Couple of neighbours. Kids. Eighteen, twenty years old. The usual, on speed and booze. Objected to having Ben and Jerry around. Guilt by association."

Crombie frowned. He didn't see Geoff's meaning. Geoff noticed.

"If your mates know you've got poofs in your neighbourhood, maybe they'll start thinking you're a poof, too."

"Surely—" Crombie began.

"True," said Pill. "The DCI'll tell you. "Queer bashers need an audience. They do it to prove they're not gay themselves."

Crombie looked at Carston, who nodded.

"They're so bloody insecure in their macho-ness," said Geoff, with sudden bitterness, "they need to stamp on the alternatives. The sexual predators like us."

Crombie felt obscurely that he was being accused of something. Carston couldn't help him. He'd seen too many proofs that Geoff was right.

"Homosexual panic," said Pill, forcing a sort of heartiness into his voice. "It's an official 'medical condition'."

"I don't understand," said Crombie.

"Happens all the time. Read the court cases. Bloke's up for assault, even murder. All he has to say is that he was propositioned by the victim. Lost control. Well, you would, wouldn't you? It's only natural. He was provoked. It was all the poof's fault."

"Is that right, Jack?" asked Crombie.

"Sometimes," Carston admitted.

"Most times," insisted Geoff.

"Insatiable, we are," said Pill, still trying to lift the tone. "Don't suppose you're a Catholic."

Crombie looked at him, thrown again by the new direction. He shook his head.

"Right," said Pill. "So you wouldn't know that the 1992 Catechism said that 'Homosexual persons are called to chastity'."

"You're right. I wouldn't," said Crombie, having no idea about what he was getting at.

"It's just the pope saying it's OK to be gay—well, not OK, but it happens—anyway, the thing is, if you are, keep your zip done up. That's the way God wants it."

"Yeah. Ask Paul and Darren," said Geoff. "You know where they live, do you?"

"Yes," said Carston.

"Right. So you've seen the neighbourhood. D'you think the folk living in their street imagine that they actually shag one another?"

Carston shrugged. It was an image that disturbed him. He was obviously as bad as the neighbours.

Geoff answered his own question.

"Course they don't. They're just two lads living together, aren't they? Probably bring women home in the early hours and shag their brains out. Nice lads."

"Are they?" asked Carston, glad of the chance to get away from the generalised accusations and back to the reason they were here.

"What? Nice lads?" said Geoff. "Yeah. They don't harm anyone. Darren's like a kid most of the time. His folks kicked him out when they found out about him. He was a wild bugger for a time."

"Aye. Till he met Paul," said Pill. "He got a lover and a father all in one."

He saw the question in Carston's face.

"Don't ask," he said. "I'm not sure I can explain. Not sure it works for straight couples. You could meet Paul in the street and his mobile would go and it'd be Darren phoning to find out where he was. Christ knows how many times a day he phones him. Needs reassuring all the time."

"Doesn't Paul get fed up with that?" asked Carston.

Pill smiled.

"I don't think so," he said. "It may be hard for you to accept it, but they're still in love. They'd do anything for each other."

The education Carston had sought from the visit was becoming a fairly comprehensive one. By the time he and Crombie left to walk home together, their mood was subdued. It was usually easy to brush aside topics associated with homosexuality, either by some flip remark, an easy innuendo or even just a shudder. Spending an hour with people who lived with what was still effectively a stigma and had to run the daily gauntlet of ignorance made both of them vow to be more aware of the harm their quips might be causing. For Carston, it was a reinforcement of a long-held attitude; for Crombie, it was close to a revelation.

It was almost a relief for them to talk about Carston's trip offshore. His awe at the environment out there made Crombie smile. Twelve years shuttling back and forth had made him immune to the enormity of the whole enterprise. For him, the platform had nothing magical about it; it was just where he worked and lived for a fortnight at a time.

"Can't see them being on Falcon much longer, anyway," he said, pulling his collar tighter around his neck to keep out the cold, damp October air. "Story is it's nearly played out. Hardly worth the trouble any more."

"Yes," said Carston. "They're shutting down soon."

"Oh. Official, is it?" said Crombie, surprised that he hadn't already heard it on the grapevine.

Carston furrowed his brow, trying to remember exactly what he'd been told.

"Er ... something about derrick and production shutdowns. For maintenance."

"For maintenance? That's a surprise."

"Why?"

"I thought you meant they were closing it for good. I mean, it's so bloody marginal nowadays, it's hardly worth the effort. Shutting it down for maintenance'll cost a fortune. Wonder what they're planning."

"Not much, by the sound of it," said Carston. "There's only going to be a handful of men out there while they do it."

Crombie stuck his hands deep in his pockets.

"Well," he said, "they must've found a way to get some more out. Maybe there's a satellite well they've been keeping to themselves."

"Satellite well?"

"Aye. Some way away from where they are. You'd be surprised how they can deviate drills nowadays. Go for miles horizontally if they want to. Find a new reservoir nearby, bang a subsea template over it, and just pump it back to Falcon. They're all at it."

Carston thought for a moment about the things Baxter had told Vicky.

"What would that mean in terms of things like redundancies and bonuses?" he asked.

"Depends," said Crombie. "Nothing really. Shouldn't make much difference. The crude still has to be processed. Why d'you ask?"

Carston shook his head.

"Just, that chap Baxter was saying things about it."

"Well, he might know something. He was out there. On the spot. Wouldn't trust him too far, though."

"Why not?"

Crombie was silent for a moment. There were very few cars about and their footsteps tapped into the dankness of the empty street.

"I'd've found it easier to say before tonight," he said at last. "Used to just sort of take the piss out of him. A poof."

Carston nodded.

"Everybody did," he said,

Crombie nodded too.

"He wasn't a popular guy, though. No point pretending. Just because of what they said back there."

"I can't make him out at all," said Carston. "I mean, know what he had in his locker? Sodium."

Crombie stopped, forcing Carston to stop with him.

"Sodium?" he said. "What the hell was he doing with that?"

"Nobody knows."

Crombie whistled and the two of them started walking again.

"Whatever it was, it wouldn't be doing any good."

"So they say."

"We avoid that sort of thing like the plague," said Crombie. "It's incredibly reactive. One of the alkali metals. Soft. You can cut it with a knife. They use it as a cooling agent in nuclear reactors."

"He wouldn't be taking it offshore then?"

"Doubt it. He could, mind you, if he wanted to."

"How? I thought you were ultra-strict about that sort of thing."

"We are. But safety officers can get away with murder."

"How?"

"Stuff it in a pack of smoke canisters. They're marked "explosives". Nobody'd try opening them."

"Is it that easy?"

"Aye. For safety officers."

They walked on, each thinking about the implications of what Crombie had said. As they turned into a busier street where the lights of shop windows seemed to steam out of the fronts of the buildings, Carston began to articulate a thought that had come to him several times over the past few days but which he hadn't allowed to develop because it was so extreme and there were so many other things to be dealing with.

"Alex, d'you think it's possible Baxter was involved in something?"

"Like what?"

"I don't know. Sabotage of some sort?"

Crombie was genuinely surprised.

"What? I doubt it."

"Hang on," said Carston. "Just think about it for a moment. He's saying things about workmates losing their jobs and him coming into more money. Could he have been planning something to … I don't know … shut down the platform? Damage it somehow? That'd mean they'd lose their jobs, wouldn't it? It would be a way of getting his own back on them."

"Well, yes, but he'd lose his, too."

"Maybe," said Carston, and immediately found himself clutching at straws. "He was a gambler, though. Maybe he had a bet with somebody about the platform closing."

Crombie's look told Carston exactly what he thought of that.

"I know. It's far-fetched, but why's he got the sodium?"

Crombie was shaking his head.

"He wouldn't need sodium if he wanted to do that," he said. "There are plenty of ways to cause problems without risking being caught with that stuff."

"Go on then," said Carston. "Tell me."

"OK," said Crombie. He walked on, his head lifting now and then as he considered the possibilities of what he was contemplating.

"Let's say he does use the sodium," he said at last, pausing as the various stages of the sabotage occurred to him, "he'd wait till there was hot work in one of the sensitive areas, on one of the lines near the separators, say. Then, after the job's finished, he manages to get a lump of the stuff into one of them. The lines are usually flushed out with water-based glycol before the system's repressurised. So the sodium reacts, the oil starts to flow and ... whoosh, he's got a fire."

"There you are," said Carston.

"Aye, but he could also get a bloody great explosion," said Crombie. "Blow the lot up. Him and all his mates with it."

Carston's mind raced with the significance of the suggestion. Could it be that Baxter was so desperate that he really was planning something that drastic? From what he'd heard of the man, he wouldn't care too much if people like Bole and the others were killed. Was it a way of committing suicide and taking them with him? Were the gambling debts getting on top of him? Was the stress of his homosexuality and their jibes about it too much? He'd asked for his pension to be paid to Vicky. Maybe that was why he'd promised she'd have money to spend. But it was too fanciful. People like Baxter didn't blow up oil platforms. That wasn't just a localised revenge; it was a major catastrophe. Hundreds of men would be... He stopped walking as another memory jumped into his head. Offshore, the OIM had told him that, for the derrick shutdown, there'd be fewer men on board. Baxter knew that. Maybe if he made his sabotage coincide with that.

He put a hand on Crombie's arm.

"Just suppose for a minute he did that, and there weren't many on the platform. What would happen?"

"They'd be evacuated right away."

"How?"

"What, out on Falcon?"

"Yes."

"Helicopter, if they're lucky. It'd take them across to Bravo. Or a lifeboat. Same thing. Depends on how serious it was."

The two of them started walking again.

"And who'd be the last to go?" asked Carston.

Crombie thought about it. "The OIM, safety officer. Probably the maintenance engineer and his crew."

It was too good to be true. Apart from the OIM, that meant Bole, Baxter and Bole's mates. Crombie had just listed the casualties that would fit Baxter's needs exactly.

"But surely," he said, deliberately playing devil's advocate, "there'd be some automatic system that would stop that happening."

"Of course there would," said Crombie, unaware of Carston's excitement and still playing a game of idle speculation. "ESDVs. Emergency Shut Down Valves. Any pressure differential triggers them right away. They're subsea. They shut off the oil and gas."

Carston was almost relieved to hear it. The scenario he'd been constructing was too monstrous. And even if it had been legitimate, it got him no further. It was Baxter's murder he was investigating, not his plans for offshore mayhem.

"Right," he said, beginning to smile at the excitement he'd allowed himself to feel. "Ah well, it was an interesting idea."

"Unless somebody over-rode them manually," said Crombie, still pondering the possibilities.

Immediately, Carston was back on alert.

"How?"

"Computer. In the control room. The whole thing's on a display there. Lets you see everything that's going on, what valves are shut, open, everything. You could over-ride the system from there."

Carston couldn't believe all the avenues that were opening in his mind.

"Or from the office in Aberdeen," he said.

"Eh?" said Crombie.

"Anstey's have got the same thing in the office. This guy Hamer showed me. Exact replica of the one on the platform. Baxter could have done it from onshore. He'd've been completely safe."

Chapter Fifteen

The next morning, he was eager to tell Ross and the team about the new turn his thinking had taken. He was still aware that it was all about the actions and motives of a dead man but he was confident that, when they did eventually pin down what Baxter had been up to, they'd open new perspectives on their enquiry.

He was pleased to find that Ross had done his usual efficient job of organising material into wall charts which let them see at a glance the various interconnections they'd established between all the individuals and events concerned. They already had it in much more detail on the computer, but there you could only get at it in little screenfuls. This was the sort of simplified overview Carston could understand. The only trouble was that the chart was full of gaping holes which needed to be bridged or plugged.

As he looked at it before starting the briefing, he was aware of a heavy panting, as if one of them had just run up several flights of stairs or was in the middle of some strenuous sex scene. He turned round. Fraser had his arms round his knees, which were bent up to his chest. He was holding them apart and panting in great, noisy gusts. Bellman, Thom and Spurle were studying him closely. Carston looked at Ross and McNeil, who were both smiling.

"What's this? Some new element in the sergeants' exam I haven't heard about?" said Carston.

"Level D breathin, sir," grunted Fraser, dropping his legs back down and taking a final deep breath.

Carston knew there were courses for everything in the force nowadays but hadn't heard that breathing was one of the topics.

"Me an' Janice go to classes. So's I can help her when the baby comes," explained Fraser.

His wife was eight months pregnant. He'd been regaling them with excruciatingly graphic anatomical details of everything he'd been learning since she'd conceived. Sometimes it made them wish he'd get back to his abysmal French.

"It's for controllin the diaphragm," he was saying. "See, shallow breathin's—"

"OK, OK. I take your word for it," said Carston. "D'you mind if we get on."

"Sorry, sir," grinned Fraser.

Carston shook his head and turned to Ross.

"Take us through what we've got, Jim," he said.

Quickly, and without elaboration, Ross went over the sequence of events for the previous week from the time the Falcon Alpha crew had come ashore up to the discovery of Vicky's body. Alibis had all been checked for the times of the two murders and, frustratingly, had left both cases wide open. Nearly all of the names he'd listed were still possibles for both crimes. The only exceptions were Bole and Baigrie, who'd been, respectively, in custody and in hospital when Vicky had been strangled.

"Did we know that Baigrie and Gallacher went to the Swan separately?" asked Carston, remembering what Geoff had told him.

Reid was sitting at a monitor. He tapped on his keyboard.

"Don't think so, sir," he said. "Neither of them mentioned it."

"Well, they did. Gallacher got to the pub later than Baigrie. There's a witness coming in this morning to make a statement. He saw Bole throw a punch, so at last we've got something more concrete on him. Jim, you and Reid deal with it, will you?"

Ross nodded and went on with his summary, following one line on his chart through the drinking spree and the queer-bashing route and another for Baxter's movements between Anstey's, Vicky's, the office and finally the dustbins where they'd found him. That was the point at which the two strands met. Another one was needed to complete the picture. It should have led from Baxter's meeting with Vicky to the time her body was found in her flat but they had nothing from which to forge any links and the fact of her death hung isolated in the patterns like a tiny, pathetic star.

"Maybe it's not connected," suggested Reid.

"Maybe," agreed Ross, "but it's a helluva coincidence."

Heads nodded all round.

"But this is all coincidences," insisted Reid. "Gallacher and Baigrie knowing Baxter, Gallacher and Baxter on the platform with Bole. They live in a small world. Oil."

"We need motives," said Carston.

"It's obvious," said Spurle. "Queer-bashing."

Carston shook his head.

"Don't think so."

Spurle flicked a hand towards the chart.

"We've got Bole in the cells downstairs, there's bloodstained stuff in Baxter's locker with his prints and DNA on it."

"Could've been planted," said Fraser.

"Who by?" asked Spurle.

"Any of 'em," said Fraser.

"What for?"

Fraser shrugged.

"That's what I mean," said Carston. "What sort of motives are behind any of this?"

"There's Baxter's gambling, too," said McNeil.

"Right," said Carston. "Come up with anything?"

"I checked the bookies you gave me. Between them, he owed nearly twelve grand."

"Twelve grand? Merde!" said Fraser. It sounded like "murd" and no-one understood it.

"They were about to close his accounts and sue him to recover the money," McNeil went on. "One of the managers reckoned he was probably in debt privately, too. Typical pattern, apparently."

"So somebody could have been after him for a payback?" said Carston.

"It's possible," said McNeil.

"Christ, this gets worse and worse," said Carston. "We'd better start asking around about his debts."

"No. I reckon it's to do with them all being pooves," said Spurle. "They all hated each other, didn't they. It's obvious. Bole hates Baxter 'cause he's a poof, Baigrie hates him 'cause he's had it off with his boy-friend, maybe Gallacher hates him 'cause of some poofy row they've had—"

Speculation was legitimate; bigotry wasn't. Carston butted in.

"But what's Vicky Bryant got to do with it?"

Spurle could only shrug. McNeil stood up and went to the chart. She tapped a name on it.

"McEwan's the only one that connects with both her and Baxter," she said. "He's maybe got a motive, too. Baxter was Vicky's regular. Sort of attached to her. Wanted his pension made over to her. They might have been making their own private agreement, cutting McEwan out. It was only what she owed McEwan that kept her on the game."

As he listened, Carston saw the legitimacy of what she was saying and realised that it was as valid as his own inventions about Baxter's proposed sabotage and a much better explanation of the double murder, which his theory didn't even confront. There were so many directions to follow.

"You're right, Julie," he said. "About time we had another go at him. You and I'll catch him at home this morning."

"Right, sir," said McNeil.

He let them all pitch in with their thoughts on McNeil's suggestion and any other ideas they had, then, before assigning them their various jobs for the day, took them through the things he'd spoken about with Crombie. They were all interested enough because it was a novel approach, but none of them showed much real enthusiasm. Ross was openly sceptical and only McNeil seemed to give it much serious consideration.

Carston's suggestion that the motive for Baxter's murder might be that one of the others had found out what he was planning sounded very lame. Nobody even bothered to ask what he was basing it on. When the briefing ended, the general feeling was it had only managed to cloud issues and multiply possibilities. Carston knew that this was no bad thing since the facile assumption of Spurle and the rest that it was a simple, understandable case of another gay getting what he deserved would lead them nowhere.

Leaving Ross to get Geoff's statement and Reid to co-ordinate the squad's movements and reporting priorities, he and McNeil left to drive to McEwan's flat. He was confident that he'd be there. People in McEwan's line of business rarely surfaced before midday.

The streets, shops and houses still seemed to be sweating out the late vapours of Autumn. It was about time the weather cleared. The north east wasn't usually this damp and people were beginning to complain about it. It still didn't keep them indoors, though. Not for the first time, Carston wondered what the hell everybody was buying all the time. The centre of Cairnburgh was always busy and people always had bulging carrier bags. Where did all the things they bought go? McNeil's voice brought him out of his musings.

"Sabotage on the scale you were talking about—that's pretty big, sir. Worth murdering for."

Carston knew that she enjoyed free range thinking as much as he did. It was partly the reason why he'd chosen her to be with him on the visit to McEwan.

"I suppose you've thought about one of the others being in on it?" she went on. "I mean, if he was getting paid for doing it, it'd sort out his debts, wouldn't it?"

"Yes. All sounds too big for one man on his own, doesn't it?" he replied. "Especially somebody like Baxter. Trouble is, he was such a loner. And, if he's the one that's got the access, why does he need anybody else?"

"Maybe it wasn't him at all. Maybe the sodium is as much of a plant as the survival suit with the blood and all the rest of it."

Carston smiled.

"Yes," he said. "I'd thought of that one. It's not a can of worms, it's a bucket."

McNeil nodded as she looked across at him then back at the road. A woman was getting ready to cross a little way ahead, the pushchair in front of her already sticking out into the street.

"Baxter seems such a … sort of midget in amongst all the rest of them," said McNeil, slowing and waving for the woman to cross. "It's just that Anstey's, Bole and his hard men, even Gallacher and Baigrie together … well … you wouldn't want to mess with any of them. Baxter seems a bit of a runt. And poor Vicky—"

She was right. Baxter and Vicky were copybook victims. If games were being played for big stakes, they were more likely to be the ones who got crushed in them. The more he thought about it, the less plausible his version of Baxter's sabotage plans seemed.

As they turned into Chapel Lane, with its hulking tenements, his mobile trilled. It was Ross.

"Thought you should know," he said. "Just got a fax from Falcon Alpha. Guy called Kemp."

"Jamie Kemp?"

"Aye. Says you asked him to check Baxter's work things."

"Yes."

"There's no personal stuff, nothing special belonging to Baxter, but he's found some other things that aren't normal."

"Like what?"

"Gas canisters with the wrong labels on them."

"How d'you mean?"

"That's what it says. H_2S and methane canisters. The labels've been switched or something. Baxter must have found them and set them aside."

"What, to use himself?" asked Carston, his sabotage theories regenerating.

"More likely to take them out of commission altogether. They were in a bag with a label on it. 'Not to be used.' In Baxter's writing."

The excitement that Carston had felt when the possibility of a grander design behind it all had first occurred to him started to prickle back inside him again.

"It's got to be something, Jim, hasn't it?"

"Aye, maybe," said Ross.

Carston smiled to himself. If Ross was prepared to concede the possibility, it meant that real evidence must be accumulating.

"We need to get up to Anstey's again. Set it up, will you?"

There was a silence.

"Jim?"

"Aye, sir. Just … er, Superintendent Ridley's been on. The Kemp guy told his OIM about the canisters and Anstey's have set up an internal investigation. The superintendent says we have to stay clear of them while it's on."

Carston's anger flared.

"Bastard," he hissed. "Look, Jim. Do what you can. Get in touch with Jamie Kemp and tell him not to use any gear that Baxter may have been using. Tell him to keep checking."

"But the superintendent—"

"Bugger him," said Carston. "He needn't know. You can make a personal call. Tell them I authorised it. They can—"

He stopped. There was no way of getting Ross to do what he asked without compromising him. Even if he gave him a direct order, Ross had to ignore it because of Ridley's instructions. Not for the first time, Carston's hands were being tied when he needed the greatest flexibility of movement.

"OK, Jim," he said. "Let's do it his way. Can you set up a meeting for me with Ridley this afternoon?"

Again there was a hesitation.

"Difficult, sir," said Ross, his discomfort obvious.

"Why?"

"The IO's here again. Wants to see you this afternoon."

Carston hadn't forgotten his indiscipline charge but he'd assumed that even Ridley wouldn't let it get in the way of an investigation.

"And Bole's changed his story," Ross went on. "I think we need to talk to him again. Could be a busy afternoon."

Carston looked out at the oily grey granite of the houses. At the best of times it was oppressive; this wasn't the best of times.

"OK," he sighed. "See what you can do. I'm going to have to talk to Ridley some time. Get me the earliest appointment you can. Grovel if you have to. The bugger's going to ruin this case if we don't."

"I'll maybe ask Andy to help," suggested Ross.

It was a good idea. Carston could never have brought himself to do it personally but the more reasonable Ross could harness Reid's negatives in their favour.

"Thanks, Jim," said Carston. "Talk to you later."

McNeil waited for him to give her the details. Her reaction, when she'd heard them, restored his mood a little.

"So, sabotage it is," she said, brightly.

"Yes, but who by?" said Carston. "Baxter's been doing all sorts of checking and re-checking out there, apparently. Now there's stuff he's marked as unsafe for use. Maybe it wasn't him who was doing the planning. Maybe he found out about it and was trying to stop it."

"So whoever was doing it killed him," said McNeil, thinking along in parallel with him.

"It's another possible," said Carston. As they got out of the car and walked up to McEwan's door, he added, "If only the police force would let us get on with our investigation."

200

Chapter Sixteen

It took McEwan a long time to let them in. The state of his clothing and the pinched redness around and in his eyes told them that they'd woken him. That was a bonus. He'd be on his guard but the fogs of whatever he'd been doing yesterday evening wouldn't have cleared. He tried to take refuge in making himself a cup of coffee but Carston's questions started the moment he let them in and gave him no time to settle.

Without actually saying so, he implied that McEwan was in the frame for Vicky's murder and that his links with Baxter, too, were suspect. McNeil was as adept at changing the angles of approach as Carston and, by the time their barely veiled accusations had sharpened his thinking, McEwan was on the defensive and desperate to satisfy them in some way or other that would deflect the attack. At one point, he even tacitly admitted that he did run a string of girls. It was a confession he'd never have made if they'd had a recorder running, but he judged that it was worth the effort of seeming to cooperate with them.

"OK, this last client you sent to Vicky," said Carston. "Who was he?"

"No idea. Stranger."

"You wouldn't tell us if you knew, would you?" said McNeil.

McEwan looked at her with a sneer.

"Nah. Professional ethics. Street cred. I'd never live it down."

"Vicky's dead," said McNeil, her voice hard with spite. "That's more important than your street cred."

He ignored her, just shaking his head by way of response.

"You're supposed to be helping us with our enquiries," said Carston. "Now you're withholding information. We could lock you up just for that."

McEwan looked at him, his face pleading.

"I've told you. I didna ken the guy."

"How did he pay you?"

"He didna. He was supposed to give it to Vicky."

"So he ripped you off," said Carston.

"No as much as he ripped Vicky off," said McNeil, the barb aimed at Carston as much as McEwan.

"But, according to you, he was a mate of Baxter's," said Carston.

"That's what he told me. On the phone. Said Baxter always said how good she was. I should bloody think so, the time he spent with her."

"What d'you mean," asked Carston.

"Punters pay for time, right?" said McEwan, feeling that he was in an area where he was in control. "They know where they are, how much. And they dinna hang around. That Baxter was a bleedin pain. Spent hours wi' Vicky. Like she was his bloody wife."

"Or maybe like she was a woman," said McNeil, "and not just a hole with fur around it."

"Ah care about mah girls," said McEwan, his accent getting broader as he strove to convince them he was telling the truth.

"Oh aye. Runnin a charity, were ye?" said McNeil, her own accent dropping to match his.

"Ah looked after 'em. Made sure they was—"

"Made sure the scars healed OK," said McNeil. Carston let her have her head. Her anger was frightening McEwan again. "Made sure their skin was ready for the next batterin."

"Ah never let punters do that," he protested. "Only if the girls wants it. Some o' them do."

"Not Vicky, though."

"No," said McEwan, quickly. "No Vicky."

"So the marks on her were what?" asked Carston. "Some sort of illness she had? A condition of some sort?"

McEwan was silent for a moment. He stood up, fetched cigarettes from the mantelpiece and lit one. It helped him to regain some control.

"That was one sick bastard. I didna ken. You get all sorts. You wouldna believe who I've had askin for—" He stopped, careful not to give away too much. "S and M, eating shit, drinking piss, golden showers, threesomes, bisexuals, everything." He stopped again and felt McNeil's eyes piercing into him.

"I told her I was sorry," he said.

"Oh, that's OK then," said McNeil.

"It's the business," said McEwan, with a flash of anger. He wasn't used to women answering him back. "You get them sometimes. You canna protect the girls all the time."

"Protect," said McNeil. "Some protection you gave Vicky."

"I told you. I couldna help that." His accent was slipping again. "It was Baxter's fault anyway. If he'd been away a bit sharper, she woulda been off wi' some other punter. He was the one who arranged a different time wi' her. It was only because o' that that she was available."

"How long was he with her?" asked Carston.

"S'posed to be from half eight. He changed it. Arrived half seven. Stayed till nine o'clock. An hour and a half, for Christ's sake."

Little associations began to click in Carston's head. In all the complications he'd been proposing about sabotage and queer bashing, he'd been missing some simple indicators.

"And how long after that did she see her next customer?" he asked.

"He picked her up at the flat around twenty past nine."

"Oh, a twenty minute break? That's thoughtful," said McNeil.

"And this was the sadist? The one that knocked her around," said Carston.

"Aye."

"And you heard it all from her? From Vicky?"

"Aye."

McNeil launched into more sarcastic accusations about the level of service McEwan provided for his girls, but Carston's mind was off on yet another tangent. It brought into consideration things that hadn't previously seemed relevant and, yet again, asked as many questions as it answered. The raised voices of McEwan and McNeil shook him out of it. They were now well into the various misdemeanours for which McNeil was confident he could be charged and he was resenting more and more that he should be

203

questioned by a woman. Especially one who showed him so little respect. Carston's voice cut across what had become their bickering.

"OK, you say you didn't know the guy who said he was Baxter's mate."

"No."

"Was there anything about his voice? Anything special?"

"No really."

"Would you recognise it again?"

McEwan shrugged.

"Dinna ken. Maybe."

"Right," said Carston. "Sit tight a minute. I'm going to phone somebody. When I get through, I want you to listen, see if the voice is familiar. He may not say much so listen hard."

He checked a list of phone numbers in his pad, took out his mobile and dialled one of them. When the person at the other end answered, he spoke for a while then said, "Yes, that's what I wasn't sure about. Can you just go over it again for me? Just to make sure I got it right."

As the man on the phone began to answer, Carston held the phone to McEwan's ear, putting his finger to his lips to remind him of the need for silence. McEwan listened and Carston could see almost immediately that he was impressed. He nodded quickly and Carston listened for himself, then thanked the person he'd called and hung up again.

"That was the man, then," he said. "The one who made the date with Vicky."

"Aye. No doubt about it."

"What about your street cred?" asked McNeil, not prepared to trust him an inch.

"If he killed Vicky, he's got it coming."

"Aye. Made a right mess of your profit margins, didn't he?"

"Would you be prepared to testify?" asked Carston.

McEwan rolled his eyes upwards and leaned his head back.

"Aw Christ, is it really necessary?"

"If you want us to get Vicky's killer, yes. So I'd like another statement from you. Would you mind?"

"I've already—" McEwan began.

"I know. But I want to make sure of one or two details. And there's the fact that you've heard the voice again. I think now would be a good time." He turned to McNeil. "You can get the full statement back at the station," he said. "I'm going to be busy with other things."

McNeil forced back her own frustration. McEwan's identification of the man on the phone had come as a surprise but there was no way she could find out any more about that until Carston was ready to tell her. She still wasn't convinced of McEwan's innocence and wondered whether Carston hadn't just given him a way of unloading the guilt onto the person on the phone. She'd have been happy to keep on grilling McEwan and only managed to content herself with the thought that she'd be able to use the time before they got back to plan her approach more carefully. What she had to do was get him to say things that they could record and use. The problem was that McEwan, too, would be able to regroup.

Carston felt none of this. He thought he now knew at least one person who was involved in Vicky's murder. The trouble was that it didn't make sense and he had no idea what the motive might be.

****

Superintendent Murray's manner left Carston in no doubt that he was there on official business. He wasn't unfriendly but his facial expressions, the seriousness of his tone, the strictness of the terminology he used and the terms of reference he established left little room for levity. He handed Carston the charge sheet. Carston glanced through it and was amazed both at the number of incidents listed there and their apparent triviality. Ridley had collected remarks he'd made at meetings, reactions he'd had to direct and indirect orders and observations from his team (mostly Spurle and Reid), about his irregular treatment of them. The latest and most serious were those concerning his cavalier responses to Ridley's instructions regarding the conduct of the Baxter investigation. The final note, almost an afterthought, deplored his treatment of McEwan. It referred to the time when Reid had seen Carston threaten him.

"I suppose that postponing this interview is out of the question, sir?" asked Carston. "We are at a fairly crucial stage of a double murder investigation."

"I know," said Murray. "But the DCC needs to collate all my material before the Police Board meeting next week."

Carston nodded.

"I've got Superintendent Ridley to waive the last charge," said Murray, looking down at his own copy of the charge sheet. "The one about the mistreatment of a prisoner. I won't have time to talk to all the janitors and the rest in the time available. But it'll be left on the record."

Once again, it was procedure. In cases of alleged mistreatment, the I.O. had to interview everyone present in the vicinity at the time, including the other prisoners. Carston made no reply. He'd decided that the less he said, the sooner it would be over.

"So," Murray went on, "let's work through these one at a time, shall we?"

As he read each individual charge and asked for Carston's reaction to it, the pettiness of what he was having to deal with must have been obvious to him. Carston was careful to remain serious and rein back his natural tendency to dismiss the whole exercise as a massive waste of their time and police resources.

The problem was that, technically, Carston was guilty as charged. Each barbed little comment, each example of how he'd bent the rules to by-pass some obstruction, each confrontation with Ridley which had resulted in the latter losing face, added to a dossier that, in its cumulative force, was very convincing. On its evidence, Carston was a subversive influence. His less than sensitive treatment of Reid was further proof that his methods worked against police solidarity. In Ridley's book, that equated to indiscipline.

As he answered Murray's questions, he was forced to recognise for himself that, over the years, by indulging in the frequent, tiny pleasures of disconcerting Ridley, he'd dug his own, made-to-measure hole. Ridley's rise through the hierarchy had made Carston's eventual put-down inevitable.

"D'you mind if I ask a question," he said as Murray got to the end of the list.

Murray looked up at him and waited.

"What's the worst that'll happen to me?"

Murray shook his head.

"I can't speculate on that," he said. "You'll have your hearing with the ACC. He'll decide."

"Yes, but you're used to these things, sir," insisted Carston, risking a call on the previous good relations there had been between them. "In your experience, what's Superintendent Ridley looking for?"

Murray shook his head again.

"It's not personal, Jack," he said, his own liking for Carston slipping briefly through his role. "It'll be something exemplary, I should think. Loss of increments, transfer to another department, maybe another force. But I've got no inside track on this. Now, can we move to your direct team? You realise that you can call any of them as witnesses in your defence."

Carston nodded then smiled.

"Yes, sir. I wouldn't want to wish it on them, though. They're mostly very good officers. Lining up on my side might queer their pitch."

"There are no sides," said Murray.

"No, sir," said Carston.

"Anyway, they're already on your side," said Murray, allowing himself a half-smile. "I've spoken to them. They give you more credit than you deserve."

As they discussed the team's results since Carston had taken charge, it was obvious that their clear-up rate had been well above the Scottish average. Carston was quick to acknowledge that much of that was the result of Ross's organisational gifts. The way he assessed information and homed in on essentials made it easier for the rest of the group to keep a clear focus. Carston also took the chance to underline McNeil's special talents for eliciting information from witnesses and even suspects. Her training in various forms of counselling had been useful in that respect but it was made even more valuable by her own natural sensitivity and instinctive feeling for justice.

"They're a good team," agreed Murray. "But we can't get away from this." He tapped the list in front of him again. "You've sailed too close to the wind too often. You're your own worst enemy, Jack."

"Not while Superintendent Ridley's around," said Carston.

"You see," said Murray. "You can't resist it, can you? Your little cracks. People don't like them." He lifted the charge sheet. "Off the record, we both know that these things are … minor indiscretions. But they've added up. And now that they're official, well … you can't duck them. And I'd really suggest, for your own good, that you don't try to joke about them."

Carston looked at him. Murray was sincere. It obviously gave him little pleasure to be doing the job but, like all their colleagues, he had to jump through the hoops the authorities had set up.

"Want my advice?" he said, picking up the papers and standing up to signify that the interview was over.

"Of course," said Carston.

"Get him to withdraw this."

"Ridley?" said Carston.

"Superintendent Ridley," warned Murray. "Yes. He can decide not to pursue it. Treat it as an internal, departmental matter."

Carston's head was shaking.

"I think it's maybe too far gone for that," he said. "I'd have to break the habit of a lifetime."

"Well, do it, Jack," said Murray, his face very serious.

He went to the door.

"I'll keep you posted," he said. "Think about it, though."

Carston nodded.

"Thank you, sir," he said.

Within a minute, Ross came in. He'd obviously been waiting not too far away. He knew better than to ask how it had gone but his silence and studied concentration on the items on his desk were as eloquent as the bluntest query.

"That's it sorted, then," said Carston.

Ross looked up at him, wanting to hear more, his expression an optimistic reaction to Carston's own lightness of tone.

"All I have to do is shove my tongue as far up Ridley's arse as it'll go and keep it there for as long as it gives him pleasure."

Ross's optimism drained away. There was nothing he could say. Where Ridley was concerned, Carston was either incurably childish, insisting on winning the playground scraps, or had some sort of death wish. He knew exactly what he had to do to stay more or less in line but seemed congenitally incapable of doing it.

"Well, from my personal point of view," said Ross, "I'd be grateful if you'd give it a try."

It was as close as he'd get to expressing what amounted to affection for his boss and Carston was aware of it.

"OK, Jim," he said. "I'll give it a little lick and see how it goes."

The two of them looked at each other as the literal image of what he'd said formed in their minds.

"Ugh," said Ross.

"Exactly," said Carston. "Now, what's the story with Bole?"

Ross was glad of the chance to move away from the slight awkwardness of the near-bonding experience.

"He's been talking to his brief. Admits everything now."

"Everything?"

"The assault. Says it was justified, though. He was provoked."

Carston closed his eyes, raised his head and gave a deep sigh. It was exactly what Pill and Geoff had been speaking about in the Swan the previous evening.

"Don't tell me," he said. "Come on. Let's go and hear it."

Ross phoned for Bole to be taken to an interview room and they went down to see him. He'd only been there a couple of minutes when they arrived but already the room stank of his sweat and old cigarettes. He looked at Carston warily. The previous anger had gone; he'd obviously been heavily coached by his lawyer. The signs didn't look good. Carston nodded for Ross to turn on the recorder. After the preliminaries, he said to Bole, "Well, I hear you've decided to come clean."

Bole said nothing.

"I'd like to hear it for myself, if you don't mind," Carston went on. "From the top please. Wednesday night, you admit that you assaulted Mr Baigrie?"

"I was provoked," said Bole. It had the flatness of a chant about it. Bole didn't even believe it himself.

"And so you assaulted Mr Baigrie," Carston insisted.

"I pushed him away. It made me mad, what he was doing."

"I see. And what was that?"

"Put his arm round my waist. Tried to… Had his arm round my waist."

Carston eased aside the thought that it would need to be a very long arm and that Baigrie must be strikingly careless about hygiene.

"He put his arm round you. In a sexual way, would you say?" he asked.

The question bothered Bole. If he answered yes, it would suggest that he recognised the sexuality of the gesture, and the only people who could do that were poofs themselves.

"I suppose that's what he thought it was, bloody pervert," he said.

"It couldn't have been him just being friendly?" asked Carston, in the tone of someone talking to a primary school child.

"Men don't put their arms round your waist," said Bole.

"Where do they put them then?" asked Carston, deeply interested in the answer.

Bole looked at him.

"I don't know. They don't. You don't … touch each other, do you?"

Carston waited.

"On the shoulder maybe," said Bole, beginning to bluster. "But not round the waist. Never round the waist."

"No. So it was a big shock to you, was it? Well, it must have been, to cause you to start hitting him."

"Course it was a shock. Any normal man would've—"

"How come you didn't mention it before?" Carston said, cutting across his words.

For an instant, Bole couldn't think of an answer, then his self-righteousness came to the rescue.

"You don't like to admit it."

"What?"

"That a poof's been… That he's … made advances."

"You're sure that's what it was?"

"No doubt about it."

"You should've told us before. It might've saved a lot of trouble."

As he nodded his regret that Bole seemed to have been holding out on them, Ross asked, "Did I mention that we got a DNA match on the blood we found on Mr Baxter's survival suit?"

Bole looked at him, uncertain how to respond.

"Aye. It's yours. So that's fingerprints and DNA. What d'you think?"

Bole shook his head.

"I'm not saying anything about that without my brief here," he said.

"Your prerogative," said Ross. "I'm not sure your excuse about Mr Baigrie extends to Mr Baxter, though."

"Or did he try to have a cuddle, too?" asked Carston.

Bole's temper was obvious in the clenching of his fists.

"OK, let's get back to the pub," said Carston. "So Mr Baigrie puts his arm round you, gives you a squeeze… That is right, is it? He did give you a squeeze?"

"He put his fuckin arm round me," hissed Bole.

"And you pulled away."

"Yes."

"Then what?"

"He wouldn't let go. I tried to shove him off me. Then I just … lost it. He forced me to do it. Wouldn't go away. I … hit him."

"Once? Twice?"

"Couple of times. No more."

"And?"

"His pal sets about me."

"Mr Gallacher."

"Is that his name? Aye."

Another of his Richter scale coughs hit him and Carston and Reid listened to the thoracic avalanches. Carston wasn't displeased with what Bole was saying. So many of the things were lies and he now had not only Gallacher's and Baigrie's testimony, but Geoff was prepared to be called as a witness, too. With any luck, he'd be able to persuade him to get even more to come forward. The more lies Bole told, the easier it would be to discredit his whole testimony. Carston took the opportunity to make him go over every bit of the story again and noted that, already, there were variants in what he said. For all that his lawyer had coached him, there was still a case for him to answer.

At last, they switched off the machine and gratefully stood up to leave as Bole began to hack up another chestful of mucus.

Carston turned to Ross.

"You can see why Baigrie fancied him, can't you?" he said.

Chapter Seventeen

When Carston phoned Alex Crombie to suggest another drink, Crombie jumped at the chance. He was due to go offshore the following day, so a normal evening in the pub was an even more attractive prospect than usual. They sat over their pints, aware that, amongst the bright, young clients in flash clothes drinking cocktails, they were something of a parody. Carston pulled down the dark grey sweater he was wearing and looked at the front of it. There were tiny specks of something on it—probably food but he preferred not to know. Crombie was wearing the same sort of sweater. He was a big man and it was tight over his shoulders and around his chest.

"D'you think we ought to take a bit more trouble with our wardrobe?" asked Carston.

"What for?" replied Crombie.

"Blend in a bit more here."

Crombie laughed.

"It'd take more than a new sweater, Jack."

Carston nodded and looked around at the other drinkers. They did seem amazingly young and the world did seem to be theirs.

A man came in. He was in his twenties, had designer stubble, spiky hair, and the walk that goes with money and self-satisfaction. He wore a full-length leather coat that must have cost at least two months' of Carston's salary but probably came out of the guy's petty cash. He called loudly to a girl in what looked like a rubber skirt who was already sitting at the bar. Instinctively, Carston disliked him. He dragged his attention to the main reason he'd wanted to see Crombie.

"I know you're going offshore tomorrow and you don't want to talk shop," he said, "but this stuff I've been asking you about Baxter and Falcon Alpha, there's more to it. I need your help again."

Crombie drained his glass, held it up and looked meaningfully at it. Carston went to the bar, waited beside the leather man and had to listen to him telling his girl about the hotel he'd booked for them in Singapore at Christmas. At last, the barmaid got round to him and he took the two fresh pints back to their table.

"See those two?" he said, indicating the couple at the bar.

Crombie nodded.

"He's going to be shagging her in Singapore at Christmas."

"Christ, you're a good detective," said Crombie.

"Elementary," said Carston. "Now then, last night you were saying that Baxter didn't need sodium to cause trouble. You said there were easier ways."

"Right," said Crombie.

"Like what?"

"Funny," said Crombie. "Since you asked me, I've thought about it a lot and there are all sorts. Just cracking a nut would do it."

"What's that? How's it done?"

"Well, the bolts through the flanges of pipes. They've got to be tightened just right. If you set too high a torque value on the ratchet, the engineer would over tighten it. It'd look OK when it was inspected but, as soon as the pressure built up, it'd give way. You'd get a leak."

"And who could do that?"

"Anybody who could get hold of the ratchet—storeman, safety guys, engineers. Problem there, though, is you'd have no control of when it blew."

"Would you with any other methods?"

Crombie nodded.

"Too bloody right, you would. It's OK for you. You'll be here tomorrow; I'll be out there with all this shit. Scares me rigid."

"I know."

Crombie's voice was quiet when he spoke again.

"Sabotage is almost built in to the bloody system," he said.

"How d'you mean?"

"I was thinking, you take where the wet condensate gas comes out of the separator, before it's processed. The whole system's pressurised but there's a bleed valve on the ball valve. If you open that little sod, the pressure of the condensate rushing out of it'll build up a positive charge. Just like stroking a cat's fur. A sort of hosepipe effect. The stuff's more like a travelling solid than a gas."

"But it wouldn't ignite, would it?" said Carston.

"That's the trouble. It could do. Easily. The charge'd get so big that it'd earth on any bit of steel or metal about the place."

"Christ."

"Aye. It'd maybe take a while, but with that sort of friction—"

"And if the emergency shut down valves had been over-ridden," said Carston.

Crombie shook his head and used his hands to repeat a gesture Carston had last seen when Jamie Kemp had been telling him the same sort of thing on Falcon Alpha.

"But there must be other protective systems," he said.

"Oh aye, especially in places like that, where you could get high pressure leaks."

There was no subtle way for Carston to introduce his next question. He tried to make it sound as if it was just following on the rest.

"How about gas canisters? What are they for?"

"Testing."

"And there's two sorts, right?"

"Basically, yes. H_2S and Methane."

"What if they got mixed up?"

Crombie's head was shaking.

"They couldn't," he said.

"Humour me," said Carston.

Crombie took a swig as he thought about it.

"Worst case scenario?" he said at last.

Carston nodded. His own beer was untouched.

"They'd knock out the gas sensors," said Crombie. "That's what the canisters are for—checking the gas detectors on the automatic systems. You squirt a bit of gas at one to check that it's working OK. But if you get 'em mixed up, you're in deep shit."

"Why?"

"Because if you use an H_2S spray on ordinary methane detectors, it poisons them. They seem to be working but they're not."

Carston found that he was holding his breath. His pulse was banging in his ears.

214

"Right," he said, "so let's get it straight. A couple of squirts of this spray in the wrong place and the automatic detection systems won't detect a thing."

Crombie was about to take another drink but he stopped and looked at Carston.

"Why're you asking all this, Jack. Sounds bloody serious."

Carston's lips were set tight.

"It could be, Alex," he said.

Their mood contrasted strongly with that of all the other laughing, shouting people around them. Carston was tugging at the sleeve of his sweater.

"If you wanted to do something like that, as a safety officer, could you?"

"What, knock out a system? Yeah, course I could."

"And open a bleed valve. And let the charge build up?"

"Jack, what is this?"

"Suppose you did. How would you get clear?"

Crombie wasn't happy with the topic but Carston's expression was intense and he could see that there was nothing idle about the speculation.

"I'd have time. Like I said, the charge'd take a while to build up. Sound the abandon platform alarm."

"And could you do it on your own?"

"Just," said Crombie. "But over-riding the ESDVs would be the problem."

Carston nodded.

"So if you had someone who could do that for you, two would be enough?"

"D'you realise you're buggering up my last night onshore?" said Crombie.

Carston smiled. There was no humour in it.

"Sorry, Alex. It's all things that have come up in connection with Baxter, like I said."

Crombie shook his head.

"The sort of stuff you're talking about, though, it's well beyond what Baxter could do."

"Why?"

"He wouldn't say boo to a goose."

"He might if the stakes were high enough."

"What d'you mean?"

Carston was reluctant to engage Crombie any further. It was all still under investigation.

"I'll tell you when I can, Alex."

Crombie nodded.

"I'd still be surprised if it was Ally Baxter. Didn't have the balls for the big time."

"Speaking of balls," said Carston, keen now to lighten the conversation, "look at him."

The leather man had both his hands on his girl's breasts. She was holding a cocktail glass to his lips as his fingers moved and squeezed. To Carston's surprise, there was no smile from Crombie.

"Lucky bastard," he said, before draining the rest of his pint. Carston still had most of his left. He shook his head as Crombie stood and pointed at his glass.

"No, I'm OK for now. You carry on," he said.

He watched as Crombie pushed through the crowd. For a big man, he was surprisingly shy and his way to the bar was littered with apologies. He still talked now and then about the pain of the separation from his wife, who'd left him for a doctor who worked in the same company as Crombie. The difference was that the doctor was never offshore.

When he came back to the table, Carston was careful to keep the talk well away from platforms, safety matters and anything connected with his job. They told jokes and picked a top ten of the women in the pub.

At last, to Carston's surprise, Crombie looked at his watch and said, "Right, Jack. Time for some sex."

"No thanks," said Carston. "I mean, I like you, but—"

"You're a laugh a minute," said Crombie.

Carston knew that Crombie had been using prostitutes since his wife left. He'd told him so. He wasn't proud of it but he'd got to know a couple of them and he and they knew exactly what it was all for. His visits to them were transactions and familiarity was even bringing a comfort into them, perhaps a sort of affection. With a trip offshore in the morning, he had to go and unload some of his needs.

More and more youngsters had been coming into the bar and their noise was making ordinary conversation difficult. The rubber and leather couple were rubbing their respective materials together even more openly as the cocktails multiplied. Carston felt a tinge of envy for both Crombie and the leather man but was simultaneously

216

glad that he didn't have to go through all the role playing that still lay ahead for them over the next few hours, or even years. It was time to leave. Outside, an unexpected pleasure was waiting. Only a dozen or so yards up the street from the pub door, a blindingly white Porsche was parked on a double yellow line.

"That has to belong to Leatherman," he grinned.

"Aye, probably," said Crombie.

"Aye," said Carston. "And if it's not him, it's some other rich bastard who deserves to be done. I think I'll phone the station. Get Sandy to send a car round to give him a ticket. Pity we haven't got any clamps."

"You vindictive old bugger," said Crombie.

"Not so much of the old," said Carston.

****

Back home, Kath had spread lots of ten by eights over the floor and coffee table in the living room. They were the publicity shots for Dot's play at the Warehouse and, as with all Kath's work, they were very impressive. She'd printed them so that the blacks were deep and glossy and the whites shone. They were nearly all individual close-ups of the cast, with a few couples and two group shots. The close-ups were mainly very tightly cropped, with the subjects' features filling the frame.

"What d'you think?" she asked, as Carston came in and stood looking at them.

On the table were pictures of Geoff and Pill. Geoff had his head angled towards the camera, looking up at it. The lighting hit his face from the right side and made him look handsome, threatening and, the only word for it, manly. She'd shot Pill in half-profile and managed to emphasise his features in such a way that they lost all their pharmaceutical associations.

"You're a bloody genius," said Carston, with genuine admiration.

She kissed him and started to collect the photos, grading them as she picked them up. Carston flopped into the sofa and pulled a couple of cushions behind his back.

"Tired?" asked Kath.

"Not really," said Carston. "It's just … every time I talk with anybody about this case, it gets more complicated."

"I thought that's the way you liked it."

Carston nodded.

"Used to. Up to a point, anyway. All the twisted motives and relationships—I suppose that's what does it for me. This is getting bigger than people, though."

Kath slid the photos carefully into her portfolio.

"What's that mean?" she asked.

Carston heaved a great sigh and talked, as much for himself as for her, about the way that queer-bashing had evolved into a suspicion of some major piece of sabotage. Her questions showed that she was genuinely interested and helped him to refine some of his arguments, especially about where Vicky fitted into it all. Since talking to McEwan, his attention had been more on her than on Baxter. The little clue he'd been given as to what had happened to her had exercised his ingenuity. In trying to work out why she'd been killed, he'd begun to guess at possible connections between her, Baxter and the person he thought was responsible. The problem was still the lack of direct evidence.

Later, they sat in bed together, Kath reading a biography of Florence Nightingale and Carston with a colour supplement he hadn't had time to read at the weekend. He flicked through the pages, finding nothing of any interest and feeling only irritation at fashion photos which were blurred, out of focus and gave the reader no idea what the clothes looked like. Equally annoying was the vogue for confessional columns. He wanted to read people who made him laugh, not self-important London dwellers who wrote as if their opinions were insights.

He'd soon had enough and, putting the magazine on the bedside table, he stretched out his right hand and gently massaged Kath's left forearm.

She looked across at him and smiled.

"Jim Murray came to see me today," he said.

"What for?"

"He's the I.O. This discipline thing with Ridley."

"What did he have to say?"

"He was worried about you."

"Me? Are they investigating me, too? What have I done?"

Carston smiled and explained what Murray had suggested about getting Ridley to withdraw the charge.

"I can't do it," he said.

218

"Why not?"

"Oh come on, love, you know him. Can you see me being nice to him? Day after day after day?"

She closed her book, put it aside and turned to rest her head on his chest, with her right arm round him. He started stroking her hair.

"You can be very, very smarmy when you want to," she said. "Lots of my friends think you're charming."

"I am, but not with Ridley."

"Is it worth forcing yourself?"

It was a simple question and, if he was honest, the answer was equally straightforward. He was beginning to think he'd had enough of the job. Recent cases had made him question the whole process of guilt and blame. On the other hand, to preserve what he and Kath had, to carry on enjoying their very comfortable lifestyle, he had to try to placate Ridley.

"Yes," he said.

"Well," said Kath, "do it."

"Easy to say when I'm lying here like this with an erection on the way."

Kath laughed and moved her hand under the duvet.

"What you need is a mantra," she murmured.

"What, Om, Om, Om," intoned Carston.

"No. Something to keep you focused. Something like 'Smarmy git'."

"Smarmy git?" he said. "Which Eastern philosophy's that from then?"

"Mine. When you feel yourself getting angry, just repeat it over and over again. It'll help you to keep a sense of proportion."

He kissed her hair. He was relaxing more and more under her fingers.

"Tell you what," he said.

"What?" she said, her head moving down across his chest.

"When I go and see him, you come and do that and I'll be fine."

Kath laughed and they stopped talking.

Chapter Eighteen

The next morning, the mantra got plenty of use. Knowing what was coming, Carston had put on his smartest suit, a charcoal grey one that Kath had chosen for him, and gone to a lot of trouble to look respectable. He knew he'd still seem shabby beside the immaculate Reid, but the aim was to be as neutral as possible. He was sure that Ridley saw his normal appearance as a sort of challenge to authority.

His over-riding need was to go back to Anstey's, but he knew that to do so would be to contradict Ridley once again. On Ross's advice, he spoke to Reid and suggested that a meeting between the two of them and Ridley would move the investigation along. It would probably have taken twenty-four hours for Carston to get an appointment; for Reid, one quick phone call was enough. They were in Ridley's office just after nine o'clock. After a fairly stiff, formal few minutes, which showed that Ridley was as aware of the awkwardness of the situation as Carston was, Carston made a deliberate effort to submerge the sarcasms that the other two triggered so easily in him. His support for Reid surprised both of them but had none of the edge that they would have expected.

"I think the answer lies at Anstey's," he said at last. "I was interviewing McEwan yesterday and—"

"Out of the question," snapped Ridley.

"Sir?" said Carston.

"We've been there too often as it is."

Carston held back the obvious retorts, about the fact that the victim and all the main suspects worked there and that they'd found bloodstained evidence and a lump of sodium in Baxter's locker.

"I told you from the start to keep away from them," Ridley went on.

"Yes, sir. I know," said Carston. "That's why I thought it might be an idea if Sergeant Reid went this time. He has very good relations with Mr Nicholas and maybe he'd be less … confrontational than I usually am."

"Huh, there's little doubt about that," said Ridley. "It's still not on, though."

Reid didn't want to miss this chance of taking a central role.

"I could make it an unofficial visit, sir," he suggested. "Say that I'm following up on something we talked about when he came here last Wednesday."

Ridley shook his head.

"No, Andrew," he said. "It's not possible. There are … other considerations."

Carston wanted to know what they were but waited. He'd given Reid the initiative.

"I see, sir," said Reid, capitulating at once.

Carston was lucky; Ridley felt the need to explain why he was depriving his protégé of a chance to shine. He spoke hesitantly, not sure of what to say, of how much to reveal.

"You see, there's … er … already an investigation… They've had a few visits from the … er … the Fraud Squad. In Aberdeen."

Carston's temper flared. Why the hell hadn't he been told this before? It was so obvious. If there was fraud going on, or even suspected, it opened up possible motives that he could never have guessed at. His own investigation could have been miles further ahead than it was. For all Ridley's concern with improving clear-up rates, his attitudes worked vigorously against them. Carston clenched his teeth and, in his head, repeated slowly, "Smarmy git, smarmy git, smarmy git". When he and Kath had talked and laughed about it, her suggestion was that he should think of himself as being and staying smarmy. In the event, it was easier to transfer the epithet to Ridley.

"Do we know what it's all about, sir?" asked Reid, to Carston's relief.

"Not really. Don't understand it, anyway. They're not getting out as much oil as they need, apparently. Seems there are ways of getting more but that'd need more investment and they're already spending a fortune in Indonesia and the Caspian. There are no funds."

It was all stuff that Carston knew. What was fraudulent about it?

"Somebody leaked some figures from an internal audit, though," Ridley went on. "They didn't add up. Projected figures for the Falcon field that couldn't be true. Showed a very positive outlook. Good forecast. All because of that, the share price has been like a yo-yo."

"Do we know who leaked the figures?" asked Carston, adding 'smarmy git' in his head because his anger hadn't yet subsided.

"No. Somebody who doesn't like Mr Nicholas, probably."

"Oh?"

"Yes. Well, he's the finance man. It's his figures that make the field look healthy."

"So he's the one who's under investigation?" asked Reid.

"No. The whole set-up," said Ridley. "I mean, for all we know, the figures may be correct. They've only been leaked because somebody doesn't like the idea of telling their bosses in the States that the future looks rosy. If they have to keep Falcon going and find funds for the Caspian stuff as well, they're going to be in difficulty."

"Mr Nicholas seemed fairly straightforward to me," said Reid.

"Of course he is," said Ridley. "Ansteys are a good company and he's a company man. Friend of mine played golf with him on the firm's outing to Carnoustie. He puts in all the hours God sends, apparently."

It was enough to make Carston want to arrest the man right away. More wheels were whirring in his head, breaking through the still echoing mantra. There was still no evidence, but the parts of the pattern which had been developing in their separate directions started to come back together. The emerging significance was as extreme an interpretation as any of the others but it had a coherence that might even appeal to Ross. The important thing now was to get a team inside Anstey's as early as possible and nudge Reid and Ridley in the right direction. Then pray that they didn't mess it up.

"I think there's a way of proceeding here," he said, tentatively. "The two investigations might well be linked."

"How?" asked Ridley.

"Well, I wouldn't want to make accusations I couldn't substantiate. But, if I could have a couple of hours to work at it, I think I might be able to suggest an approach."

"Some other maverick effort," said Ridley.

"Oh no, sir," said Carston. "In fact, it'd be better if Sergeant Reid handled it. He is nominally in charge, after all."

Again, Ridley looked quickly to catch any hint of sarcasm. Carston continued to be charm and consideration personified.

"What form will the work you'll be doing take?" asked Ridley. "You realise I can't have you making any sort of contact with anyone at the company."

"I appreciate that, sir," said Carston. "No, I just want to look at some regulations. I think some of them have been bent and people have been getting in the way. It would help if I could have your permission to get in touch with Aberdeen and get them to fax some things to me, too."

"You're not getting involved in their investigation."

"Of course not, sir."

"Couple of hours?" asked Ridley.

"At the most, sir," said Carston. "I think there may be more than one charge. It might help the Aberdeen squad. They'd probably appreciate it."

It was the final bait. The prospect of having Reid collect vital evidence and maybe even tie up the case was very attractive to Ridley. If, at the same time, he could further the Fraud Squad's investigation, it would do him and Reid no harm at all. For the first time in ages, he liked the sound of what Carston was saying.

"Alright," he said. "Two hours. And you bring whatever you get straight to me, right?"

"Right, sir," said Carston.

He stood up to go.

"Why the change?" asked Ridley.

"Sir?"

"How come you're suddenly cooperative? Wouldn't be to do with the indiscipline charge, would it?"

The bastard. It was so hard for Carston to sustain his blandness.

"In a way, sir," he said.

"Ah," said a self-satisfied Ridley.

"Made me think a bit more about working with the squad, respecting the rules."

"Good, good. That's what they're there for. Flights of fancy are all very well, but…" he lifted some folders from his desk, "this is what it's about in the end. Procedures."

"Yes, sir. Thank you, sir," said Carston.

By the time he was out of the office and on his way downstairs, the words "smarmy git" were screaming through his brain like a Japanese bullet train.

****

As soon as he got to his office, he phoned the Queen Street headquarters in Aberdeen and spoke to Donnie McIntyre. They were old friends. McIntyre's attitudes to the hierarchy were as relaxed as Carston's but he was much better able to hide them. As a result, he'd made Superintendent and, in promotional terms, was now well ahead of Carston. He was also co-ordinating the investigation into Anstey's and Carston used their friendship unashamedly to ask fairly direct questions about what the Fraud Squad thought was going on there.

He was excited to find that it complemented the theories he'd been forming and was convincing enough to get McIntyre's interest in a possible collaboration. First, though, he had some homework to do. He told McIntyre exactly what he was looking for and arranged for the relevant information to be emailed directly to archives. Next, he went down to the basement where the computing experts worked and worried at them until they produced the print-outs of all the files on Baxter's stick. Cracking his password had been simple. He'd used his date of birth backwards. No wonder it had been so easy to delete his files from the offshore computer.

Carston brought the papers back to his office to scan them. They all seemed to be tables of statistics about pressures, equipment replacements, induction schedules and the like. It was the sort of material that Alex Crombie would be familiar with but it seemed to offer little of interest to Carston. Then, to his delight and disbelief, he came to a file called Vicky. The name jumped off the page at him. Below it were solid blocks of text. No tables, no statistics, just words. At first, as he started reading, he was expecting references to Vicky herself or perhaps letters and notes Baxter had written to her. But there was no mention of her and no clear meaning came through. Carston wondered if the words had somehow become garbled in transcription. There were complete sentences, each of which made sense, but which didn't necessarily follow one from the next.

Gradually, as he read on, the words released their true significance and the character of Baxter began to form again for Carston. It was clearly his voice—a single mind weaving complaints and experiences into a monologue that outlined the misery his life had been on Falcon Alpha. They were all there, Bole, Gellatly, Milne and the rest. Their taunts, jokes and cruelties were chronicled along with Baxter's own reactions to them and assessments of their characters which were filled with as much bile as they'd heaped on him. It was a long, sad record of days and days of suffering. And woven through the pettiness were other pieces of information that began to excite Carston and link into a sub-plot that very quickly came to dominate everything else. It was the mother-lode.

He finished reading, a broad smile on his face despite the continuing woes through which he was wading, then got on to the archivist, Alan Saunders. He told him about McIntyre's email and the Vicky file and asked him to look out everything he had on some specific offshore regulations and send it up with the print-out of the email as soon as possible.

While he waited for it to arrive, he first went through the Vicky text again, highlighting passages to make it easier to decipher, then spent the rest of the time studying Ross's chart and sketching out his own version of people's movements and connections. It all fitted together perfectly. It was mostly speculation, of course, but the Vicky file gave it an impetus which was hard to resist.

By ten thirty, he was looking at his watch and forcing himself not to call Saunders back. He wandered about, picking up sheets of paper, half-reading what they said and putting them back again. He stood for ages at the window, watching the grey figures on the slippery pavements and marvelling, for the umpteenth time, that they all seemed so purposeful.

A knock at the door made him start. Constable McHarg came in with the booklets and files he'd been waiting for.

"You asked for these, sir," he said.

"Yes. Put them on the desk there."

He slumped visibly as he recognised the size of the task ahead. The sheaf of documents was over six inches thick.

"Who got that together, Tolstoy?" he said, leaning forward to pick up the fax from Aberdeen which was on top.

"No sir," said McHarg, deadpan. "Sergeant Saunders."

Carston flicked a quick glance at him.

"Ah," he said. "I suppose Tolstoy's been moved on, has he?"

"Dinna ken, sir."

"OK McHarg. Thanks, lad."

McHarg went out, shut the door, and Carston swallowed to get the word "lad" out of his mouth. He hated saying it. It made him sound like a telly cop. McHarg liked it though; it gave him the feeling that he was a part of the station community. Maybe it made him think he was in a TV series too.

Chapter Nineteen

Carston took off his jacket, hung it carefully on a hook, loosened his tie and sat down to plough through material he knew would be as dull as a Ridley joke book. He forced himself to read it thoroughly, only skipping sections when he was sure that they weren't relevant to what he was looking for.

He took lots of notes, jotting down figures, measurements, extracts from reports and surveys and the odd sentence from newspaper clippings. He also skimmed back through the forensic reports they'd received, and was particularly pleased by the analysis of the paint flecks that Brian McIntosh had scraped from the crescent-shaped wound in Baxter's skull, and by the presence of some carpet fibres he'd found in the slashes across his genitals.

By the time Ross and McNeil arrived, he was testing another part of his theory. They found him kneeling in a corner of the office, measuring a red fire extinguisher. He got up and, although he cursed when he saw the dirt on the trousers of his best suit, the expression on his face told Ross that his mood was good.

"OK," he said. "Get Reid in here, too. We've got some work to do. Then, if Ridley can manage to see past the end of his nose, we're all going for a little trip to Aberdeen."

While McNeil went to fetch Reid, Ross filled the coffee pot and spooned in the grounds. By the time the other two came back, it was bubbling and popping away. He poured mugs for all of them. McNeil took hers and leaned back against the window sill. Reid was sitting at a desk, his laptop fired up and a pencil and pad in front of him. Ross sat down and turned on his own computer.

"Right," said Carston. "We're going to be taking some artificial aids to Aberdeen with us. If that's a problem for any of you, now's the time to say so."

The three sergeants looked at one another to check whether any of them had any idea what he was talking about. They obviously didn't. It showed.

"We're dealing with experts here," Carston went on. "We've got plenty of circumstantial evidence and I'm dead certain we'll get more once we point the Grampian scene of crime boys in the right direction. But it wouldn't hurt to give ourselves a little edge. Nothing illegal, of course. Just a touch of strategic misdirection."

Ross and Reid looked uneasy, Ross because he knew how dangerous Carston's excursions outside normal procedures could be, Reid because he lived by those procedures. McNeil, on the other hand, felt a little pulse of excitement. Despite one particular misjudgement she'd made on a previous case, she was convinced that the usual plodding adherence to the rules, although desirable, added weeks or more to an investigation. She also distrusted predictability in anything.

"I suppose you'll be taking responsibility for it, sir," she said, a smile on her lips.

Carston looked at her and noticed the glint of amusement in her eyes. She couldn't possibly be flirting with him right under the eyes of the others, but it felt like it. He dismissed the thought at once, inwardly deploring the evidence that he was becoming a dirty old man.

"Don't I always?" he said.

He flicked back through the pages of his own pad until he found the beginning of his notes.

"What I'm going to do is give you a quick overview of what happened last week, then you're going to get a file together to take to Aberdeen. Reid, this is your chance."

Reid looked up from his screen.

"I've had a word with Superintendent McIntyre. Told him how our investigations have overlapped with his. He's happy for us to act together on this. I've told him you're going to be our lead man when it comes to tying it all up. Think you can handle it."

"Yes, sir," said Reid.

McNeil and Ross looked at one another. Ross gave a barely perceptible shrug of the shoulders.

"But—" Reid began, before stopping again.

"Well?" said Carston.

"I'm slightly concerned about the ... misdirection you mentioned."

"Don't worry. We'll come to that. If you don't like it when you hear it, you can opt out. If you want to stay in, we'll do it the hard way."

Reid just nodded. He wasn't convinced.

Carston picked up some of the printed material he'd been looking through and handed it to Ross and McNeil.

"This lot's for you two," he said. "I've marked up the ones we need."

They both looked quickly through the papers and read some forbidding titles: Geneva Convention on the Continental Shelf 1958 Article 5(5), Convention on the Prevention of Marine Pollution 1972, UN Convention on the Law of the Sea 1982 Article 60(3), Oslo Commission Guidelines for the Disposal of Offshore Installations at Sea, Environmental Protection Act 1990, the Radioactive Substances Act 1993, the Dumping at Sea Act 1996.

"What d'you want us to do with them?" asked Ross.

"Lift out the bits that are relevant to what we need so that we don't have to heave through all of them again when the time comes."

"How do we know what's relevant?" asked Ross.

"Christ, you want everything done for you, don't you?" said Carston, with a smile. "Right. What happens when a platform starts running down?"

"Makes less money," said Ross.

"Yes. And so they have to close it down and get rid of it. And it's not cheap. You can't just take it to the dump. You've got to get permits and approvals from the government, plug the wells, get rid of any hydrocarbons that are still there, dismantle the platform, take it ashore and then clear the site."

"Wow," said McNeil, still riffling through the pages in front of her. "Some operation."

"You wouldn't believe it," said Carston. "There's the International Maritime Organisation, another thing called OSPARCOM, that's the Oslo and Paris Commission, the London Convention—it just goes on and on. What it comes down to, though, is that, before long, Anstey's are going to have to remove

Falcon Alpha down to a depth of 55 metres below the surface so that it's not a navigational hazard. Or, depending on which regulations you read, they may have to get rid of it altogether."

"They knew that ages ago, though," said Ross. "It's built in to their licences. They have to say how they're going to get rid of it before it's even built."

"That's right," said Carston. "Doesn't help when it comes to the crunch, though, does it? It's bad news. You want your bankers and shareholders to think the cash is still pouring in. If you start talking about shutting something down, it sounds like failure."

Ross's head was shaking.

"I can't see that," he said. "You buy into it right from the start. Nobody believes a well's going to go on forever."

"Right again. That's why companies start getting their decommissioning plans developed long before production starts falling. They do conceptual and feasibility engineering studies, look at options—it's all part of their overall strategy." He pointed at the documents he'd given them. "It's all in there. But have a look at this, too."

He held up a copy of the fax he'd received from Donnie McIntyre in Aberdeen.

"Anstey's projections from the past five years. Hardly a mention of decommissioning anywhere. And yet everybody knows it's running down. And that's what got the Fraud Squad interested."

"Maybe it's my inexperience," said Reid, "but I don't see how it connects with our case."

"Me neither," said Ross.

McNeil nodded to show that she, too, was in the dark.

"Well, you can all be thinking about that while we're on our way to Aberdeen. D'you think you could go and have a word with Superintendent Ridley, Reid? Tell him I've been in touch with Superintendent McIntyre and that he's very keen for us to liaise with them on this. Jim and Julie will get all this ready for you and we'll hit the road as soon as we get the go-ahead."

It was all going very quickly and Reid was still worried about the orthodoxy of Carston's strategy, but the fact that he himself would be in charge of tying it all up made him keen to sell the idea to his boss.

"Right, sir," he said. "D'you want me to go now?"

"That would be good," said Carston.

He held his smile as Reid got up and left the office.

"He may be convinced, but I still don't see it," said Ross.

"Think about it, Jim," said Carston. He picked up the fax again. "In spite of all this, when the decommissioning happens, it's going to be hard for the management people in Aberdeen to make their period in charge seem like a success. So somebody's got to do something."

"Who?" asked McNeil.

"Well, who's been rocking the boat?"

"Baxter," said Ross.

"Right. He talks about redundancies for others, bonuses for him. He's got sodium in his locker and he's been mucking about with gas canisters offshore in a way that could lead to the whole platform going up in smoke."

"Sabotage?" said Ross, his tone revealing the enormity of the suggestion.

"Yes. At first, I wondered whether it was some sort of gesture thing—you know, a glorious suicide, taking all the folk he hated with him. But that would've been hard to achieve on his own. That's why we're going to have a chat with them all again. So get going on your bits of paper. I want to be away as soon as Ridley gives us the go-ahead."

It was twenty minutes before Reid reappeared. He'd had to be at his most persuasive with Ridley and only the personal glory it would bring had kept him at it. But it worked and they were cleared to leave. Carston rang McIntyre, asked him to set up the meeting and arranged to see him at Grampian HQ. He also suggested that McIntyre should get a search warrant and told him the sort of things the officers who enforced it should be looking for. At first, McIntyre was wary of the approach Carston intended to take.

"If you're going to be telling him all this, we should caution him," he said.

"Technically, yes," said Carston. "But if we do that, he'll have his lawyers in and we won't be able to bring up half the stuff we want to. I need to see his reactions."

"Bit thin, Jack," said McIntyre.

"I know, Donnie, but wait till you see it. We've nearly got enough already to put him away. When your lads have finished the search, we'll be quids in. Trust me."

McIntyre held out a little longer but, in the end, agreed to go along with the plan, saying only that, if Carston went too far at any stage, he'd stop everything and reinstate the proper procedures.

Carston gave Ross and McNeil another hour to collate their information and they, he and Reid were on the road by two thirty. As they drove along beside the grey and glittering Dee, Carston outlined the approach he intended to take during the meeting. Ross and Reid were grateful that his strategy wouldn't stray too far outside normal procedures. McNeil was amused by it. All three of them were content to play the roles that Carston had sketched out for them.

****

When they heard how many were coming, Nicholas and Hamer opted to see them in the boardroom. It was a long, well appointed place and a secretary had put a tray of fresh coffee and biscuits in the middle of the highly polished table. Around the walls were photographs of platforms silhouetted in sunsets, waves breaking against steel and generally heroic images of men dragging the reserves out of the invisible wells miles below them.

The two Anstey men were well aware that this was not just another fact-finding, evidence-gathering visit. The search warrant had set Hamer blustering but there was nothing they could do about it, and McIntyre's teams had begun work right away, concentrating on the locations that Carston had suggested might be most productive. McIntyre himself had opened the meeting by moving straight into the whole question of decommissioning and the related finances, which turned the focus immediately on Nicholas. He was as controlled as ever, quoting figures and using impenetrable jargon to defend the statements he'd been producing and show that the costs of getting rid of the platforms were built into all his projections. It was when Carston introduced Baxter's name and hinted at their suspicions about him that his façade slipped a little.

"You're suggesting he was going to blow up the platform," he said.

"Seems that way," said Carston. "Problem is, he couldn't do it on his own."

"Oh?"

"No. Releasing condensate, letting it build up a charge … all that. It couldn't happen unless two other things were fixed. The gas protection system had to be out of action and the Emergency Shut-Down Valve had to be kept open. He'd covered the gas. He had canisters all ready to stop it working. But he still needed somebody to over-ride the ESDV."

"Nobody out there would do that. It would be suicide," said Hamer.

"No need to," said Carston. "You could do it here. On that computer mimic you showed us."

"I see," said Nicholas, who seemed amused by the idea. "And who's he going to get to do that? Al Qaeda, maybe? Was he a Muslim, too?"

"I can't believe anyone would think seriously about deliberately blowing up a platform," said Hamer.

"Maybe he just wanted to damage it," said Carston.

"What does that achieve?" asked Hamer.

"Well, whether it's completely destroyed or just badly messed up, it's no good as a platform, is it? So who picks up the tab?"

"The insurance, of course," said Hamer, apparently unaware of the implications of what he was saying.

"Exactly. So, once the publicity's died down, you can clear out and you've still got plenty to spend in Baku or wherever. Nice little earner, in fact."

"And that's what Baxter was up to, is it?" said Nicholas. "Doing the company a favour."

Carston just looked at him. Nicholas held his gaze.

"But he'd kill so many people," said Hamer, still well outside the loop the rest of them had entered.

"No," said Carston. "The platform was due for a maintenance shutdown. There wouldn't be many on board and there'd be time for them all to evacuate. He's there with them, remember. Wouldn't want to risk losing what he'd be getting from the scam."

"What scam?" asked Hamer.

"Oh, come on, Mr Hamer. The platform goes up, Anstey's say goodbye, Baxter's colleagues are redundant, but he gets a big pay-off. Everybody's happy except the guys who've been making his life a misery."

"I take it you've got evidence for all this?" said Nicholas.

"Oh, lots," said Carston, with a smile. "Would you mind, Sergeant?"

The question was directed at Reid, who nodded, stood up and left the room.

Carston reached across for a biscuit and took a bite before turning to Nicholas again.

"By the way, what was it Baxter said about Vicky?" he said.

Nicholas was quiet for a moment, then said, "Vicky? Who's that?"

Carston noticed the light flush that was spreading on his neck. He put his biscuit in his saucer and slowly flipped through the pages of his notebook. McNeil, Ross, McIntyre and his two sergeants all waited. They knew this was Carston's show for the time being. He found the page he was looking for.

"Strange," he said. "I've got it down here." He began reading, without giving the words any undue emphasis. "'He wanted her named as his next of kin, so that she'd get his pension.' That's what you said."

"Oh, right. Her name was Vicky, was it? I'd forgotten."

"You'd forgotten?"

"Yes."

"Really? That's funny."

Carston looked at his notebook and read again.

"'Me: So he gave you her name. You: No.'"

Nicholas looked around at the others, then back at Carston.

"Is this some sort of accusation?" he asked.

"Oh no," said Carston. "Not yet."

He took another bite of his biscuit.

"D'you remember what else you told me about her?"

"No," said Nicholas.

"Lucky I took it down then, isn't it? You said Baxter was angry. Some guy had used a whip on Vicky. That upset him. Said he was going to find the man, get him."

"Yes, right. I remember that."

"Yes. There's a problem, though."

Nicholas looked at him, waiting, maintaining his control.

"She didn't see the guy with the whip until after she'd finished with Baxter. Baxter couldn't have known anything about it."

"You're mistaken. He told me. How else would I know?"

"Maybe you saw them for yourself," said McNeil.

Her voice surprised everyone except Carston. Nicholas looked at her but said nothing.

"When you went to see her, maybe," she added. "You know, after you'd phoned her pimp to arrange it."

To Carston's surprise, Nicholas smiled. He turned back from McNeil to look again at Carston. His movements were slow, calm.

"When you started with all this," he said, "I wondered whether our lawyer should be here, just in case the company's interests were involved. I'm glad I didn't. We don't pay him to listen to stories."

Carston smiled back, nodding slowly. The silence held for a moment, then was broken as the door opened and Reid came back in. He was carrying a holdall and a large transparent evidence bag containing a red fire extinguisher.

"Ah, thank you, Sergeant," said Carston. "I'll take the holdall. Just leave the other bag there."

Reid put the evidence bag by the wall beside the door, handed the holdall to Carston and sat back in his seat again. Carston unzipped the holdall and took out a memory stick, some sheets of A4 and an evidence bag containing a Stanley knife. He put them on the table in front of him and rummaged inside the holdall again. After a few moments, he drew out the corners of some smaller evidence bags, glanced at the labels on them, then looked up at Nicholas again.

"Your way with figures may be good," he said, "but I wonder whether you're as clever when it comes to hairs and fibres. You'd be amazed how many our forensics team found in Vicky's flat. And on Vicky. And on Ally Baxter."

Nicholas said nothing but Carston noticed that, while he was managing to maintain his stillness, his fingers had started playing with a pen on the desk. In the end, it was Hamer who broke the silence.

"I don't see what this has to do with the company," he said, rather plaintively. "Or sabotage."

Chapter Twenty

Carston was grateful for Hamer's interjection. He wanted to keep shifting the focus.

"Yes, of course. The company," he said. "Sergeant Ross?"

Ross flicked open his own notepad and ran his eyes over the top page.

"Yes, sir," he said to Hamer. "After all, if it's your insurers who have to pay up, we're talking about savings of several billions in the end, aren't we? The sort of figures that'll go down pretty well in America."

"Well, I suppose so, but none of this is making sense," said Hamer. He was flushed and sweating.

"Can I ask you about Alistair Baxter?" asked Ross.

"What? Yes, I suppose—"

"It seems he was something of a gambler."

"Was he? I didn't know. That sort of thing only becomes a problem if it interferes with a man's work."

"Yes. With respect, though, he was in a position of some authority. Somebody with fewer scruples than yourself might think that that's the sort of weakness that could be exploited."

"I don't see why," said Hamer.

"Really?" said Ross. "A man with serious debts. A vulnerable man, no friends on the platform. I'd have thought it was quite easy to string him along, promise him a big payout, make him feel he was part of some big, important plan."

"Human resources consists of biographical facts, not speculations," said Hamer. "I don't recognise the man you're describing."

Ross turned over a few pages and tapped the notes on the one at which he'd stopped.

"No, it's not speculation," he said. "It's facts."

As Ross continued to paint his picture of Baxter, based on the musings that Carston had taken from the Vicky file on the memory stick he'd found, Carston himself was watching Nicholas. Even though the focus had shifted to Hamer, his fingers were still twirling the pen and he still held himself in that unnatural stillness.

"He'd had enough, basically," Ross was saying. "He was stressed out before but then, trying to plan a way to disable the platform … well, it got worse. He was getting … twitchy. That day he came ashore, we think he had an argument."

"He did. With Bole," said Hamer.

"No, later than that," said Ross. "During the evening. You see, he wanted to set up whatever he was going to do so that it coincided with the maintenance shutdown but his … partner … wasn't ready. Made some excuse about unfinished paperwork. Baxter didn't buy it, though. It was going to be this trip or not at all. That's what he said."

"What do you mean, 'said'? How do you know he 'said' anything? And who did he say it to?" asked Hamer.

"We know he said it," said Ross. "We've got his word for it. It's all in the file."

"Yes, and as for who he was saying it to, well, that's why we've come. Just want to confirm it," said Carston, his voice light, cheerful, contrasting strongly with Ross's measured delivery. "What do you think, Mr Nicholas?"

Nicholas shrugged and shook his head.

"But he phoned you from here, the night he was killed, didn't he?"

"Yes."

"Why?"

"Why what?"

"Why did he phone you?"

"He told me about the woman."

"Vicky," said McNeil, intent on making him acknowledge that "the woman" had a name.

Nicholas looked at her and said nothing.

"He phoned you to talk about his girl-friend?" said Carston, sounding surprised.

"Yes."

"Nothing else?"

"No."

"And you were at home?"

"Yes."

"Is that where Sergeant Reid got you when he phoned later?"

"Yes. It was late. I was getting ready for bed."

"You sure?" said Carston.

Nicholas was still again, the pen motionless in his fingers. Suddenly, he smiled.

"No, you're right. It was another call I got at home. When the one from the sergeant came through, I was here. I'd forgotten some paperwork. I had to come and get it."

"Yes," said Carston. "Mobiles are a godsend, aren't they? Bit of a bugger, too, though. Give you away, don't they? We know you were here. We checked the phone company's records."

Nicholas laid the pen carefully on the desk and leaned forward.

"Look, this isn't just an interview," he said. "Am I being charged with something?"

"Good grief, no," said Carston. "We're just trying to bring all the pieces together, let a little light in."

Slowly, Nicholas eased himself back.

"Is that when you talked to Mr Baxter about Vicky?" Carston went on. "When you came in for your papers?"

"I told you. We talked about it on the phone."

"So he wasn't here, then?"

"No."

"He wasn't filling in his own paperwork? The stuff Mr Hamer mentioned."

"No."

Up to this point, Carston had stayed relaxed, conversational. Now, he started to increase the tempo, press harder.

"He didn't tell you all about her, about how she knew everything about the scam, about the phone calls and chats he'd had with her?"

Nicholas shook his head.

"He did want more money, though, didn't he? A bigger share."

Nicholas was still again.

"Worked out what you'd be getting: millions, a special bonus from the States, seat on the board. It made his fifty grand cut look very silly. How much more did he ask for? Two? Three hundred thousand?"

To Carston's annoyance, but not to his surprise, Nicholas smiled. It had more nervousness in it than confidence. Carston returned it, nodded, then picked up the bag containing the Stanley knife.

"Horrible things, these, aren't they? You should see some of the effects they have on people's faces. Or genitals."

Through the thick plastic, he pushed the button to slide the blade out of the handle.

"Quite useful for us, though, sometimes. You'd be surprised at what gets lodged down the sides of the blade as it's pushed in and out of the handle. You can tell where it's been, what it's been cutting—not just flesh but … well, carpets, all sorts of things. It's usually easy to place it. Not just at the scene of the crime but where it's been kept, who it belongs to, even."

If anything, Nicholas's smile got broader. Carston slid the blade back and put down the bag.

"And, you know, even if we can't find the knife, bits of the material from it get lodged in the wounds, so we can still link the body with the location where the knife was kept."

He stood up and went to pick up the bigger evidence bag; the one with the fire extinguisher inside it.

"Same with this, he said. "Bet you wonder what it's doing here, eh?" he said, laying it on the table.

Nicholas shrugged.

"Surprised to see it?"

"Should I be?"

"Not an obvious weapon, is it?" said Carston. "Not easy to pick up, swing round. What did you do, throw it at him?"

Nicholas turned to McIntyre and his two sergeants, the remains of the smile still on his face.

"I hope you're taking notes. Your colleague's making some very serious allegations," he said.

McIntyre looked at Carston.

"Yes, probably threw it," said Carston. "Had a row. He threatens to shop you, turns to walk out, and you … well, you have to stop him, don't you? You couldn't have that. All the plans, all the money… And your reputation. The first finance director to decommission a platform for free."

Nicholas held up a hand to stop him. Carston bent his head, waiting for a reply. Nicholas had second thoughts and shook his head.

"Of course, there wouldn't be any fingerprints on it; you'd have wiped them off," said Carston, as if they were mates in a pub, involving in a game of "let's just suppose—". "But it's the same as the Stanley knife; you can't get rid of every trace. There'd be fibres, deposits that place the extinguisher at a specific location, Baxter's blood—"

He was counting the items off on his fingers in a slow enumeration.

"We've all seen CSI," said Nicholas, interrupting him, irritated by his delivery. "I know what you're looking for. Bits of my DNA—" He pointed at the extinguisher. "Flakes of paint or something else from that in Ally's head, the right shaped wounds... Go ahead, check it out. You'll be disappointed."

"No, no," said Carston. "This isn't yours. It came from my office. We haven't found yours yet. Same with the knife. That's not yours either."

Nicholas's smile fell away. The stillness returned.

"But you knew that, didn't you?," Carston continued. "That's why you're so confident that we haven't got the things you were talking about. But we will have. Very soon. Even if we don't manage to find your knife or your extinguisher. I mean, you can't bang something like this into somebody's skull without—"

He broke off to add a little aside.

"You were right, by the way. It was his skull. Good guess."

He grinned his congratulations at Nicholas and went on.

"Makes helluva mess, though, doesn't it? All the slippery stuff coming out all over the tiles. That's what the carrier bag was for, wasn't it? To keep it all in. And the survival suit, to keep stuff off your car. Waste of time, by the way. There'll be traces, however careful you were. And I bet our team's found blood in the corridor outside your office already."

"And we're taking samples from the extinguisher holder there too. For the flakes of paint," said Ross.

Carston lifted the fire extinguisher again and laid it on the floor beside his chair.

"You know, all in all, you haven't been very lucky with this, have you?" he said. "One minute, you're in line for a fortune and a step up the ladder, the next, some little scumbag is threatening to pull the plug." He stopped, as if he'd suddenly thought of something. "The phone call was lucky, though, wasn't it?"

Nicholas said nothing. None of this was being recorded. They hadn't charged him. They hadn't yet produced any actual proof. Carston turned to Reid.

"You did tell Mr Nicholas that it was a case of queer-bashing, didn't you?"

"Well, I didn't use that actual terminology—" He stopped as he saw Carston's expression change. "But yes, I think I made the offences clear."

"Yes," said Carston. "So that was a bit of a bonus, wasn't it? I mean, you've got this body, all nicely wrapped up, but nowhere to put it. You know he lives in Cairnburgh, so it'd be better to dump him there. But what if somebody sees you? How would you explain being there at that time of night? Then your fairy godmother calls and it's all sorted. You can dump him in Cairnburgh, the police have arrested the guy who had a fight with him earlier. The guy's been out queer-bashing, Baxter's a queer. Q.E.D. Too good to be true, isn't it?"

He was putting on a performance, deliberately turning it all into a seemingly light-hearted anecdote. Only Nicholas knew how close to the truth it all was. He kept his head lowered but looked up at Carston with loathing.

"Do you find it pleasurable talking that way about a murder victim?" he said.

The smile disappeared from Carston's face and the bantering tone was dropped.

"No, Mr Finance Director," he said. "There's no pleasure in it. No relief in thinking of him dumped among some rubbish bags, having his skull hammered to pulp and gristle to hide the mark the extinguisher left, having his genitals slashed with a Stanley knife. No, I don't get any pleasure from that. Did you?"

He stopped and held Nicholas' stare. Nicholas' eyes dropped away.

"And you were wrong about Bole and his pals, too," said Carston. "They all knew how to spell faggot."

The flush that had begun on Nicholas's neck had spread to his face. Superintendent McIntyre leaned forward in his chair.

"This has all been kept at this informal level deliberately," he said. "To give you every opportunity to answer the questions we have. Obviously, we need to revisit it all in much greater detail and that'll be back at the station. So perhaps—"

"Excuse me, sir," said McNeil. "Sorry to interrupt, but there is one more thing."

McIntyre looked at her and nodded, then turned back to Nicholas.

"You mentioned the company lawyer earlier," he said. "Do you want to change your mind? Do you think he should be here?"

"No," said Nicholas. His voice was barely audible now.

McIntyre nodded to McNeil.

"No, you're right," she said. "Just stories, isn't it? You said so."

She pushed a sheet of paper across the table for him to look at. It was a list of phone numbers, with dates and timings. Some were highlighted.

"Recognise this?"

Nicholas glanced at it and shrugged.

"The calls Mr Baxter made during his last trip. You had a look at them, didn't you?"

"No," said Nicholas.

"Yes. That's where you got Vicky's number. Never answered, though, did she?"

She was guessing but she was doing it with conviction. Carston was impressed. She was in control.

"Had to try this one instead." She jabbed at one of the highlighted numbers. "Dave McEwan. Nasty individual. Her pimp."

Nicholas shook his head.

"Yes," McNeil insisted. "He'll testify. He listened to you on the phone. Recognised your voice."

McNeil knew that, as far as Nicholas was concerned, Vicky was an afterthought. Something inconvenient, something to be discarded. That really pissed her off.

"This scam you had going with Baxter would've been the biggest story since the Brent Spar. There'd've been journalists crawling all over it, waving their cheque books around. Vicky knew everything. She wouldn't be able to resist. It would've got her out of… You went to her flat on the Thursday. She was in a red dress, remember? Waiting for you. Ready to sell you a bit of happiness. Probably offered you a drink, but never got the chance, did she?

Only a woman, wasn't she? In the way. What did you use? A tie, wasn't it? We've got fibres from it, we know the pattern, material, colour. The pathologist even told us how you did it."

As she went on, there was no passion in her voice. She forced herself to suppress the anger and pity she felt for Vicky and kept her tone neutral, cold. It gave her words even greater power.

"Round her neck from the back. No time for her to get her fingers inside it. Your left forearm against the back of her neck. She was fighting. Scratching at the tie. We've got the evidence. You leaned backwards, pulled the tie higher, lifted her head. The ligature mark stretches into a vee at the back. We don't know how long it took. Long enough for her to know that she was dying. After, you wanted it to look as if a punter had done it. You slit her dress, pulled her pants down. That's when you saw the marks."

Nicholas suddenly shook himself out of his silence.

"Prostitutes are murdered all the time," he said.

"Aye. You were counting on that, weren't you?" said McNeil, the ice still in her voice. "The thing is, though, there's usually a reason for it. The punter gets his sex then doesn't want to pay for it. Or the strangling's just taken things a bit too far. Or they want to rob her. But Vicky didn't have sex before she was killed. There was money there, but nobody took it. So where's the motive?"

The silence seeped back. The police officers there had all been briefed so none of it was surprising. Hamer had long since given up trying to understand it. Nicholas lowered his head. For some moments, he just looked at the carpet between his feet. When he looked up again and spoke, he was calm.

"A prostitute, a gay employee, and I killed them both. And I'm implicated in a plot to blow up an offshore platform. I must say it sounds rather fanciful."

"Yes, it does, doesn't it?" said Carston.

He took yet more sheets of paper from his briefcase and laid them on the table.

"You deleted all the files from Baxter's computer on the platform, didn't you?" he said.

"No," said Nicholas.

"Oh don't be tiresome," said Carston, sounding disappointed with him. "Our IT boys'll be able to trace the deletions back to a terminal onshore, maybe even the one in your office."

"There are lots of terminals here," said Hamer, trying to play some sort of role in what was going on.

"I know," said Carston. "But we know who used them for this particular job." He tapped the papers in front of him. "This is what he deleted. It's one of Mr Baxter's files from the platform. Called Vicky. It's a sort of diary he wrote. He kept a copy on a memory stick. It's all there. The things he had to put up with. And, of course, all the things Mr Nicholas had asked him to do. I think he wrote it as a sort of insurance policy."

He turned to Nicholas.

"You were right to want to get rid of it," he said. "It's lethal. Cast-iron. Dates, times, equipment. It's all here."

Nicholas was still again, giving no sign that he'd accepted the overwhelming evidence that he'd been presented with.

"I think it's time to get on with some formal procedures," said McIntyre. "You still haven't been charged. D'you want to say anything before we go down to the station?"

Nicholas looked at him, shook his head, then turned to stare at Carston.

"Say goodbye to your job," he said. "When this nonsense is over, I'll make sure you're kicked out for it."

"Better join the queue," said Carston.

McIntyre's sergeants moved to lead Nicholas away. He shrugged off their hands and strode out ahead of them.

Hamer was completely lost.

"Thank you for your help, Mr Hamer," said Carston. "We'll let you know what's happening as soon as the paperwork's started."

Hamer just looked at him, then at the others.

"Right," he said. "Yes. So I can—"

He gestured towards the door. Carston nodded.

"Yes. Bye then," said Hamer.

He stood for another moment, way out of his depth in it all, and finally left them.

"Can I have a word?" Carston said to McIntyre.

"Sure."

"I'll be out in a minute," said Carston to his three sergeants. They dutifully collected their files and papers and went out to their car. Reid took the fire extinguisher.

"All yours then, Donnie," said Carston, when only the two of them were left.

"He was right, you know," said McIntyre.

"What?"

"Bloody far-fetched."

"Yes. Have you got enough on the fraud to take to the Procurator Fiscal?"

"We have now."

"Good. By the time you've interviewed him, we'll have plenty more. I'm sure they'll find Baxter's blood somewhere. Probably in the corridor outside Nicholas's office. I'm not sure about the fire extinguisher and the knife. He was pretty confident that we didn't have them. He'll have ditched them somewhere deep. But there'll be paint traces round the holder. It'd be worth checking all the company cars, too, starting with Nicholas's. There'll be contamination somewhere. That survival suit won't have stopped it."

"While I'm working my guts out, where are you going to be?"

Carston smiled.

"I'll get everything we have from Vicky's flat and get it to you ASAP. And I'll get one of my sergeants to tidy everything up and work with you."

"The lassie?" said McIntyre.

"No chance," said Carston. "She's all mine. Sergeant Reid's your man. He's one of Superintendent Ridley's protégés and he needs the experience."

"So he doesn't know his arse from his elbow."

"Not yet. But he's learning. Anyway, he's a star when it comes to shuffling paper and doing stuff with computers. He should be OK. If he's not, you can chew his balls off."

"I will."

"Good. He can make a start with you right away."

They shook hands, thanked one another and went out to the car park. Ross, McNeil and Reid were standing beside their car.

"Good job, everybody," said Carston. "Listen, Reid, I know it's short notice but would you be happy to stay in Aberdeen this evening? Get things started? Superintendent McIntyre will need to start processing all this right away."

"No problem, sir," said Reid.

"Right, then. You're with me," said McIntyre.

They said their goodbyes and Reid followed McIntyre to his car.

"I'll drive for a change," said Carston.

The air hadn't yet thickened but the orange spread of sodium lights was already anticipating the twilight as they pulled out of the Queen Street car park and turned west to head for the North Deeside road.

"So we're giving the case to Aberdeen, are we?" said Ross. He was sitting in the back seat. McNeil was beside Carston in the front.

"Yes," said Carston. "The murders are ours, but Donnie's squad's already got a big file on him. Why? D'you want to get involved in negotiations with them?"

"No, thanks."

"The important thing's to get the bugger locked up," said Carston. "Which reminds me, let's make bloody sure we cross every t and dot every i before we pass anything on to Reid. I think Donnie'll keep tabs on him but we need to be squeaky clean with what we send him."

Neither of the others answered. Carston's willingness to leave Reid in charge puzzled both of them. It added to the rather subdued mood. They all felt a little flat, with none of the elation that should have come from having untangled the mess. The need to pass it on to other people somehow undermined the achievement. McNeil glanced across at Carston.

"D'you no mind handing over a collar, sir?" she asked.

Carston sighed and nodded.

"In a way," he said. "But if I have to play politics to hang on to it, I'm not bothered. The important thing is we've got him."

Ross wondered briefly whether Carston was being more political than he'd like to admit. The probability was that, by giving the glory to Reid and Ridley, there'd be less haste to discipline him. He might even seem to be toeing the line for a change. He also thought that, by involving Reid in the little deceptions that had helped to unsettle Nicholas, he'd made sure that no news of it could get to Ridley without Reid himself being implicated. Ross had never doubted that Carston was clever. He knew he could handle Ridley and the rest, but surely he'd never use their techniques to get what he wanted. Would he?

McNeil stole another quick look at Carston's profile. He was a good-looking man. When people like Spurle, Reid and Ridley got on his nerves, his eyes flashed and his mouth set tighter, but normally his face was open and when he looked at you, you knew he was really listening to what you said. From what she could see of them, his eyes looked sad and yet she was sure that a smile was playing at the side of his mouth. Carston's peripheral vision told him that she was looking at him. He turned to her and his smile got wider. To her embarrassment, McNeil felt a blush come into her cheeks.

****

Carston dropped them off, then drove to Gallacher and Baigrie's house. Bole's lawyer had been pressing ever more strongly for his client's release and Carston was afraid that, for all the evidence against him, for all the witnesses now prepared to identify him, he would probably get away with a suspended sentence or maybe even be acquitted. Carston wanted to tell Gallacher and Baigrie face to face that the chances of him getting what he deserved were slim.

Gallacher opened the door and showed him in to the sitting room where candles and incense were burning and failing to hide the unmistakable smell of cannabis. Gallacher was still in his standard office suit and tie and both he and the unusually smart Carston made a curious contrast with Baigrie. He'd been released from hospital that afternoon and, although he still wore a patch over one eye and the other looked full of blood, he'd showered and put on a dazzlingly white one piece outfit which shone like satin but was probably viscose.

As they talked, Carston was aware of an edge of hysteria in him that never quite broke the surface but forced a shrillness into his always camp delivery. As he made unfunny jokes about changing his favourite colour from aquamarine to black, saving a fortune on television licences, having a poodle as a guide dog and so on, the rhythms of his speech were too fast and the laughter forced past the words in nervous snatches.

Gallacher sat beside him, his hand on his thigh, stroking and occasionally patting it. He was even more sensitive to the distress underneath Baigrie's stream of chat. His smiles conveyed his solidarity but in his eyes, Carston saw the occasional cloud of anxiety. This was the first day of their new life together. As Baigrie's blindness advanced, the strains would at times be intolerable. It made Carston even more bitter about the news he'd brought them.

"So he'll be getting away with it," said Gallacher when Carston told them about Bole's claims.

Carston raised his hands to suggest that it was anybody's guess.

"The way his brief's been coaching him," he said, "the jury'll probably accept his plea of provocation."

"And the new witnesses you've got, Geoff and the others, they'll make no difference."

Carston noticed that, unlike on previous occasions, he made no reference to Baigrie's condition being proof enough in itself of Bole's guilt.

"You know better than I do what the defence'll do with them."

"It'll be a convention of queens," said Baigrie. "All girls together to protect one of their own."

"Something like that," said Carston.

"Exactly like that," insisted Gallacher. "The whole truth and nothing but the truth. Huh."

"You weren't exactly forthcoming with that, though, were you?" said Carston, feeling that he was being included in Gallacher's scorn.

"What d'you mean?"

"You didn't tell us you'd gone to the Swan separately. That meant neither of you had an alibi for the time Ally Baxter was murdered."

"You learn to hedge your bets," said Gallacher. "With the chips stacked the way they are, there's no point in playing it straight."

"Same as Bole," said Carston.

"No," said Baigrie. "Not the same at all. Why's he lying? What's his reason? Just bloody self-preservation. Doesn't matter what happens to other people as long as he gets support for his pig ignorant attitudes."

There was nothing Carston could add. Baigrie and Gallacher's withholding of information was as damaging to their cause as Bole's manipulation of public prejudices. Every day, they experienced the need to dissimulate, but that was no more a justification for being uncooperative than Bole's selfishness. If they were looking for genuine acceptance, intolerance either way was a bad starting point.

After a final apology, he stood, shook hands with both of them, wished them well and left. As Gallacher showed him to the door, Baigrie remained sitting, a dazzling white splash in the plush, gaudy splendour of their sitting room. It was hard to dispel the image of him sitting there day after day until the twilight already in him had developed into the full night that was the legacy of Bole's frenzy.

The sombreness of Carston's mood stayed with him, even when Kath greeted him with the news that Ridley himself had phoned to say that he was off the hook. In the light of Carston's most recent success and as a result of the support expressed by many of his colleagues, Ridley had decided to drop the charge. Carston knew damn well that it had little to do with him and lots to do with the kudos he'd generated for Ridley and his glove puppet Reid in the eyes of the people at Grampian headquarters in Aberdeen.

As he sat with his arm round Kath, watching Channel Four news and thinking back over the past week, there was little satisfaction in him. Recognition and approval were so all important to Ridley and yet he, Carston, didn't give a toss about them. His focus was on making the connections, thinking things through, solving the mysteries. In this case, handing the glory over to Ridley was part of his victory, but it gave him no real pleasure. Pushing everything else aside was the depressing truth of Baigrie's condition. Bole would be released, Baigrie's sea blue eyes would soon be useless. What was the point of untangling motives if justice was so arbitrary? That was the question that kept coming into his mind. And he had no answer for it.

****

Out on Falcon Alpha, Steve and Jamie were standing in driving rain, checking the emergency supplies on level three. The waves had been building for a few days and the spray driven off them mixed with the rain to sting their faces. Onshore, though, in Cairnburgh's biggest club, it was hot and it was techno night. The beat was solid and far from intricate but bubbles and folds of sound kept wrapping around it and leading the dancers deeper inside the music.

McEwan, in an olive green Paul Smith outfit, with a loose Tommy Hilfiger shirt, was dancing with two women. They were both young, with dark hair into which they'd scattered some sparkly dust. One wore a pale apricot top over tight silver trousers, the other, the taller of the two, had on a white mini-dress which looked as if it had been painted on her. They were loving the music, smiling broadly at its effects and moving in and out of its rhythms.

McEwan danced between the two of them, brushing first against one, then against the other, trailing his hands down their backs and across their stomachs. The music slipped briefly into a softer register, ready to start building once again. McEwan reached out his arms, took their hands and pulled the two girls into him. He kissed each of them, then moved slowly back, releasing his hold. The two girls looked at the small white tablets he'd left in their hands and their movements, smiles and laughter became even brighter.

The End

ABOUT THE AUTHOR

Bill Kirton was born in Plymouth, England but has lived in Aberdeen Scotland for most of his life. He's been a university lecturer, presented TV programmes, written and performed songs and sketches at the Edinburgh Festival, and had many radio plays broadcast by the BBC and the Australian BC. He's written four books on study and writing skills in Pearson's 'Brilliant' series and his crime novels, *Material Evidence*, *Rough Justice*, *The Darkness*, *Shadow Selves*, and the historical novel *The Figurehead*, set in Aberdeen in 1840, have been published in the UK and USA. His most recent publication from Pfoxmoor is a hilarious satire of the spy and crime genres, *The Sparrow Conundrum*. His short stories have appeared in several anthologies and *Love Hurts* was chosen for the *Mammoth Book of Best British Crime 2010*.

Two of his books have won awards. *The Sparrow Conundrum* was the winner of the 'Humor' category in the 2011 Forward National Literature Awards and *The Darkness* was second in the 'Mystery' category.

His website is http://www.bill-kirton.co.uk and his blog's at http://www.livingwritingandotherstuff.blogspot.com/

BY THE SAME AUTHOR

THE JACK CARSTON MYSTERY SERIES

Material Evidence:
"…a fine debut with intense plotting, strong characters and just the right touch of acid in the dialogue … Fine Rendellian touches … a cracking page-turner."
—Aberdeen Press and Journal

"…Add to the cast of characters a good sense of pace and an excellent plot that kept me guessing and you'll see why I liked this book."—Cathy G. Cole

Rough Justice:
"…a thoughtful and thought-provoking book … It ought to bring Bill Kirton the attention he deserves." (Sunday Telegraph)

The Darkness:
2nd Place, 2011 Forward National Literature Awards, Mystery

"…a wonderful, thrilling, dark, compassionate book"
—Gillian Philip, author of Firebrand

"…clever, tightly constructed, immensely satisfying and peopled with a cast of completely believable characters, who don't let you go until the final word"
—Michael J. Malone

"…a dark, intense ride … a book that keeps you guessing right until the exciting conclusion."
—P. S. Gifford

Shadow Selves:
"…a thoroughly engrossing medical mystery with a surprise ending that was totally unexpected."—Chris Longmuir, award winning author of *Dead Wood*

HISTORICAL FICTION

The Figurehead:
"Profound, detailed, incredibly written, *The Figurehead* is definitely a kind of book one wants to go back to again and again..."—Maria K.

SATIRE

The Sparrow Conundrum:
1st Place Winner, Humor, 2011 Forward National Literature Awards

"...The Sparrow Conundrum is the demon love child of Spike Milligan and John Le Carre. I absolutely adore this one— hysterically funny, with this weirdly tender wickedness."
—Maria Bustillos, author of Dorkismo: the Macho of the Dork and Act Like a Gentleman, Think Like a Woman

"...You have combined the elements of The Tall Blond Man with the One Black Shoe with The Biederbecke Affair and thrown in Happer from Local Hero for good measure. It is killingly funny, and for those who love farce—from Scapin to Noises Off—this is utterly brilliant, divine, and classic, and couldn't be bettered."
—M.M. Bennetts, author of May 1812 and Of Honest Fame

CHILDREN'S BOOKS (written as Jack Rosse)

Stanley Moves In
"...Stanley in all his obnoxious glory ... it's hard not to like Rosse's charming tale of this out-of-the-ordinary fairy."
—Melissa Conway

The Loch Ewe Mystery